T0272652

MURDER AT THE HACIENDA

Also by Amanda Allen

Santa Fe Revival mysteries

SANTA FE MOURNING
A MOMENT IN CRIME
DEATH COMES TO SANTA FE *

* *available from Severn House*

MURDER AT THE HACIENDA

Amanda Allen

SEVERN
HOUSE

First world edition published in Great Britain and the USA in 2024
by Severn House, an imprint of Canongate Books Ltd,
14 High Street, Edinburgh EH1 1TE.

severnhouse.com

British Library Cataloguing-in-Publication Data
A CIP catalogue record for this title is available from the British Library.

ISBN-13: 978-1-4483-1101-9 (cased)
ISBN-13: 978-1-4483-1536-9 (e-book)

All Severn House titles are printed on acid-free paper.

Typeset by Palimpsest Book Production Ltd.,
Falkirk, Stirlingshire, Scotland.
Printed and bound in Great Britain by TJ Books,
Padstow, Cornwall.

Praise for the Santa Fe Revival mysteries

"Colorful, playful, and engaging"
Booklist on *Death Comes to Santa Fe*

"Maddie is a winning heroine, and the period details will appeal to those enamored of 1920s speakeasies"
Publishers Weekly on *Death comes to Santa Fe*

"A likable heroine and a flamboyant cast of supporting characters"
Booklist on *Death comes to Santa Fe*

"Santa Fe, a place of beauty and artistic inspiration, provides the perfect backdrop for the sympathetic sleuth"
Kirkus Reviews on *Death comes to Santa Fe*

"Allen perfectly captures the serene enchantment of Santa Fe. Her gutsy heroine has plenty to work with in a mystery that keeps you guessing to the end"
Kirkus Reviews on *A Moment in Crime*

"A satisfying read for Maddie fans; it's also a good bet to give fans of Jessica Fellowes' The Mitford Murders"
Booklist on *A Moment in Crime*

About the author

Amanda Allen wrote her first book at the age of sixteen – a vast historical epic starring all her friends as the characters, written secretly during algebra class. She's never since used algebra, but her books have been nominated for many awards, including the RITA Award, the Romantic Times Reviews Reviewers' Choice Award, the GDRW Bookseller's Best Award, the National Readers Choice Award, and the Holt Medallion. She lives in Santa Fe with two rescue dogs, a wonderful husband, and far too many books and royal memorabilia collections.

ONE

December 1924

'What will you do for Christmas, then, Señora Maddie?'

'Hmm?' Maddie Vaughn-Alwin snapped back to earth at the sound of Juanita Anaya's voice. She'd been thinking of the just-begun painting that waited in her studio, and her mind was so swirling with colors and lines and shadows there was no room for anything as solid as Christmas plans.

Or for washing dishes. Maddie blinked down at the dripping bowl and dish towel in her hands, suspended above the kitchen sink, and she laughed.

'I'm afraid I'm useless at anything today, Juanita,' she said with a rueful smile at her housekeeper and friend, who was efficiently chopping vegetables at the kitchen table, the dogs Buttercup and Pansy waiting at her feet for any scraps. Maddie finished drying the bowl and tucked it away in the cupboard. 'What did you say about Christmas?'

Juanita shook her head. 'I always know when an art exhibition is coming up, Señora Maddie, your head goes right up into the clouds! You do remember what month it is?'

Maddie studied the wintry scene outside the kitchen window. Her garden was glistening with frost, a sugary dusting of snow over the sleeping flowerbeds and bare trees. Her friend and neighbor Gunther Ryder's house was empty beyond the slatted fence. He'd been away on a writing retreat somewhere in the countryside for a few weeks and she missed him. She usually loved the quiet and pale peace of midwinter, but for some reason now she felt a bit restless. 'It's December, of course.'

'And Christmas is in December.'

Maddie laughed again. 'I *do* remember that much. I might

have been working hard in the studio lately, but I notice time fleeting past.'

And fleet it had in the last few months, ever since the Montoya murder and Fiesta time. The weeks had passed quietly for once, eaten up in painting and fantasizing about her wedding to Dr David Cole.

'You do remember that the twins and I are going to the pueblo next week?' Juanita reached for potatoes to peel, and shook her head again. 'We'll take Pansy with us, Ruby can't do without her lately, and Eddie is staying here to work at La Fonda. He'll be able to sleep at a friend's place closer to the hotel.' Juanita and her children – Eddie who was nearly grown, and the little twins, Pearl and Ruby – were like Maddie's own, chosen family, but they had decided to go stay with Juanita's once-estranged, now-reunited family at the pueblo for the holidays. 'I'm so afraid Dr David will be terribly run off his feet at the hospital, and you'll be alone. Don't you have any plans?'

Maddie held out her hand to admire her engagement ring in the pale-yellow sunlight, watching the sparkle of the sapphire and its surrounding diamonds. She smiled every time she looked at it, but it was true David had been very busy at work lately, with the hospital short-handed. They didn't see each other nearly as often as she would like. The lot of a (future) doctor's wife, she supposed. 'Not solid plans, no.'

She thought of Christmases in her childhood, the enormous tree in her parents' Fifth Avenue house, with its shimmering ornaments she wasn't allowed to touch. The goose on the Christmas-day table, services at Grace Church, silent hours spent in her grandparents' stuffy drawing room. Ice skating in the park – that part was nice. Christmases had been so different in Santa Fe since she moved there and built up her own home, with wonderful, cinnamon-sugary smells coming from the kitchen, carols on the gramophone while the twins danced to the music, dogs barking, tinsel sparkling.

'I doubt David will work quite all the time,' she said. 'Maybe I'll find a tree, and he and I can cook something . . .'

Juanita looked horrified. 'You? Cook? In my kitchen?'

Maddie tilted her head as she studied the sparkling, spotless kitchen, the pale-green tiles and polished wood floor, the new icebox. 'I know what happened last time, Juanita, but I swear I wouldn't try to make coq au vin again. Just something easy. Like . . .'

'Boiled eggs?'

Maddie laughed. 'Fair enough. It might be all I know how to cook, but you have to admit my eggs are quite good. And my toast, too, since we just got that spiffy new toaster.' She pointed out the chrome-shiny new gadget, put in pride of place on the counter.

'Eggs and toast aren't a proper holiday meal,' Juanita said with a worried tsk. 'I'll leave you some things in the icebox. I'm just worried.'

'Oh, Juanita, don't be! You must go and have a lovely time with your brother's family. Pearl and Ruby have been talking about nothing except playing with their cousins lately.'

'It makes a change from all their chatter about your wedding.'

Maddie giggled to think of the twins' ideas. Twenty-foot trains, sprays of gardenias, doves in flight. 'They're very helpful, yes. When you get back, we'll set a real date and they can get planning in earnest. For Christmas, just think about your family and don't worry about me. I'll find something to eat, and I won't burn the house down. David and I will find a way to have a nice holiday.'

Juanita still looked doubtful. 'If you say so, Señora Maddie.'

'I do!' She kissed Juanita's cheek and gave her a reassuring smile. As reassuring as she could, anyway; she would miss them all terribly. 'You need this time with your brothers and their families. And didn't you say Frank Altumara is going to be there?'

A rosy-pink blush touched Juanita's cheeks, and she patted at her coronet of braided dark hair before she reached for her paring knife again. 'You know he's just a friend.'

Frank had been a gorgeous actor on the movie set when the scandalous Bishop murder happened, and he also just happened to have been Juanita's youthful suitor, before she married. They'd been writing to each other ever since, and Maddie kept hoping something else would bloom – though she wouldn't like it so much if Juanita moved off to California!

'Of course, if you say so,' Maddie said. 'Tell him hello from me, and I want to hear all the movie gossip when you get back.' She glanced at the clock on the wall over the door. 'I have to run. I said I'd drop those sketches off at the museum.'

'Stop in at Kaune's grocery and get some more potatoes for dinner. Dr David said he'd eat with us, and I do worry they're not feeding him well enough at his lodgings.' Juanita always worried about everyone, but she seemed especially fond of David – and who wouldn't? He was handsome, kind, funny, and very bad at looking after himself, working long hours at the hospital and out at Sunmount, the TB clinic in the foothills.

'I'm sure he would never miss your shepherd's pie.' Maddie left Juanita to her cooking and went to fetch her coat and hat. As she went through the rooms, she paused to admire it all, as she did all the time. Her home, her refuge, her place to just be *herself.*

She'd loved the house ever since the first time she saw it, though it had been in a rather dilapidated state back then. Months of care and scrubbing had made it new again, with its thick, white-painted walls and dark viga ceilings, cozy fireplaces faced in blue tiles. Bedrooms, sitting rooms, and a welcoming dining room, filled with carved-wood Spanish furniture piled with bright embroidered cushions, shelves filled with books and pottery, splashes of brilliantly colored paintings on the walls. She'd added modern plumbing and electricity, but left everything else alone. It was all she'd ever wanted for herself.

She hurried into her own bedroom at the end of the corridor, a small but pretty and girly space, with an old Spanish bed hand-painted with roses and ribbons, crowned with a pink and white striped canopy. The same silk draped the windows, keeping out the winter cold. A dressing table draped in more pink was lined with crystal bottles and pots, silver-backed brushes and framed photographs – Juanita and the twins in the garden, Maddie and David in their engagement portrait, and her late husband, Pete, impossibly and forever young in his uniform before he left for France. She wondered if she would have to change it when David moved in, but imagined he wouldn't even notice.

She glanced in the mirror to smooth her wavy brown bob of hair, put on her hat and touch up her lipstick. As she reached for her fur-collared coat and the portfolio of sketches, Buttercup pushed the door open and whined to go along. 'OK, just this once,' Maddie said, and snapped on the dog's lead. 'I'd like the company.'

It was cold, but still and dry, the breeze smelling of woodsmoke and pine as Maddie and Buttercup strolled to the end of Canyon Road and turned toward the plaza. It felt like snow in the air, with its crisp, blue-tinged snap, and she noticed holiday decorations popping up everywhere. Wreaths on doors, swags of greenery, loads of firewood sliding past on sleds, ready to cheer up everyone's Christmas Eve bonfires.

As she walked, she imagined the painting she'd started working on in her studio. The image, progressing so well in its line and color in Maddie's mind, halted and reversed, like pencil marks erased. Her footsteps faltered in mid-stride, the heels of her new spectator pumps clicking into silence on the cobbles. Buttercup, cavorting so happily on the end of her lead, glanced back reproachfully.

'Sorry, darling,' Maddie told her. 'On our way in a trice, I promise.'

She opened the alligator handbag dangling from her elbow and dug around until she found her always-present notebook and little pencil. She flipped past lists of wedding ideas, many of them supplied by Pearl and Ruby, and Juanita's grocery shopping needs to a few line drawings. Just ideas to remember for the painting. She sketched them out and nodded with satisfaction.

She tucked the notebook away, gave a quick tug to Buttercup's lead, and continued on their little stroll, trying to forget about paintings, weddings and murder and just enjoy the clear winter sunshine.

She was grateful for the quiet days after all the uproar around Fiesta and Ricardo Montoya's death, of course she was. It was lovely having her peaceful home back again. She had just rather liked feeling *needed*, useful, that's all.

She reached the turn of the lane and paused to glance up at the sky from under the brim of her new blue felt hat. The cathedral lay ahead, its square stone bell towers mellow and golden in the winter light. A glorious image.

Buttercup gave a low but insistent bark, and tugged at her lead. She had been promised a walk, she knew there was a treat waiting at Mrs Nussbaum's tearoom, and she *would* have it.

'Sorry, Buttercup darling,' Maddie said, bending down to scritch the dog's pale ears. 'I know you hate to stop once you get near the plaza. You have people to greet, leaves to munch . . .'

'Maddie! Madeline Vaughn, is it really you?'

Maddie spun around at the sound of her name being cried out. Surely she knew that voice! It had been the terror of every field hockey player's heart at Miss Porter's School, especially that of reluctant athletes such as herself.

Katrina Wilton. Yes, it *was* her, leaping out of Maddie's girlhood memories and hurrying across the street, waving madly. Maddie was astonished – it seemed so many people ended up in her little southwestern town these days. Her old beau William. Now Katrina.

She hadn't changed much from their school days. She was still tall, broad-shouldered, a bit awkward, but so cheerful faced she made everyone near her smile. Her blonde hair, darkened a bit with streaks of light brown, was unfashionably long, looped up in braids under a wide-brimmed brown hat. She wore a tweed suit, beige jersey and black lace-up shoes with warm lisle stockings. A pile of parcels slipped and slid in her arms.

Maddie felt her heart lighten at the sight of her old friend. She'd always rather adored Katrina, despite those fearful school games. Katrina was always kind, always helpful, always ready to laugh and jolly everyone along.

'Katrina! Whatever are you doing here?' Maddie called, hurrying to meet her. Buttercup trotted along, always happy to meet a new friend. 'Gosh, is it really you?'

They met at the picket fence edging the plaza, and Maddie leaned in to give Katrina a quick *bise* on both cheeks. But Katrina dropped her parcels and caught her in a sudden, squeezing hug, almost lifting her heeled shoes off the ground.

Maddie laughed and wrapped her arms around Katrina in an answering hug as Buttercup whined at their feet.

'Oh, Mads, it *is* grand to see you again,' Katrina said. She let go of Maddie and tilted her head back to study Maddie's stylish blue suit and fur-trimmed coat. 'And just look at you! Such a fashion plate. New Mexico seems to agree with you.'

'You look spiffing, too.' It wasn't *quite* true. At first glance, her old friend truly hadn't changed a bit, with her healthy good looks and lively brown eyes. But up close she looked rather tired, lines of strain lining those eyes and her lipstick-free mouth, her usually rosy complexion now pale. Her old, hearty cheerfulness, so much a part of her, seemed to have a strange, strained quality. 'Whatever are *you* doing in Santa Fe? The last I heard you had gone to be a nurse?' Her mother had been quite scandalized. A *Wilton* girl, working? But that was before Maddie ran away to be an artist, which was even worse.

'Oh, I married a local boy. Alfonso Luhan. Al. Hadn't you heard? I met him in New York during the war, when I was doing my nurse's training and he was about to be sent to France. We've been away for a few years, in California, but his family owns a rancho called Los Pintores in the country here, and they wanted him to come home. Thought we might as well try it. They say the air here is very healthy.'

'Los Pintores. Yes, I've heard of it; it's said to be one of the largest and loveliest in the area. And you married their son?' Maddie tried to remember what she knew of the Luhans, an old family who had owned their land for hundreds of years as a grant from the Spanish crown. They seldom came into town, but she knew they had a few sons.

Katrina laughed, which sounded a little forced and rusty, as if her formerly plentiful laughter didn't get used much now. 'Funny, isn't it? I always thought I'd be a spinster, running about doing good works, but here I am. I'd heard you became an artist! We were always sure you would at school, your drawings were so lovely.'

'Yes, I am! Just starting out, really, but I've had an exhibit or two at the Museum of Art here, and some portrait commissions.'

'That's wonderful!' Katrina's smile faded a bit, and she added, 'I was ever so sorry to hear about Pete. What a terrible thing the war was.'

Maddie thought of those dark days, the time of being lost in a deep hole, and she glanced away, blinking. 'Thank you, Katrina. It was such a blow.'

'You were such a handsome couple. All of us Miss Porter's girls envied you.'

'Did you? How funny, as I always envied you, and your wonderful skill at games. I do miss Pete so much. But time can be a wonderful healer . . . and I *am* engaged again. To a handsome, sweet doctor. So, I do agree this is a healthy place to be.'

'Engaged! Oh, Mads, that's so wonderful. Is he gorgeous? I'm sure he must be. Is he . . .' She paused, as if searching for words. 'Is he from some old local family, like my Al?'

'Yes, he's gorgeous, but he's not local. He's from England, actually.'

Katrina's eyes widened. 'Could he be Dr Cole? Oh, he *is* dishy, if an old married lady like me can say so.'

'You know David?'

'Not so well. We're – well, the truth is, we're here in Santa Fe for a few days so Al can see some doctors, find out if they can help him. Your Dr Cole sat in on a consultation. How kind he was!'

'Katrina. Is everything all right?' Maddie asked gently, concerned by the worry she saw drifting over her friend's face.

'I . . . not really. The war. He can't quite get over it, you see, and . . .' Katrina ended up on a choked little sob, making Maddie even more worried. The old Katrina never, ever cried.

'How about a cup of tea? I was just headed to Mrs Nussbaum's tearoom over there, she makes lovely cinnamon toast.' Buttercup gave a yip at the sound of her favorite place.

Katrina glanced down. Her face lit up, changing from the verge of tears to complete joy in an instant. Maddie had forgotten what a first-rate animal lover her old friend was. Katrina knelt down to greet Buttercup, who ecstatically licked her nose and curled close. Buttercup always knew when people needed her; she was a fierce friend and protector to Maddie and the twins and anyone else in trouble.

'What a handsome fella, Maddie! Is he yours? Just look at that adorable widdle nose.'

'Yes indeed, but the fella is a girl. Buttercup. I rescued her on a walk one day when she'd gotten herself rather stuck in an arroyo.'

'I'd love to have a little lap doggo myself. It does get a bit lonesome at Los Pintores.' Katrina sounded wistful. But her cheerful smile was quickly pasted back on again, and she gave Buttercup a kiss on the top of her fuzzy head before gathering up her parcels and standing. Dust streaked her tweed skirt. 'Let's go have that cuppa. Al is at the hospital; he won't be done until after lunchtime. I'm longing to hear more about your gorgeous doctor, and all you're doing here! Oh, Mads, you are a sight for sore eyes. I'm so glad to see you again.'

'And I'm glad to see you.' Maddie led her into Mrs Nussbaum's tearoom, a haven of white wicker and copious green plants, smelling of spices and fresh bread, warm and cozy. Buttercup flopped down, flat on her belly on the wood planks of the floor, ready to snooze and wait for treats. The tea and toast quickly arrived as Maddie and Katrina chatted about old school days, their families, art and books.

'I really can't tell you how very happy I am to see you, Mads old thing,' Katrina said as she reached for the last piece of toast. 'It's been a beastly few months since we came here. And I'd hoped coming home would do Al some good!'

Maddie was really worried now. Katrina, always so positive and cheerful, looked at the end of her rope. 'Your husband is really ill? All the doctors, you said.'

Katrina sighed. 'Yes, ill. The war hit some men hard, they can't let go of what they saw. When we first met, he was so happy, so strong and merry. We had so much fun! Now – now he can't sleep, can't eat. He won't talk to me much; he just seems to drift further and further away from me.'

'Oh, Katrina, I am so sorry.' Maddie thought of the men she'd seen in the hospital in New York, where she volunteered just after the war. Pale, ghostly men who drifted through the corridors, not seeing what was around them, haunted by nightmares and visions of the horrors they'd been through. It made her heart ache to know Katrina's husband was one of them.

'We usually rub along all right. Living in California, where it's warm and there's the ocean. He can forget, sometimes. But he always talked about New Mexico like it had some kind of magic, the mountains and deserts, the huge sky. I imagined being here, with his family, could be a good thing.'

'And it's not?'

'Not much. It's all just . . .' Katrina's voice trailed away as a waitress brought more tea. She dug into her battered tapestry handbag and came up with a silver cigarette case. 'I don't usually smoke – constricts the lungs, you know. But sometimes a girl's gotta do what a girl's gotta do, yes?'

'Go right ahead, Katrina darling. You were saying Los Pintores isn't doing your husband much good?' She tried to remember if she had ever met the Luhans, but all she could remember was a stern-looking Don Victor Luhan, owner of the estate, and a pale, pretty wife at a Fiesta dance. She hadn't met them, but they seemed to be an object of much respect in town. People like that were not always the most forgiving of perceived weaknesses, of letting the family image down in any way.

'Yes.' Katrina exhaled a long, silvery plume of smoke, and slipped Buttercup a bit of toast. 'The country air does seem a benefit to him. It's so quiet there, and we go on long walks. Their housekeeper is an excellent cook, too, and she can tempt him into eating a bit more. But his family! There have been . . . incidents.'

Maddie frowned. 'Incidents?'

'Quarrels with his father, mostly. Don Victor Luhan. Oh, he does remind me of my old grandpapa! You remember him? The Admiral?'

Maddie shuddered to remember that cold-eyed old man. 'Sure I do. He would show up on family days at school sometimes and bark at all of us.'

'Well, Don Victor likes to bark, too. He is so particular about how everything must be in his house, he's such a tyrant. Al's brothers can escape – Sam works the land and Ben is at university – but Al and me, and his sister Helena, are stuck there listening to it all. Al can't work now, with his lungs and his nightmares, and I only have a little money of my own from my grandmother. My parents send a bit once in a while, but they're a bit tight these days, too, since Pa doesn't agree with owning stocks and shares. We won't have much until Don Victor pops off, and I'm sure he'll outlive us all, so we're stuck there for now.'

'The cranky ones always do seem to live to be a hundred,' Maddie murmured. 'Is there no hope for Al's health?'

Katrina shrugged and stubbed out her cigarette as she refused to meet Maddie's eyes. Maddie feared her friend was trying to be brave, trying not to reveal a deep despair. 'Who knows? Your handsome Dr Cole and his colleagues seem hopeful, which is nice. Al didn't want me to hang about while he was having his exam today.'

'If anyone can help, or know where you can find the best help, it's certainly David.' Maddie reached out to touch Katrina's trembling hand. 'I'm sure it will all work out. Can I help in any way?'

Katrina nodded and flashed an overly bright smile. 'Could you maybe – oh, no, it's too much.'

'Tell me! I want so much to help, I do.'

'Well. Are you busy for Christmas?'

Maddie thought of Juanita and the twins leaving for their pueblo, her quiet sitting room. 'Not at all. What are you thinking of?'

'They're having a house party at Los Pintores. They say it's quite a holiday tradition. Al's brothers will be there, and a friend or two of theirs, as well as my parents-in-law and maybe a few neighbors. It's very beautiful there, really, and could be inspirational for your art! There's also a writer coming too, staying in the casita while he does some research on a new novel. A Mr Gunther Ryder. I'm not much of a reader, I'm afraid, but they say he's very good.'

'Gunther's there?' Maddie cried. That son-of-a-gun. Her neighbor and best friend *had* been rather quiet lately, which wasn't like him, and just said a few mysterious things about a new project and a writing retreat.

'You know him?'

'Quite a coincidence! He's my neighbor. He is certain to cheer you up; he is such fun.'

'Then you certainly must come, too. Do say you will. It would be so nice to have someone in *my* corner out there for once.'

'Come to Los Pintores for Christmas?'

'Yes. I know I make them all sound wretched, but it's not all that way. Helena is lovely, and Sam is a brick. And the land is so beautiful, with the river nearby. You could bring your doctor! I'd love for him to spend more time with Al, if he can. And Buttercup, of course.'

Maddie turned this over in her mind. She was truly worried about Katrina and wanted to help. And getting away with David for the holiday did sound enticing. 'Of course I will, Katrina. It sounds so Christmas-y indeed!'

TWO

'On the third day of Christmas, my true love gave to me – five gold rings!' Maddie sang, then paused. 'No, no, that's not right.' She laughed and kicked at a melting clump of snow.

David laughed with her as they made their way through the frosty slush of the winding streets, past the Loretto Academy where Pearl and Ruby went to school, dark and closed against the purple-black winter sky. Arm in arm, leaning happily against each other, they paused to take a deep breath of the minty-cold air. The cathedral bells tolled in the distance.

'It's nearly time for Los Posadas,' Maddie said, the time two weeks before Christmas where the faithful lead a parishioner dressed as Mary and a tiny baby around the plaza on a donkey, begging for a place to stay. They were always turned away, until they found a spot in a courtyard at the Palace of the Governors and were given hot cider and biscochitos. It was always beautiful, with music and farolitos lighting the night, the whole town gathered together. 'Surely that makes my songs not too early!'

'My grandmother used to say never before Christmas Eve,' David said. 'And not gone before Twelfth Night.'

'So did my nanny, but she can't see me now! I love my own life here, and I love when I sing Christmas songs!' She threw her arms out wide and spun around and around. 'Five gold rrrrrrrings!' David laughed and caught her up in his arms to spin her around and around, making her laugh even harder. As he slid her to the ground, their lips met, soft and sweet and full of promise.

'I can't wait to spend every Christmas from now on with you, Maddie,' he whispered.

'Despite my off-key tunes?'

'*Because* of your off-key tunes. No one has a way with "Yes Sir, That's My Baby" like you do.'

They walked on, arm in arm, content just to be together. Life felt just right in that moment.

'You know, David darling, I don't think I've ever been so happy,' she said. 'I never imagined there *could* be this much happiness!' She held tight to his arm and let memories, old and new, good and bad, wash over her. When she was young, she'd never have dreamed she could break away to live her own life, where and how she wanted. Find just the right man. Now here it all was.

'Neither did I. Not in a million years,' he said quietly, and she feared he was thinking of the war, of the way he'd lost his first wife.

'But I can't quite stop thinking about poor Katrina.' Maddie remembered Katrina's tired face, the defeated droop of her shoulders. She loved Al as much as Maddie loved David, and she was full of fear for him.

'Your old friend and her husband?'

'Katrina was always so light-hearted and merry! And so very kind to everyone. They don't deserve this.'

'I've seen so many lads come home like him. Is that really a life at all?'

David hadn't told her much of *his* war, patching up the wounded in inadequate field hospitals, but Maddie knew enough to worry about him deeply. 'I hope you're not terribly disappointed I told them we'd visit for Christmas. I know how much we love a Santa Fe holiday. Bonfires, lights on the plaza, the music . . .'

'I *do* love a Santa Fe Christmas – especially with you. But I want to help your friends as much as you do, if I can. War does such hellish things to a person. Maybe I can point him toward the right doctors, the right treatments. And we'll have next Christmas here at home.'

'As Dr and Mrs Cole!' Maddie shivered at how strange that sounded, at the thought of all the changes, good and bad, coming for them. She was glad to see the front steps of La Fonda up ahead, the carved doors opening to welcome them, her second home in Santa Fe.

The flagstone-floor foyer, dotted with brightly cushioned Spanish chairs and tables, the long reception desk, was quiet at that hour, just a few people milling about. Maddie paused to take off her snow boots and fur-edged coat, exchanging them for a spangled shawl and stylish new bottle-green T-straps. She glanced at a tin-framed mirror and smoothed her brown bob, tied back with a green ribbon bandeau, and shook out the skirts of her green gored-skirt dress, edged with sequined flowers.

A new frock, from the box sent by her cousin Gwen in California. Maddie thought it rather the bee's knees, and hoped David might admire it, but he seldom paid attention to clothes. He thought she looked best in a painter's smock, the darling man.

She took his arm and they turned toward the lobby, all high carved viga ceilings and colorful murals, tall silver vases filled with holiday greenery. Wreaths and ribbons hung along the stairway. One direction led to the restaurant and elevators, the other to the bar. Maddie was quite looking forward to the hotel's specialty – a gin Orange Flower in a teacup.

'Mrs Vaughn-Alwin!' a voice called.

Putting orange blossoms and holiday plans out of her mind, she turned to smile at Anton, the Swiss concierge and all-round seer of everything at La Fonda. He always took care of every tiny detail of the hotel, from the carpets to the vigas to the food and the sheets, and always made sure Maddie's favorite table was ready at the restaurant. He hurried toward her, dodging around the bellhops with their carts, the befuddled tourists with maps, just to shake David's hand. Anton was always the very image of fashion in his perfectly tailored dark suit, his pomaded gold hair and Van Dyke beard, his monocle in place so he wouldn't miss a thing.

'Anton,' she said, returning his continental *bise*. 'How lovely to see you again. It's been much too long. I had to quite scramble to finish my pieces for the January art museum opening, and David has been so short-handed at the hospital, so many new patients.' David did try to reassure her, but she couldn't help but worry the days of the flu were coming back upon them.

'Indeed, this is always the strangest, busiest time of year here in Santa Fe!' Anton said. 'And shall we see you here for our Christmas Eve party?'

Maddie remembered – or sort of remembered – last year's party, there being a lot of very nice champagne. Dancing, a jazz band. Will Shuster breaking the elevator from riding it too much. Usual stuff. Wonderful stuff. 'I'm afraid not! I'm going to visit an old school friend, she married a Luhan and lives at Los Pintores. I'll be here for New Year's Eve, though! Couldn't miss that. Gunther should be back then, too, so things will be ever so jolly.'

No party was complete without Gunther, especially the gathering of the year – New Year's Eve dancing at La Fonda, with sunrise breakfast at the White sisters' El Deliriro estate.

Anton smiled and rubbed his hands together in satisfaction. 'Yes, yes! Santa Fe is never the same without Mr Ryder. My champagne stores have built up shockingly without him. Isn't he also at this Los Pintores?'

'Yes,' Maddie said. 'To try and settle down and finish his latest novel; it's terribly late. Poor Gunther, he's having such fits about it.'

Anton shook his head ruefully. 'Ah, Los Pintores. I would have recommended he take a room here; he'd get more peace and quiet. I hope you'll all return very soon, Mrs Vaughn-Alwin.'

Maddie tilted her head to study him curiously. 'Really? Why? I hear it's very beautiful up there.'

'Oh, it is. For one who enjoys such a . . . rural style.' Which Maddie knew Anton did not, nor did Gunther. 'A lovely old house, lots of history, beautiful artworks. And in the summer Mrs Luhan wins so many prizes for her roses and attends so many parties – or used to. Don Victor Luhan is quite the homebody, unlike his wife. It's just so far from town and, well, one does *hear* things . . .'

'Things?' Maddie whispered. She had no doubt Anton heard everything that happened five counties away.

'The family is not all completely in harmony, that is all. But with four such grown children, what should one expect?' He flashed her one of his wide, professional smiles. 'Nothing terribly interesting, I fear, nothing to keep you from having a fine holiday. Now, your table is ready, and I must see to those pesky old invoices in my office! Go, enjoy yourselves, my dears. Plan your wedding!'

David took Maddie's arm and they made their way out of the lobby toward the bar before dinner. La Fonda was getting to be quite the place in town for meetings, and it was certainly one of the most elegant, though not in the stuffy, every-bit-perfect way of her mother's New York haunts. It was built in the style of a Spanish hacienda, on the site where hotels had stood since the 1600s, centering on an open courtyard with a multi-tiered tiled fountain at its center, open to the blue sky above.

Maddie glimpsed the fountain, the ghostly shapes of wrought-iron tables and chairs beyond the tall doors of hand-painted glass panes. She herself had done a few of those, scenes of roses and lavender in her garden.

In the summer, everyone liked to lounge out there in the sun, but in winter weather everyone stayed under the covered portal on the south, with its large fireplace.

The corridors around the courtyard were filled with painted Spanish furniture, much like Maddie's own house, cushioned with sheepskin and with bright Navajo rugs on the floors, warming the whole space.

Maddie glimpsed Eddie, Juanita's son, as he carried some bags toward the elevator. He waved and called her name, and she waved back, marveling at how tall he had become, how far he'd traveled since she'd first met him. Juanita used to worry he would get into criminal trouble around town; now he was working steadily at La Fonda, winning promotions. Anton said he would go far, and Maddie couldn't have been prouder if she'd been his true auntie instead of honorary.

She held David's hand, whispering little sweet nothings together as they neared the bar tucked at the end of the lobby. It was dark and cozy there, except for a man playing guitar on the small stage, pale amber light glowing above the oval bar, people gathered in red leather booths and on sheepskin stools.

They waved at a friend milling around – Olive Rush, the tall, energetic organizer of all things artistic. An Eastern heiress who, like Maddie, never quite fit in that life and had to come to New Mexico to discover herself, threw them a kiss. She was never sleeping, always in her Navajo velvet skirts and an elaborate turban of her own design, always moving and planning. Maddie waved back, and turned away since she knew if she talked to Olive, Olive would recruit her to some more work, as she always did with everyone.

They went to hop up on leather bar stools, where David struck up a conversation with a fellow doctor to his left, analyzing a case as he often did while they were out, and Maddie ordered an Orange Blossom disguised in a tea cup from Marco, the usual evening bartender.

'I hear you're off to the Luhan place for Christmas,' he said, pouring and mixing like an alchemist.

'Word gets around fast.' She laughed.

He shrugged. 'It's La Fonda! Wouldn't you rather stay here for our party? Gonna be a humdinger. They got the Pips Morrison Five to play for the dancing.'

'Anton said the same thing,' Maddie said. She was tempted by that dancing, but she'd already promised Katrina. 'Is there something dangerous out there? At Los Pintores?'

Marco handed her the drink and glanced around as if to see if anyone was listening. Everyone was already floating happy on that gin, chatting and laughing. 'Not dangerous, I'd say, just . . . weird. Everyone's been scared of Don Victor for decades – his family's always held a lot of power here, and if he thinks you're behaving improperly or not taking care of your property like you should, you might find your holdings under threat. My uncle did.'

'How can one man do that on private property?' she asked.

'He has lawyers. And he has the freehold on a lot. His family's original land grant was huge. Mostly it's his family, though, the way he keeps a tight grasp on them. Ben, the middle son, he's off at university, but no one's really seen Helena since she left Loretto, and that's too bad! She's a real looker. Señora Luhan used to enjoy a party herself, but we never see her, either. But mostly it's the ghosts . . .'

'Ghosts?' Maddie whispered. She loved a good spooky story.

'They say a woman got pushed down the staircase at Los Pintores once at a party, and you can still hear her scream. When she does, it means something bad will happen to the family. There's a white horse that runs the fields, a little girl who stares in the window . . .'

'My goodness,' Maddie whispered. Family feuds and ghostly horses, too. It would be an interesting holiday indeed.

But there wasn't another minute to shiver deliciously over haunted corridors, for she was caught up in the foxtrot across the small dance floor, amid all the other whirling couples. She danced and laughed until her feet quite ached in their new T-strap shoes, and she had to pause. She went to lean against the paneled wall to cool off for a moment, and studied a new painting hanging there. A tempestuous storm moving in over the mountains, roiling clouds against a blue-gray sky. Garish purples and slashes of black tried to enhance the drama, but only distracted.

'Ghastly, isn't it?' someone said. 'The hotel should have consulted me before choosing it.'

Maddie turned to see her friend Olive Rush standing there, a teacup in hand. Tall, draped in a pleated red velvet Navajo skirt and blue satin turban, Olive was always a distinctive figure dashing around town, her portfolio of paintings usually under her arm and a mission at the museum or studio in mind.

'Olive, darling!' Maddie said. 'It . . . it's not that bad, really. I do like what they've done with the color of the sky there.'

Olive snorted. 'You're always too sweet, Maddie, my dear. I would say it's garish, doesn't capture the spirit of the place at all. And we have so many stunning pieces at the museum I'd be happy to loan! I must speak to Anton at once.' She took a sip from her cup, studying Maddie over its gilded edge. 'Marco tells me you'll be spending the holiday at the Luhan place.'

'Yes. Word does get around. My old school friend Katrina is married to Alfonso Luhan, and she asked me out there for a few days. I think she's feeling lonely so far from town.'

Olive grimaced sympathetically. 'Who wouldn't be? Poor girl. I've heard it's utterly dismal out there these days. And it used to be rather jolly! Be sure and take hot-water bottles, and a fur if you have one.'

'David is going with me. Should he take a mink, too?'

Olive hooted with laughter. 'Then you'll be sure to keep each other warm! Our favorite lovebirds.'

Maddie laughed, too, even though she felt the warmth of a blush wash over her cheeks. His kisses *were* rather shivery-hot. 'You say it used to be jolly? Have you been there often?'

'Not for some time, and never often. Isabella Luhan used to consider herself quite a patron of the arts, and she invited me to parties two or three times. Trying to get some artistic salon together.'

'Was she a useful patron, then?' Maddie found herself more and more curious about this odd family, after what Katrina and Marco had told her.

'Hmm, yes – and no. Her taste was atrocious. She would have adored that painting over there! And she could never quite decide which arts she wanted to support most – writing, painting, theater, music. She even tried to get a dance troupe here once. But money could sometimes be got out of her, if you knew how to go about it. And she knew how to throw a party! Such luscious food, the best champagne, music and dancing, tea in the garden.'

'What happened then? Katrina told me it's quiet as tombs out there now.'

Olive shrugged, the long fringe on her embroidered shawl shimmering. 'Who knows? Time does march onward. Her husband, Don Victor, never did seem to appreciate art. Or fun, for that matter. He probably put his foot down and made her stop all the socializing and spending. He was certainly strict on his children, insisting they always march to the beat of *his* drum, always be perfect to his own standards. Then their son was injured in the war, and Isabella became quite a recluse.'

'I am sorry to hear that. That poor woman.' Maddie thought of the Christmas that lay ahead of her, quiet and dull, with a tense, unhappy family around her. Her heart ached even more for Katrina.

'Do you think all the Luhan clan will be there, then?'

'I think so. Alfonso has a sister and two brothers, I believe.'

'It shouldn't always be *too* boring, then. Helena Luhan used to be quite the wheeze when she was at school here at Loretto, gave the nuns fits with her pranks! Always sneaking away to get into trouble.' Olive frowned as she studied the colorful whirl of the dance floor. 'I would just stay away from Don Victor as much as possible if I were you, Maddie dear.'

'I certainly will. He sounds utterly dreary. I'll just be there to help Katrina, if I can.'

'Well, do take your sketchbook with you, along with that fur. No matter what, it's stunningly beautiful country out there. The sky and trees, all those colors – even in winter.' A frown flickered over her long face, and she gently touched Maddie's arm. 'Just be careful, yes? We need your art for the new museum show this spring.'

Before Maddie could ask what exactly she needed to be 'careful' about, David came to her side. He slipped his arm around her and kissed her cheek, making her smile. If he was with her, the holiday couldn't be too dreadful.

'Ah, love's bright dream,' Olive said happily. 'I am glad you're going to Los Pintores with our Maddie, Dr Cole. You'll keep an eye on her, won't you?'

'Always. It's my very favorite thing to do in life.' David beamed down at Maddie, making her feel all warm and aglow again. 'Would you care for one more dance before we go into dinner?'

'I would utterly love that.'

'Go, go!' Olive said, shooing them off with her turquoise-laden hand. 'Enjoy yourselves.'

Maddie certainly intended to. Yet even as she whirled in David's arms, the music spiraling them higher and higher, she felt a touch of trepidation at the thought of the upcoming holiday. What had she really let them in for?

THREE

'Look, I think we're nearly there!' Maddie said, waving the map she was meant to be reading toward a crooked sign etched with the words *Los Pintores*.

David turned off the main road and through a pair of wrought-iron gates that led on to a graveled driveway. It wound up and around, bouncing over ruts made worse by the recent snowfall, and Maddie glimpsed the river running past stands of towering cottonwood trees, dark juniper and piñon forests beyond, a pond with a summerhouse, horses in a paddock, several outbuildings.

At last, they emerged on to a circular drive that skirted an empty fountain and there was the hacienda itself. Very elegant, three stories in a square, the roof dotted with chimneys, a covered portal all around the second floor. It was painted a pale beige with blue trim around the many windows and tall doors. A low, stone wall surrounded the house and its gardens, holding back the rest of the sweeping estate, the looming woods. She could see that in the summer there would be climbing roses and spreading lilac bushes, but now all was dusted with snow and iced with frost.

It was all designed to impress, a handsome oasis against a majestic backdrop of natural beauty, and Maddie had to admit she *was* rather impressed. She could just imagine the Christmas parties they must have there, as Katrina said they were a tradition. Light and music spilling out of the windows.

Yet there was something else, something strange about all that grandness. Something disquieting. A silence seemed to hover over it all, like a bubble of ice, some tense sensation of waiting, watching. It rather gave her the shivers, and she thought of Marco's tales of ghosts. She could well imagine it was not the place for a shell-shocked man.

Buttercup seemed to feel it, too. She gave a little whimper, and crowded closer to Maddie as they circled an empty stone fountain and came to a stop on the oval drive in front of the carved double front doors.

As Maddie stepped out on to the gravel, wrapping her coat closer against the chilly wind, the elaborately carved, heavy front doors opened and Katrina came bounding out.

'Mads, you're here at last!' she cried as she ran down the steps, her long brown cardigan flapping around her, tendrils of hair escaping her coronet of braids. 'And your sweet doggo! And Dr Cole, of course. My, you are even more handsome than I remembered!'

David actually blushed, his cheeks turning rosy above his short, golden beard, and Maddie giggled to see it. 'Er – thank you, Mrs Luhan. So pleased to be here. I want to hear all the shocking tales of Maddie's misspent school days.'

Katrina gave a hoot of laughter. 'Oh, I do have a few of those. All the girls on our corridor came up with such wheezes, do you remember, Maddie? Those were the days. Well, come in, come in! We're all gathering in the sala, it's getting bally cold out here. Will the snow fall soon, do you think? We could go sledding.' She caught up a wriggling Buttercup under her arm and led them inside.

They stepped into a darkened foyer, with a sweeping staircase ahead of them and doors to either side. Perhaps that was the staircase the ghostly lady tumbled down to her death? Paintings hung on the whitewashed walls, dour-looking Luhan ancestors and landscapes of the house and garden in brighter, sunnier times, while a faded, flowered carpet runner ran up the stairs. A maid appeared to take their wraps and quickly vanished again.

'Come on,' Katrina said. 'Everyone is in the sala upstairs, it's really the only warm room in the house.' She dashed up the stairs, turning on a landing to go along a corridor toward a pair of double doors. 'The bedrooms are on the next floor up, but the sala and dining room are here.'

The sala, the grand salon that was always the heart of such old haciendas, was a long, vast room, the wood floors covered with more patterned carpets, faded tapestry chairs and settees lining the walls along with glass-fronted bookcases and gilt-framed paintings, none of which looked very good to Maddie's artist eyes. But the dark wood vigas of the ceiling spoke of many warm, cheerful fires from the two fireplaces at either end of the room, their surrounds painted in scenes of flowers and vines Maddie recognized as work by her friend Olive Rush, and she remembered Katrina had said Isabella Luhan liked to be seen as a patron of the arts. There was a glorious grand piano, and stunning blackware pueblo pottery arrayed on carved tables. A Christmas tree was up in one corner but not decorated, while pine and holly garlands wound around the windows and paintings, a beribboned wreath over the fireplace.

Maddie paused for a moment in the doorway, struck by how much like a stage set it all was, just like the outside of the estate. It all seemed so *organized*, like something by Shaw or Wilde, if they had set plays on a New Mexico rancho. The players were gathered in neat groupings near the fire, as if posed.

A fire crackled in the tiled grate, with a tea table laid out beside it such as she hadn't seen since visiting the Plaza Hotel with her mother. Sèvres porcelain tiered plates arranged with sandwiches, cakes, rolls, a silver samovar, gilt-rimmed cups thin as eggshells and painted with lilies of the valley.

And the characters were as carefully arranged as the refreshments. Two young people, a woman and man, sat in a window seat. A very thin lady, pale-fragile except for her red-rouged cheeks and lips, silvery-blonde hair piled high atop her head, lounged on a velvet chaise, wrapped in several cashmere shawls. Her eyes, also a pale blue, seemed barely lined, and beneath her wraps she wore a stylish tea gown of mauve chiffon, with fine pearls draped around her neck.

A very distinguished-looking gentleman in a well-cut gray suit, the waves of his salt-and-pepper hair echoed in a pointed beard, hovered solicitously behind her. Maddie wondered if he was Katrina's curmudgeonly father-in-law, as she couldn't quite remember what Don Victor looked like from that Fiesta dance.

'This is my mother-in-law, Maddie, Señora Isabella Luhan,' Katrina said. She deposited Buttercup on the needlepoint hearthrug, where the pup sniffed curiously under a tile-topped table. Katrina poured Maddie and David cups of tea. 'And her doctor, Dr William Pierce, who has come all the way from Denver for Christmas. Mama-Isabella, this is my very old school friend from New York, Madeline Vaughn-Alwin, and her fiancé, Dr David Cole. Perhaps you know each other, Dr Pierce?'

Dr Pierce smiled faintly. 'I don't believe so, though the name sounds familiar. You are at Sunmount, yes?'

'Yes, indeed,' David answered. 'Though I also consult at the hospital in Santa Fe.'

'But you are not, I think, from New Mexico. Your accent . . .'

'From Brighton originally, yes. I've been here for several years, it's quite an astonishing place.' David bowed low over Isabella's hand, making her giggle happily.

'Yes, astonishing,' Dr Pierce said faintly, giving Isabella a rather disapproving glance. Perhaps the doctor thought giggling at handsome men wasn't healthy for her or something. 'I was originally from Connecticut myself. I was a surgeon, but now mostly a private physician in my semi-retirement. Isabella has visited my clinic a few times, and was most kind to invite me for the holiday.' He flashed her an adoring smile to replace the disapproval, and she beamed back.

'I couldn't do without you, Willie darling, and you know it,' she said. She glanced at Maddie and gave a faint smile. 'I had a terrible case of the flu in 1918, you see, Mrs Vaughn-Alwin, and I just haven't been the same since. So very tired all the time, and such headaches! Willie has quite saved me.'

'How dreadful for you!' Maddie exclaimed, thinking of the terrible flu cases she'd seen in her volunteer work. It seemed maybe some of Los Pintores's air of sadness was because of all the illness within its walls.

'We are so glad dear Alfonso met a lady with nursing experience, too,' Isabella said. She held out her cup for Katrina to refill without a word of request. 'Such a help. And you were friends with Katrina in New York?'

'Yes, we were at school together,' Maddie answered. 'Katrina was so much more popular there than I was! I was always in the corner scribbling away in a sketchbook while she made friends with everyone and led all our games.'

Isabella tilted her head as she studied Maddie closer. 'Ah, yes. You are the artist, correct? I think you did Catalina Montoya's portrait.'

'I did. She was a wonderful model.' And Maddie had also helped catch the killer of Catalina's husband. But that didn't seem to be a good topic for tea talk.

'She is a such a dear lady; I see her whenever my health permits me to visit Santa Fe. We were at school at Loretto together. Poor Catalina! Such trials she has known lately. But I hear she is soon to remarry? Very swift. Well, I look forward to seeing the portrait soon. I am quite the connoisseur of art.' She waved a thin, beringed hand at the landscapes and sea scenes on the walls, their heavy gold frames glinting.

'Oh, Mama, I'm sure an artist from New York isn't interested in your fusty old oils,' the young woman in the window seat said disdainfully.

Maddie glanced over at her, and the man who sat beside her. They were both extraordinarily good-looking, the lady fashionably whippet-thin in a cream sweater and tweed skirt, her blonde hair cut in a sharply angled bob, the man equally blond, equally striking.

'And that,' Isabella said tightly, 'is my terribly rude daughter Helena. The Sisters at the school at Loretto didn't do her much good, I fear.'

'They certainly did! I became terribly good at climbing out of windows and hiding, and such things. Very useful. Except out here in the middle of nowhere,' Helena said with a cheerful, red-lipsticked grin. 'How d'ye do, Mrs Vaughn-Alwin. I want to hear all about the parties in Santa Fe these days, as I moulder away here in the silence. Oh, but do be warned, never sit in that armchair by the fire, it's Papa's and he won't let anyone else use it.' She waved toward a red velvet chair, which was indeed empty.

'You could be in Santa Fe all the time, Helena, if you did

your duty and married properly,' Isabella snapped. The flush in her cheeks rose higher, and Dr Pierce leaned closer to soothe her.

'Where would be the fun in that?' Helena snorted.

'Besides, you'd probably be married off to someone with another rancho, and still be stuck in another quiet hole,' the man beside Helena said. 'Too dull. I'm Benito, by the way, Ben, youngest son of the house. Studying law at Princeton, for my sins, and home for the holidays. Ever so happy to see new faces here. My father is in his library, and brother Sam is out checking the fields before the snow falls or some such. I brought home a friend, Felipe, jolly fellow, rather keen on Helena, but for some reason he insisted on taking a look at the estate with Sam. I guess they have to make sure the McTeers aren't making mischief.'

'The McTeers?' Maddie asked.

'Just neighbors to the south,' Dr Pierce said. 'I doubt we'll see them out in such weather. Lazy Scots.'

Ben laughed. 'Not so lazy as all that, are they? Their estate is thriving while we sink down. It's all so Montague and Capulet around here.'

Maddie's curiosity was piqued by the promise of a feud, but she couldn't ask more as the sala door opened and a lady in rustling black bombazine hurried in, a tray of more sandwiches and cakes in her hands. She was plump, with threads of iron-gray running through her tightly pinned black hair, but it was obvious she'd once been very pretty. Maybe attractiveness was in the water at Los Pintores. She glanced over the gathering, her lips pursed as if she rather disapproved of it all. Maddie thought of Juanita's ready smiles and cheerful conversation, their laughter in the kitchen, and was doubly glad she'd found someone like Juanita and her family.

'More refreshments, Señora Isabella,' the woman said as she plunked down the tray. 'Señor Sam will be hungry when he comes in.'

'Thank you, Marta,' Isabella said faintly, waving her away. 'Could you refresh the samovar, too, please?'

'Oh, goodie, chocolate buns, my favorite,' Katrina said, with a flash of her old heartiness. 'Come on, Maddie, have a few more cakes, you must be famished after your drive.'

Maddie realized she was, rather, despite the picnic Juanita had packed for the journey. Juanita never quite trusted anyone else's housekeeping and had sent far too much to eat. 'I am, yes, but . . .' She glanced around, seeing that Alfonso and his other brother weren't there yet, nor was the fearsome Don Victor. 'Should we wait for the others? Or perhaps Alfonso is rather tired today?'

Katrina peeked at the doorway, a glimmer of uncertainty dimming her cheerfulness for an instant. 'I'm sure he's right as rain. Just went out for a little walk.'

'The fresh air will certainly do him good,' Dr Pierce said. 'He must raise himself out of his torpor for more exercise.'

'He wanted to be alone for a while,' Katrina said. 'We should get some of those chocolate buns before Helena and Ben snaffle them all up!'

'We certainly wouldn't!' Helena protested.

Maddie glanced at the tea table to see the best cakes were indeed being 'snaffled' by Ben and her own traitorous fiancé. David gave her a guilty little smile and offered an almond scone.

'You have to try the lemon tarts,' Helena said as she came over to fill her teacup. 'Marta is a wonder at them! She's been with us forever, and I used to steal them from the kitchen all the time when I was a child. I would get tremendously scolded!'

'Not much has changed, eh, Helie?' her brother said, nudging her teasingly.

David wandered over to talk shop with Dr Pierce, and Maddie shared some of the Santa Fe gossip with Katrina, Helena and Ben, laughing with them over the White sisters' grand new swimming pool, and the time the poet Witter Bynner drunkenly tumbled in while declaiming a new verse and dressed in Grecian robes. Suddenly, the door swung open and Alfonso Luhan appeared there, looking around at them as if he'd never seen them before in his life.

'Al!' Katrina cried and hurried to take her husband's thin arm. 'How chilled you are! Do come sit by the fire and have some tea.'

Maddie was rather shocked at the contrast between tall, strong Katrina and her husband. Al Luhan was quite handsome, with soulful dark eyes and wavy black hair, high, carved cheekbones and a movie-star blade of a nose, but he was very thin, stooped like an old man as he leaned on a cane. His heavy, beige wool sweater, a fisherman style with threads pulling loose and a hole at the elbow, hung from his shoulders as if they were a wire hanger. He glanced over them, the expression in his eyes vague and far-away, as if he didn't really see them.

Katrina held his hand tight between hers as she led him into the room. 'Darling, this is my old friend, Maddie, who I've told you so much about. Maddie Vaughn-Alwin, this is my husband, Alfonso. Al. And this is her fiancé, Dr Cole, who you remember from Santa Fe.'

Maddie put on her brightest smile. 'I'm so happy to meet you, Señor Luhan. Any man who can win Katrina's heart must be very special indeed!'

Al took Maddie's offered hand in a firm, warm grip, much stronger than he looked. 'Call me Al, please. It's about time Katrina invited friends here for a bit of fun. She's always so busy playing nursemaid to me.' Katrina led him to a chair near the fire, where Dr Pierce hurried to check his pulse. 'I say, Katie old bean, I'd love a cup of tea. You're quite right. It's getting so cold out there, I wouldn't be surprised if snow came in soon.'

'Of course, darling.' Katrina rushed to pour the tea and fill another plate with sandwiches and those tempting lemon tarts. Buttercup trailed hopefully behind her. 'Shouldn't you rest before dinner? You were out there a long time.'

A look of irritation flashed over Al's face. 'I'm not tired at all. I walked all the way to the south wall and saw Sam and Felipe riding back this way. I'm just hungry, and I want to talk to your friend Maddie. Let her know she's most welcome, and we aren't all so loony all the time.'

Katrina handed him the plate. 'If you're sure . . .'

Al caught his wife's hand and kissed it, drawing her to sit down on the arm of his chair. 'I'm sure. Do sit down, Katie, and eat one of these chocolate buns you like so much. I'm much stronger today. I saw that writer fellow, Ryder, on my walk, and he kept me most entertained. I wish I could write stories like him. Escape into words.'

'Oh, Gunther is still here? How spiffing,' Maddie said. She'd be happy to see a familiar face, especially if it belonged to her best friend and neighbor.

'He's livened things up here no end,' Helena said. 'We'll have such a jolly Christmas with company like this.'

'Mind you, Papa isn't so keen to have guests, especially artists and writers,' Ben said. 'If Mama didn't consider herself a patron of the arts, he wouldn't have allowed it.'

Maddie felt rather uncertain about the whole thing, despite the fine lemon tarts. 'Perhaps we shouldn't have intruded . . .'

'Nonsense,' Al said. 'This is our home, too. We should have our own friends visit.'

Amid the tense silence, a strange noise arose from the corridor outside the sala – music. Singing! Liveliness! '*When the wintry winds start blowing, and the snow is starting to fall, then my eyes turn westward knowing, that's the place I love best of all!*'

Helena's eyes brightened with excitement, and she patted at her hair. 'Sounds like Felipe and Sam are back!'

Ben leaned close to Maddie and whispered, 'My sister is quite enamored with Felipe, I believe.'

'And does he like her, too?' Maddie whispered back, happy there might be a bit of romance in the air for the holidays.

Ben shrugged. 'Who can tell with Felipe? He's a charmer with all the ladies, but Helena is no dummie, so there must be something there for her to be excited to see him. It would be a good thing for Helie, though. Get her out of here.'

Two men appeared in the sala, one tall and sun-browned despite the winter weather, his dark brown hair streaked with gold as if he spent much time outdoors, dressed in denims and with a quiet demeanor. The other man was one of the most handsome chaps Maddie had ever seen, with shining chestnut curls wind-tossed around an angelic face. He was the singer, it appeared, throwing his arms wide and finishing: '*A sun-kissed miss said don't be late, oh that's why I can hardly wait, c'mon open up that Golden Gate, California here I come!'*

Everyone applauded, especially Helena, who rushed to take his arm. 'You were marvelous!'

He bowed low to the right and left. 'Thank you, all! We shall be here every evening, taking requests.'

Isabella's pale cheeks blushed a bright pink, and she reached out for Felipe, who kissed her hand. She ran her beringed fingers lightly over his cheek, as if he was one of her sons, too, and said, 'Let me introduce you to all our guests, who I'm sure must have guessed who you are. And this is my son, Sam Luhan. This rancho could never do without his work.'

She introduced Maddie and David, and Sam nodded before going to find a lemon tart. Felipe, though, came to sit next to Maddie.

'Tell me, Mrs Vaughn-Alwin, what is your favorite song?' Felipe asked as he snapped up the last lemon tart.

'I just heard "Somebody Loves Me" at a party in Santa Fe, it was spiffing.'

'Excellent choice indeed. I can tell that you, Mrs Vaughn-Alwin, are a lady of great taste and refinement, as well as great beauty.'

'Also an engaged woman,' Helena said crisply, catching his arm between her hands. 'To a doctor, no less. This is Dr David Cole, and Maddie is the future Mrs Cole.'

'Doesn't mean we can't have a song, does it?' Felipe said with a teasing grin. He and Helena burst into singing, dancing around the sala in a mad gallop. 'Everybody loves my baby, but my baby don't love nobody but me!' Ben went over to the piano and played along, the song getting louder and louder. Maddie closed her eyes and swayed along, laughing.

'What the devil is going on here?' a drum-like voice boomed across the sala, like an angry referee at a Harvard–Yale football game. The music jangled to a halt, throttled in mid-note, and the dancers skidded to a stop.

'Nertz,' Katrina whispered, as Isabella whimpered and Dr Pierce quickly took her trembling hands.

Maddie's eyes flew open. She glanced hesitantly over her

shoulder to see a man who was surely Victor Luhan looming in the doorway, his round, jowly face brick-red with indignation, as if a spot of fun going on in *his* house was an abomination. His eyes, an extraordinary pale blue gray under bushy black brows, glowed with fury.

A woman stepped up beside him, and she was also quite the vision in a very different way. Platinum-blonde curls peeped from beneath a little white hat trimmed with red, looping ribbons and bobbing feathers, and she wore an ultra-stylish suit of a startling bright-cherry color. Her stockings were actually rolled below the knees, like a teenaged flapper in a speakeasy, drawing attention to red high-heeled shoes. A white fox fur piece was slung over her shoulders, watching them all with a glittering glass eye. It seemed to smirk just like its owner as she surveyed the gathering. Her white-gloved hand reached out to brush Victor's thick fingers.

Maddie peeked at Isabella on her chaise, but she didn't even look at her husband as she whispered with Dr Pierce. Helena and Felipe were poised to take their next dance step, as if frozen.

Al, too, had gone completely white and icy still. Katrina clutched at his hand, her eyes bright with fury, and Al started to shake uncontrollably. Buttercup cowered behind Maddie as David hurried to Al's side.

Helena shook back a gleaming wave of her golden bob and said, 'What is *going on here*, Papa, is a bit of music for the festive season. I'm sure even you have heard of music.'

Victor stomped his foot, making the wooden floor tremble. 'That racket isn't music. And I do not appreciate my sala being turned into a cheap vaudeville hall. Isabella, I thought you could keep control of things for a mere few hours while I worked, but I see I was very wrong. I live in a house of good-for-nothing parasites! Useless wasters.'

Isabella fluttered in her chiffon sleeves, her cheeks pink again. 'Oh, Victor. I never thought – that is . . .'

Victor gestured impatiently, violently for her to be silent, and she sank back on her chaise cushions with another whimper. The doctor laid a gentle hand on her shoulder and glared at Victor.

'Whatever, Isabella. I should have known not to leave you to manage so much as a house fly. No wonder our children are such weaklings. I just hope there is some tea left for my secretary, Mrs Upshaw, after her journey.' He took the blonde's arm and led her toward the tea table as she leaned against his shoulder and simpered. 'Or has Katrina eaten it all again? One would think she was riding herd all day and not babying an invalid along.'

'You can't talk to her like that!' Al burst out. His hands curled into tight fists, and he pulled away from Katrina's restraining touch.

'Darling, please don't,' Katrina pleaded. 'You mustn't upset yourself; it doesn't matter at all.'

'It does! This is our home, too. You can't be treated in this way,' Al ground out. 'I won't take it any more!'

'Your home!' Victor scoffed. 'A home I maintain while you all lounge about.'

Al started to shake as if he stood in a gale wind, and Katrina reached for his hand again. 'Come on, let's go up to our room. You can have a lie down before dinner, yes? I'll read to you.' She tugged at him, trying to urge him from the chair.

'Let me help you,' David said gently. Kate shot him a grateful smile, and David glanced back at Maddie before they led Al out of the sala. She nodded and waved, gesturing that they would talk later.

'You see, Mrs Upshaw,' Victor said, almost jovial now as he handed the blonde a plate of sandwiches. 'My son is a useless layabout now, won't support his wife as he should. So, the girl eats me out of house and home!'

'That isn't true and you know it,' Ben retorted. 'Sam does most of the work around here, and Katrina has to take care of her husband.'

'And I pay for your schooling, young man,' Victor scolded, waving his finger at Ben. 'I expect you to make the most of it soon, get a proper career and stop this gallivanting. How did I raise such a useless family?'

Mrs Upshaw simpered again. 'You do work ever, *ever* so hard, Vicky sweetums.'

Maddie felt a hot wave of anger rush over her as she watched

Victor eat cake and smirk with his 'secretary.' Al had fought and sacrificed for his country. While his father sat here on his comfortable estate, apparently terrorizing everyone.

She opened her mouth to shout something furious, but a gentle touch on her arm stopped her.

She glanced back to see the housekeeper, Marta, who had brought in the refreshments. The woman still looked rather stern and stony, but there was a glimmer of sympathy in her faded gray eyes. No doubt she saw such scenes every day at Los Pintores.

'Your room is ready, Mrs Vaughn-Alwin, if you'd care to follow me. Everyone will be dressing for dinner soon.'

Maddie drew in a deep breath. 'Yes, of course. Thank you, Mrs . . .'

'Sanchez. I am Marta Sanchez.' She turned and walked toward the door, and Maddie scooped up Buttercup to hurry and follow, eager to be out of there. Marta led her from the landing up to the third floor, where Katrina said the bedchambers were. It was a long corridor, lined with straight-backed chairs and small tables, closed doors hiding who knew what, and an incongruously frivolous sprig of mistletoe hung at one end, in front of a window.

'You're in the Blue Room, if that suits. There's a bath just across, if you'd like to wash. And a small sitting room just over there, if you ever need a quiet spot.' She gestured toward the end of the corridor, expressionless. 'Most visitors do appreciate that, even if we don't have many to stay here lately.'

Maddie nodded, grateful there would be somewhere to escape until Christmas was over. 'You are very kind.'

Marta sighed. 'I have worked here at Los Pintores for a long time, Mrs Vaughn-Alwin. A very long time.'

Maddie wondered what all Marta could have seen, and she shivered to imagine. Marta opened a door off the upstairs landing and led her inside. It was a lovely room, with whitewashed walls hung with floral watercolors, blue and white striped curtains at the window that looked down to the kitchen garden and the trees beyond. A carved bed was draped with blue brocade and piled high with fluffy pillows, while a white armoire and dressing table flanked a small fireplace.

A tall, fashionably slim girl in a blue housemaid's frock, her glossy chestnut hair bundled into a white cap, was hanging up Maddie's gowns in the armoire. Her lipsticks and perfumes, her silver-backed brush, were already neatly arrayed on the dressing table.

'Oh!' the girl gasped, her blue-gray eyes wide with dismay. She quickly laid one of Maddie's scarves, a pretty blue silk, on the dressing table bench. '*Tia* – I mean, Mrs Sanchez. I did mean to be done with this before you came back.'

Aunt? Maddie glanced between them. Not much resemblance there, with Marta shorter and round, her graying hair scraped back tightly, and the lovely, wide-eyed girl. But she knew many hacienda families employed other families, sometimes for generations, around Santa Fe.

A small smile cracked Marta's stern expression as she studied the girl. 'All right then, Rosa. Just remember what we talked about – efficiency. Mrs Vaughn-Alwin, this is my niece, Rosa, who has just started her work here at Los Pintores after she finished at school. She can assist you if you need anything.'

'I'm very pleased to meet you, Rosa,' Maddie said. She set down Buttercup, who leaped up into the center of the bed, sniffing and circling in the fluffy counterpane before plopping down.

Rosa bobbed a wobbly curtsy. 'I'm glad to meet you, Señora. I will work ever so hard for you, I promise.'

Marta straightened some of the brushes and bottles laid out on the dressing table. 'Do you need Rosa to press a gown for dinner, Mrs Vaughn-Alwin?'

'Oh, yes, please. The blue velvet, I think.' She wanted to be warm and cozy in that strange, cold house, and the velvet was her heaviest frock.

'It's ever so pretty,' Rosa said as she draped the dress, sapphire blue trimmed with creamy lace, over her arm. 'It would go ever so well with that blue scarf.'

'You're very right. But I think I might need a fur coat unless there's a fireplace in the dining room!' Maddie said.

Rosa giggled. 'There is, Señora, but I'm not sure it helps

much. You're ever so lucky to live in town! There's no getting away from the winter winds here.' She bobbed a curtsy and hurried out with the dress. Buttercup leaped up on the bed and crawled under the blankets, making a little lump near the pillows.

'I wish I could join you, Buttercup,' Maddie sighed. 'That little circus downstairs is quite enough to wear a girl out.' It made her even more grateful for her own peaceful, pretty little house. Maybe she should have stayed there.

And there was still dinner to get through before she could climb into bed with her new Agatha Christie novel. And then the next few days. Yikes.

She sat down on a blue-striped slipper chair next to the window and unfastened her shoes, kicking them off. She thought of poor Katrina and her husband, the wilting Isabella and her devoted doctor, the blonde secretary and her staring fox fur, Ben and Sam, Marta and Rosa, all stuck here. It could be rather funny in a play, a drawing room full of dysfunctional family, but not so merry around a dinner table.

There was a quick knock at the door, and Gunther peeked inside, his red hair glowing like a beacon in the cold. His smile was just as bright, and Maddie jumped up to go and hug him. Buttercup barked happily in greeting.

'Maddie, dearest, I heard you were here! At last. I've been positively crawling the walls all by myself in this madhouse. And I thought my own insane family back in New York could prepare me for anything!' He set up the tray on the dressing table and expertly mixed everything up in his engraved silver cocktail shaker. 'I thought you could use something a little extra-extra before dinner. I know I could.'

'Darling, you absolutely read my mind,' Maddie said gratefully. Gunther's special mixtures could cure any woe. 'Tell me what is the gossip about all the Luhans?'

Gunther plopped down in the chair across from her and took a long sip. 'My love, we don't have the time to begin . . .'

But, of course, he *did* begin. 'Doesn't this place absolutely give you the shivers?' he asked, as they clinked glasses and Maddie took a wonderfully warming sip.

She shuddered a bit, as the first taste of a Gunther Special was always strong. 'I heard there are ghosts here, and I think I believe it. I thought you wanted to come here for some peace and quiet to write?'

'So I did. And Isabella Luhan offered me one of the casitas for a while, though I'm staying in a room down the hall for now, since it's so cold. Bone-chilling.' He sat down at her dressing table and crossed his legs, his green silk cravat gleaming like a sprig of Christmas holly. 'But I really should have stayed home. You know there's a *ghost* here!'

'It's so old, surely there's a beastie or two wandering around.'

Buttercup peeked out from her blankets in alarm, and then scooted right back.

'The main one is Señora Constanza Luhan. Helena told me there was once a party here, a hundred or more years ago, and too much local cider was consumed. They make it from their own apple orchard, and it's famously potent. Constanza and her husband argued at the top of the stairs when he thought she danced too close to a neighbor, and she fell right down – or he pushed her. She died right at the foot of the stairs! They say you can still hear her screams.'

Maddie thought of the steep staircase, the tension between everyone in the house, and took a deeper drink. She didn't relish the thought of how dark it would be there at night. 'Surely the living people here are scary enough.'

'Blimey, the living are always scarier, darling, we know that all too well. And there is such an atmosphere here, isn't there? No one seems to like each other very much. I'm sure it must be better in the summer, when there are more farm workers about, and everyone can escape the house. But in a cold winter . . .'

'We're all stuck, and unhappiness just seeps into the walls,' Maddie murmured, thinking of her own family's cold, lonely, ritual-laden holidays in New York.

'Exactly! I should use that in my next story. Maybe I'll put in a haunted house, too.' He poured out the last of the drinks into their glasses. 'You can see why I just can't get much work done. Creativity doesn't flow in a place like this.'

Maddie nodded. She went to the window and gazed out into the darkening evening, the sun already sinking amid streaks of dove-gray and rosy-pink, the gardens disappearing and the trees looming beyond. Suddenly there was a beam of light, a door opening somewhere below, and a figure dashed out through the gloaming. White and fluttery, vanishing as quickly as it appeared. Helena? Rosa or Marta?

Or maybe the ghost of Constanza.

FOUR

Dinner was sure to be something out of Dante, Maddie thought, leaning closer to the dressing table to powder her nose. If there was some way to shimmy out of it, have a tray sent up to her cozy room instead, that would be glorious. But she couldn't abandon Katrina, or David, who had been so good to come to Los Pintores with her. That was the reason she was there anyway, to support her friend. At least she felt pleasantly fizzy from Gunther's cocktails.

She tossed the powder puff down and reached for her tube of Elizabeth Arden lipstick. Whatever did a girl do before cosmetics? They were like armor in a jeweled compact, protecting one's true, vulnerable face from the outside world.

She glanced out the window. Beyond the dark reflection, snow fell in steady white sheets from the starless sky. Whoever she'd glimpsed out there earlier had surely gone. The whole estate was wrapped in silence.

There was a soft knock at the door just as she put the cap on her lipstick. 'Come in!' she called, almost hoping it was Gunther with his silver shaker again. But she couldn't be squiffy at dinner; she would need her wits about her with that lot.

It was Rosa, this time in a black dress and neat white apron, like she was in some old-fashioned English country house. 'Do you need help with your gown, Mrs Vaughn-Alwin?' she asked shyly.

'Oh, jolly good. I was just wondering why I ever brought frocks that fasten up the back!' She gave her brown bob, fastened at the sides with jeweled clips, a quick pat, and tossed away her dressing gown. It landed on Buttercup where she lounged on the bed, and the pup snuffled and rolled over indignantly.

Rosa took up the blue gown, with its slashed and puffed sleeves à *la Renaissance*, its lace trim and full skirt perfectly pressed by her earlier, and carefully lifted it over Maddie's head. 'It's ever so pretty, Mrs Vaughn-Alwin, if I may say so.'

'Of course you may say so, and thank you very much, Rosa! You must see lots of lovely frocks at a big estate like this.'

'Oh, no, they hardly ever have parties here now,' Rosa said as she smoothed the folds of the skirt and started fastening up the little pearl buttons. 'With . . . well, with everything, they don't entertain much. My aunt says they used to have grand gatherings here, before Mrs Luhan became ill and the war came along. I don't remember them at all.'

'Have you lived here long, then?'

'Since I was tiny. Mrs Sanchez is my aunt, and she raised me after my parents died.' Rosa found a pair of gloves and lace shawl in a drawer and handed them to Maddie.

Maddie wondered what all Rosa had seen in her time at Los Pintores, the secrets she must know. Rosa was a pretty girl, quick with her work and kind. Surely she'd like to get out of there.

'I'll come back after dinner to help you, if that suits?' Rosa said.

'Yes, of course. Thank you so much for your help, Rosa. Your aunt is lucky to have you.'

Rosa gave her a shy smile, her gray-blue eyes glowing at the compliment. After she left, Maddie headed downstairs, leaving Buttercup snoring on the bed. She headed toward the sala, where they were meant to gather for cocktails, but she must have taken a wrong turn along another corridor and was distracted by a hum of voices and 'thwack-thwack' noises behind a half-open door.

Curious, she pushed open the door all the way and found herself in a billiards room. The stuffed heads of trophies – deer, wild boar, moose – hung on dark wood-paneled walls. *Ugh*, Maddie thought as they stared down at her with their glassy, disapproving eyes, just like Mrs Upshaw's fox fur. Buttercup would hate this room. Maddie would have to keep the pup far away from it all.

'Mrs Vaughn-Alwin!' Ben Luhan called cheerfully. *Too* cheerfully? Maddie noticed an empty bottle of brandy beside a full ashtray on a marble-topped table. 'Glad you came to join us.'

Ben, Felipe, Gunther and Sam were there, dressed in evening suits, brandy glasses on a table nearby, but luckily Don Victor was nowhere to be seen.

'Please, call me Maddie, everyone!' she said.

Gunther waved her over toward the leather-upholstered settee where he lounged. 'Do come in, Maddie, please, and save me from all this talk of sports-ball. We need your lovely presence.'

Maddie laughed, and studied the men gathered around the billiards table as Sam lined up a shot. They all seemed rather more relaxed without their parents around, chuckling and joking. She went to sit next to Gunther and examined the room. Dark-paneled walls echoed the forest-green rug and curtains, and those animal heads seemed to stare at them all most disapprovingly. 'I was looking for the sala, but this is surely more fun. Is it a strictly masculine retreat in here?'

'Not at all,' Sam said, grinning when he made his shot very neatly. 'We want to hear about those schoolgirl pranks you and Kate got up to. Save us from Felipe here yammering on about football.'

'I never *yammer*,' Felipe said with a good-natured laugh. 'I discourse fluently about very intellectual topics.'

'I fear I have few tales of pranks. Katrina was the head-girl sort, and I was busy scribbling in my sketchbooks. There were just one or two aberrations . . .' She smiled at Ben as he handed her a glass.

'Some brandy?' he said. 'It's the good stuff, no bathtub gin at Los Pintores. It's the one good thing about my father.'

'Thanks so much.' The amber-colored brandy did look rather nice, and she didn't want to be stuck with Isabella Luhan in the sala just yet. 'But don't stop your game on my account. I'll just watch while I have a wee sip.' She glanced uncertainly at the mounted heads. 'If they would just stop staring at me.'

Ben went to line up his shot. 'You mean the wall of horrors? They're Papa's, of course. The great hunter. I think there are nicer trophies to be had.' He gestured toward a glass case behind the settee, displaying silver cups, blue ribbons and, of all things, a cricket bat, as well as some of Katrina's old horse show prizes.

'Cricket?' She peered closer at the bat. It looked to be a rather ordinary piece of wood to her, the handle worn smooth, the edge nicked from all the balls it once smacked into. The initials AEL were burned into the handle.

'Ben is a *college man*, as was Al,' Sam scoffed. 'Ben is at Princeton, and Al went off to Harvard before he left for war. Both of them hitting things with bats while I ran this place.'

'I do play a bit of cricket, which is harder than you seem to think, Sam,' Ben said defensively. 'I also study a lot, so I can help you with the business side of this place when I come back. But I think I'll jolly well miss it all when I'm here all the time! Friends and parties, theaters, games, dining societies . . .'

'Civilization,' Felipe said.

'You're at Princeton, too?' Maddie asked.

'Yes. I knew Ben when we were at St Michael's school here, and we went off to college together,' Felipe said, tossing back a silken curl of chestnut hair from his brow. He really was quite matinee-idol, Maddie thought. 'I don't play cricket, though. Tennis for me, and theatricals once in a while. No rowing; I can't swim at all.'

'Felipe makes a lovely Juliet,' Ben teased. 'But they don't give any prizes for what he *really* excels at. Courting the ladies.'

Felipe laughed, and his cheeks slowly stained rosy-pink. 'Ben, really. You'll give Mrs Vaughn-Alwin entirely the wrong impression of me.'

'None of the rest of us can get a look-in when he's around,' Ben added.

'No fear of that here,' Maddie said, finishing off her drink. 'I can usually take the measure of a man on my own.'

They all laughed, ribbing Felipe for his romances, and Sam refilled everyone's drinks.

'I did hear the beauteous Felipe is set on wooing the fair Helena,' Gunther whispered. 'That's why he's here. Pitching the woo.'

'Really?' Maddie whispered back. She thought of how Felipe and Helena had danced in the sala, Helena all smiles, Felipe gallant. Marrying one's brother's college roommate did seem like a natural thing to do. A Christmas romance. 'She's receptive to his, um, woo-pitching, then? It sure seems like it.'

Gunther laughed. 'What do you think, darling? The lad should be in the movies. Look at those cheekbones.'

A gong rang out, brassy and bossy, and the laughter faded in the billiards room.

Sam straightened from his shot and put his cue away, reaching for his dinner jacket. 'Dinner is served. Come on, friends – our *dear* papa does get cranky when people are an instant late for meals.'

FIVE

Dinner proceeded much as Maddie expected – or feared – it would. Victor expounded on how politics in Santa Fe was all really downhill, no one had any values any more, no one cared about what was really important – land and money, of course, and the men who held them for generations. Los Pintores was a grant to the Luhans from the Spanish king in 1710! He deserved to be heard. He deserved to be in charge.

Isabella sat at the other end of the table beside her doctor, wearing another floaty silk and chiffon gown of sea green and a magnificent triple strand of pearls. She picked at the filet in mushroom sauce on her gilt-edged plate and steadily drained her wine glass, looking even more like the pale, swooning heroine of a Victorian poem than she had before.

The secretary, Mrs Upshaw, sat to Victor's right, clad in a truly eye-popping gown of orange satin trimmed with coral and green beads, diamonds flashing in her ears. They caught the candlelight as she constantly nodded at Victor's words, even once bursting out with, 'You're darned right, Vicky – I mean, Mr Luhan.'

'Wherever did he find her?' Helena whispered, loud enough that Maddie heard her two seats away. 'She's a lot, even for Papa's taste.'

'In a traveling vaudeville show, I'm sure,' Ben muttered.

Across the table, Katrina was murmuring to Al, her expression frantic while his was frozen. Maddie worried all was not well.

'I will not tolerate whispering at my table,' Victor boomed. 'Were you all raised in a barn? You were certainly not! In my day, there was respect . . .'

'We tried to get Maddie to tell us about your schoolgirl hijinks, Katrina,' Felipe said, and Helena gave him a grateful smile for the interruption. He briefly squeezed her hand. 'But she said you were much too proper. Head girl, in fact.'

Katrina laughed when she saw her husband give a flicker of a smile, and smoothed back some of the loose tendrils of her braids. 'I was head girl, true, but not always quite so proper. Remember the poetry teacher, Maddie, and the hot-water bottle? That *was* a wheeze. I never saw anyone so furious as she was when she was all soaking wet! I was so sure they would write to my parents about it.'

Victor suddenly pounded his fist on the table, making the silver and crystal rattle. Katrina jumped and flushed bright red. 'That is exactly what I am talking about! Young people have no respect today, no moral fiber. So-called ladies pulling pranks on innocent bystanders, wasting their feminine education, growing up to smoke cigarettes and dance all night in those – those speakeasies. How can they ever be fit mothers to future leaders? You see why we sent you to the nuns at Loretto, Helena. They tolerate no such nonsense.'

Helena rolled her eyes, while Mrs Upshaw, who certainly looked like she'd spent a night or two in a speakeasy, fidgeted in her brocade-cushioned chair.

'Are we suddenly in a Dickens novel? Moral fiber?' David whispered to Maddie.

Maddie pressed her napkin to her lips to stifle a moral-less giggle.

'Oh, Victor,' Isabella murmured, turning her wine glass around in her thin hand. 'We do have guests to consider . . .'

'Guests who are the very people who need to hear this!' Victor shouted. 'They're the generation who are leading this country to doom.'

Isabella slumped back in her chair. 'I feel so very faint.' Dr Pierce reached for her hand to check her pulse, murmuring soothingly into her ear.

'Well,' Helena said, ignoring her father's scowl as she drained her wine glass and waved to the maid for more. 'I don't know about the rest of you, but I could sure use a gasper. The nuns taught me how to smoke properly, you see. Anyone care to join me?'

Maddie tried to hold back another bubble of laughter. It *would* be nice to escape that stuffy room. 'Thanks awfully, Helena. I think I will.' When she put her napkin down beside the half-empty plate, she noticed a little pink smear on the white damask. *Oh dear*, she thought. Surely lipstick meant Society Was Doomed. Her feminine education wasted.

She followed Helena, Ben, Sam, Al and Katrina into the sala, where Marta was laying out coffee in a silver service. They sat down as close to the warm fire as possible, Katrina near Al on one of the chaises as he watched the flames in brooding silence.

'I'm really sorry, everyone,' Katrina said, her cheeks red with agitation. She twisted her hands in the lap of her brown silk skirt. 'I never should have asked you here, ruining your holiday just to keep us company!'

'Papa is usually better behaved in company,' Helena said. She leaned closer to Felipe as he lit her cigarette, and she smiled up at him. 'I don't know what's happened to him tonight.'

'Must be the drink,' Sam said. 'I saw a crate of wine bottles in his library.'

'I'd say it's the secretary,' Ben added.

'Surely he does want to impress *her*,' Al said faintly. 'But what makes her different from the others before her?'

'We're just happy to see you, Katrina darling, really,' Maddie assured her. Her friend obviously needed support now.

'Otherwise we would be too lonely in our quiet houses, with only Christmas cocktails for company,' Gunther said, reaching out to pat Katrina's hand. 'Here we get dinner *and* a show!'

Katrina laughed on a little hiccup.

'We all have horrid relations we must tolerate,' Maddie said.

'We certainly do,' Felipe muttered. 'Why do you think I'm here, and not with my family in Taos?'

Helena shot him a sympathetic glance, a soft touch on his arm. 'We just have to ignore Papa and have ourselves a little fun! Like we always do.'

'Yes,' Sam said. 'If we get enough snow tonight, we can go sledding on the south slope tomorrow.'

'Oh, I don't know if I should go out . . .' Katrina began, glancing uncertainly at her husband.

'Go on then, Katie,' Al said hoarsely. He looked quite

exhausted, slumped in his chair, his face grayish in the moonlight. 'You love a spot of exercise, and you've been stuck inside here with me for too long.'

'It's settled, then,' Helena said. 'And no parents allowed!'

SIX

'Is this spot all right, then?' David asked the morning after that uncomfortable dinner as he led Al to a cushioned iron seat under the portal, near a patch of watery-pale sunlight. The early sky was lowering, a pale gray color as more snow threatened at any moment, and a brisk breeze had blown up. Buttercup trotted behind them. 'You have a lovely view here.'

And it was. The snow-dusted trees looked like a painting against the pale gray sky, with a pond and summerhouse in the misty distance. Maddie was sure it would be spectacular in the summer, all green and gold.

'It's fine,' Al said dully, not looking up.

'Are you sure you should be outside, love? It's getting rather cold,' Katrina said as she fussed with the blankets covering him.

'*Gillipollas*, Katrina!' Al shouted. 'I'm not some elderly invalid you need to wheel around Sunmount. I'm just tired. I like the fresh air here. You should go upstairs and change your clothes before you go sledding, so you won't look like a dishrag next to Maddie and Helena.'

Maddie and David exchanged a quick glance over Al's head. They could surely both see Katrina needed all the help she could get.

Katrina just laughed and twitched the blankets firmly into place. 'Now that's a fine how-d'ye-do, isn't it? I slave my fingers to the bone – to the bone, I say! – and all I get is "Kate, you're an old dishrag." Why don't you just be quiet, Alfonso Luhan, and take your medicine already?' She pulled a brown bottle out of her pocket and held it out to him with a little shake.

Al grinned up at her and took the pills from her fingers. 'I'm sorry, Katie. My father's nonsense just drives me mad sometimes. And the holidays are the worst. I should be doing so much better for you.'

Katrina kissed his cheek. 'I know he's horrid, my love, but we can't worry about that too much right now. We need to try and have a happy Christmas. Now, I'm going walking for a while, with Maddie and David who are off for a walk with the sweet doggie. Will you be all right here? You can call for Marta if you need to go inside.'

'I'm fine, really. The clear air will do me good.'

'Come on, you two,' Katrina said, taking Maddie and David's arms to march them down the portal steps into the garden. 'Let's leave this grumbling old bear to his medicine.'

They went through the gate in the low adobe wall that encircled the house gardens to the path beyond. In the distance they could see the sledders flying down the slope. 'Thank you for all your marvelous help,' Katrina said quietly. 'Truly. I couldn't face this Christmas here without you.'

'We're just happy to see you, Katrina, really,' Maddie said. They laughed as David dashed off after Buttercup, who glimpsed a bird that must be caught. He waved back and called that he would go check on Al.

'You are such a lucky duckie, Mads,' Katrina said as they walked past the pond and its pretty summerhouse. 'David is a brick. And so handsome!'

Maddie laughed, and felt that familiar warm, gooey feeling deep inside when she thought of David and his kind heart, his inner strength. His bright blue eyes and thrilling kisses. 'Don't I know it. He's been an utter dream lamb. After Pete . . .'

Katrina gave her hand a sympathetic squeeze. 'I'm so happy for you, Maddie dearest. You deserve it. When is the wedding?'

'In the spring, I think. You and Al must come! It won't be a large event at all, but my wonderful Juanita will surely bake a scrumptious cake.'

Katrina smiled sadly. 'You couldn't move it up a bit, I daresay, so we could escape back to Santa Fe a little sooner?'

'Is it so very bad, darling?'

'Not as bad as it could be, I suppose. Victor isn't home a great deal, and Isabella keeps to her rooms, so I mostly run the house.' Katrina kicked at a snowdrift, sending a soft white cloud into the air. 'It is really beautiful out here, isn't it? I love getting away for walks, it's so peaceful.'

Maddie looked around. She saw a few outbuildings, Gunther's little writing casita, a laundry house. A beautiful chapel with stained-glass windows. It seemed like its own little world, all quiet and still.

'If not for my martinet of a father-in-law and Gothic maiden Mama-Isabella!' Katrina said with a laugh. 'Al's siblings are rather nice, though Sam works terribly hard and Ben is away at college most of the time. Helena is just bored, I think. But I'm so glad you came to visit, Maddie, really. Though no doubt you're wondering just what sort of asylum you fetched up in.'

David came back to them, wrapping his muffler closer around him as the wind picked up. He held Buttercup under his arm. 'I think Al is resting comfortably now,' he said. 'His pulse seemed steady, and he's in a good humor.'

'Lovely!' Katrina sighed. 'You two are the best tonic. I do worry so very much.'

Maddie took Katrina's arm as they walked on toward the hill. 'How is he, really, Katrina?'

Her booted steps slowed. 'He's – well, he's better off than some of the poor boys we've seen in hospitals. He only uses the wheelchair sometimes now, and we try to get walks in everyday, just like this. Build up his strength. But he's always so nervous, so jumpy, and he has such fearful nightmares. And . . .' She glanced away.

'And what?' David asked gently. 'You can say. I was there, in France.'

'Sometimes he has these hallucinations,' Katrina whispered. 'He thinks whoever is there is a Hun. He fights them.' She rolled up the cuff of her tweed coat to reveal a line of bruises, purple against her freckled skin.

Maddie gasped, her mind racing with fear. 'Katrina! Darling, you can't do all this alone. You need help.'

'I know, I know!' Her voice was thick with tears as she jerked down her sleeve. 'But who can help, who can understand? No one, it seems.'

'You saw Dr Richards in Santa Fe, yes?' David said,

frowning thoughtfully. 'He has a good reputation with cases like this.'

'Yes, but nothing going, I'm afraid. His treatment could only *maybe* work, and it's frightfully expensive. We don't really have a bean right now; it's why we still live here. There will be some when Victor pops off, which he's much too disobliging to do.' She gave a bubble of almost hysterical laughter. 'He will outlive us all.'

'Let me see what I can do,' David said. 'It's not my area of specialty, but I know a few others I could contact.'

'And you can come stay with me in Santa Fe whenever you need an escape. You and Al both, I have a lovely guest room. Juanita's cooking would have you right in a trice!' Maddie added.

Katrina flashed a weak smile, and David handed her a clean handkerchief. 'You help out just by being here, really. Now come on, let's stop being such gloomy gusses! It's Christmas. Things will work out somehow, I just know it,' she said with a reflection of her cheerful self. 'Now, shall we go try the sledding, Mads? If you'll stay with Al for a while, David?'

She leaped up and strode out toward the snowy slope, and Maddie had to follow, Buttercup at her heels. Everyone called out cheerful greetings as they reached the summit, and Ben handed Katrina a spare sled. She dashed and bumped down the trail, whooping in delight. It was nice to hear.

'See?' Helena cried, offering to partner with Maddie in the next run. 'I knew it would be the most fun to get out today!'

Maddie wasn't sure she'd say it was the *most*. The wind was cold, grabbing at her coat with icy fingers, and snow caught in her eyelashes and melted on her cheeks in fine, sugary flakes. But she had to agree it was nice to get out of the house, to breathe some fresh air and feel free from its silent corridors and tense rooms for a while. Felipe and Ben laughed, birds twittered as they soared overhead, and it was a relief.

Yet there *was* still that cold. Maddie shivered and glanced around the scene from their vantage point there on the hill. She saw smoke from the chimneys of what must be the neighbors' house, curling around the treetops, and in the other direction the casitas and outbuildings of Los Pintores, all seeming to say they weren't quite as alone out there as it seemed. For good – or for ill.

As Helena polished up the sled, Maddie glanced back at Ben, who was laughing with Felipe as they kicked at the snow and watched Katrina climbing back up the slope. 'So that's your neighbors' house over there? The ones your father dislikes?'

Ben glanced over at the chimneys, the flat tiled roof. 'The McTeers, yes. But it doesn't mean anything, really, this silly idea of a feud. You may have noticed, Maddie, that my father dislikes just about everyone and everything. Women with lipstick and nail polish, cuffs on trousers, sauce on chicken . . .'

'The French?' Maddie laughed, thinking of the interminable dinner conversation.

Ben laughed, too, and kicked at the snow. It didn't sound very jolly, though. 'So you *have* noticed.'

'Hard not to.'

'It wasn't always like this here, you know. My father used to be away a lot, business in Santa Fe and Albuquerque, sometimes even in Denver, and my mother would have parties here. So much fun! Music and food, talk . . .' His voice faded as if he remembered it all too wistfully, and Felipe gave his shoulder a sympathetic clap that made him smile again, a quick flicker.

'I'm sorry your mother is so ill,' Maddie said, thinking of Isabella and her chaise. 'If I had known, we wouldn't have intruded . . .'

'Of course not! We're glad you're here. And I know Mama is, too. She wants to have parties like she used to, I'm sure. If she had the strength,' Ben said.

'And now she has to have a doctor on call at all times? How sad.'

'Dr Pierce, you mean?' Ben said with a grimace. 'Never mind about him. He's a bit like what Mrs Upshaw is for my father, that's all.'

Maddie was shocked. 'You mean – your mother and Dr Pierce are – are . . .'

Ben laughed. 'Having a torrid affair? No, I shouldn't think so. That would take planning, and Mama doesn't have the energy.'

'He just seems to give her something missing in her life?' Felipe suggested, his handsome face covered with concern. 'She deserves better!'

Ben frowned in thought. 'Yes, I think so. Something missing in her life, like Mrs Upshaw gives my father – unquestioning flattery and constant agreement. You have to pay for stuff like that, though, when your spouse can't give it.'

Maddie thought it all sounded terribly sad and lonely. No wonder Los Pintores always felt so cold, despite its beauty. 'And what exactly does Dr Pierce give to Señora Isabella? That kind of constant agreement?'

Ben scuffed at the snow again, looking as if he was thinking of this, thinking of his parents as people, for the first time. 'Something like that, I imagine. She used to have lots of beaus, you know, artists and writers who would flock around her. She married young, and I guess she missed all that. I'm just glad I'm away from all this most of the time.'

Maddie wished she could get away from the messiness of being human sometimes, too. Escape seemed to be what everyone at Los Pintores sought. 'And what will you do when you graduate?'

'Who knows? I'd like to write, maybe. My father says it should be the law, and Sam could use help here. I just don't want to come back here, really. Not permanently, not for my real life. I'd just be in Sam's way, no matter what he says.'

Maddie remembered seeing Sam heading out for the fields as they sat on the portal, and thought he worked all the time, even in winter. Did he like it, did he want to do it? Or did he, too, want to run? 'Sam likes it here, then?'

'He likes it fine, I guess. He's good at it, the estate has done well under his care, and I know our father is happy to leave the work to him, even though he complains about it all the time. Sam seems to appreciate the land; he belongs to it in his way. Not like Helena over there.' Ben gestured to his sister, who was idly rolling snowballs next to her sled. 'Poor old Helie. She just wants to have fun!'

'Like you,' Felipe teased, and Ben laughed.

'Helena just wants to have a life, nothing wrong with that,' Ben said. 'Maybe she could use a Dr Pierce to help pass the time.'

Helena tossed a snowball at her brother and giggled when it landed with a splat on his shoulder.

'She seems happy enough to me, right now anyway,' Maddie said.

Ben brushed the snow off his shoulder, watching as Felipe bounded over to return the volley and start a snowball fight with Helena. 'I'm glad I could get Felipe to come home with me for Christmas. Having company sure lightens things up!'

'Come on, Maddie! Let's give this sled a try,' Helena called, pushing Felipe into a snowbank.

Maddie glanced up and saw a man standing just beyond the low stone fence, watching them intently from under a hat pulled low. He was wrapped in a brown greatcoat, but he seemed very tall and powerful beneath the layers, golden hair like a Viking's sticking out from under that hat. He held a pitchfork perched lightly on his shoulder, a veritable battle sword. He turned and strode away, and she wondered how long he had been there.

'And that's one of your neighbors?' Maddie asked, gesturing toward the retreating figure.

Ben looked to where she pointed. 'Jim McTeer, the son. I met him once at a shop in Española; he was pretty quiet but seemed like an all right sort of fella. Polite. He and his father have really improved that land. The Candelarias neglected it so much the last few years. We should be grateful to them, keeping up the neighborhood and all that.'

'But your father doesn't think so?'

'Of course not,' Ben said with a laugh. 'You remember what we said about how my father disapproves of everything? Newcomers are one of the reasons the world is going to ruin, y'know.'

Helena stomped toward them. 'Come on then, you slow pokes! What are you hanging about chatting for?' She ducked when Felipe tried to land another snowball on her in revenge.

'Maddie saw Jim McTeer lurking around over there,' Ben said.

Helena scowled. 'I'm sure he wasn't *lurking*. Who has time for such things? He's just interested in the land; we're his neighbors, after all. Now, get moving!' She gave Ben a playful shove and grabbed Maddie's hand to tug her on to the sled.

As they jostled for seats, the sled rocking in the snow, Maddie turned back to glance at Helena. To her surprise, a thoughtful expression had replaced her merry smile. That faded, though, as they launched themselves down the hill, speeding faster and faster in forgetfulness.

Later that day, washed and warmed after snowy adventures, Maddie ventured down toward the kitchen in search of hot tea or cocoa and a treat for Buttercup. Her nose still tingled from the snow, and she felt a bit lighter, more cheerful after their laughing sled runs.

Until she saw Dr Pierce standing in the corridor just outside Isabella's suite, studying himself in a silver-framed mirror hanging there. She remembered what Ben said, about how the doctor was paid to give Isabella approval, attention. Was it more, though? Could it really be? He was a handsome man, if a bit too slick for Maddie's taste, and obviously skilled in soothing his patients.

'Dr Pierce,' she said. 'How is Señora Isabella today?

He glanced up, and for an instant she thought wariness or maybe even irritation flickered over his face, before he smiled charmingly. 'Mrs Vaughn-Alwin. So kind of you to ask. She has rather tired herself out, after the late evening yesterday. She was quite unable to sleep. I warned her against such exertions in entertaining, but she won't hear of slowing down. She insists on a fine holiday for her family, such a kind and unselfish heart she has.'

'Indeed,' Maddie murmured, though she wasn't sure 'kind and unselfish' were the very first words to describe Isabella. 'It's a lovely home for entertaining. She is a fine hostess.'

'But parties can be so injurious to a weak heart, a delicate constitution. And with everything happening around her . . .' His words faded, replaced with a disapproving frown. Maddie wondered if he meant the goings-on with Don Victor's secretary right under his wife's roof.

'Does she have a weak heart? I am so sorry to hear that.'

Dr Pierce shook his head sadly. 'Mrs Luhan is a very brave lady, she never complains. But she does suffer from many painful ailments, I fear.'

'She's fortunate to have you with her, Dr Pierce. Has she been your patient for a long time?'

'Not so very long. I wish she had come to me sooner; I could have assisted her so much more. Yet she does not like to burden anyone.'

'Not long, then?'

'A few months, since the summer. I flatter myself I have been of great help to her. I keep up with all the most modern theories of medicine, and can integrate caring for the whole patient, which is key.'

The *whole* patient? 'I am sure she is very grateful for it.'

'I fear I cannot help her with all her worries, though. Her children are an anxiety to her; she cares so much for their happiness. And such a large house to run. Such a burden.'

'You help her find the strength, I am sure, Dr Pierce. She speaks so very highly of you.'

He smiled and preened a bit. 'I do my best, as I do for all my patients. They are very loyal to me, as I am to them.' He leaned closer, his expression suddenly sharpening in some way. 'I know you have many friends in Santa Fe, Mrs Vaughn-Alwin. If perhaps one or two of them might be in need of medical assistance . . .'

Maddie couldn't think of anyone she disliked enough to sic the doctor on them. Before she could answer, Marta came up the staircase with a basket of fresh linens in her arms, muttering under her breath.

'I will keep that in mind, Dr Pierce, thank you,' Maddie said. She went down the staircase, smiling at Marta as she passed, and thought of what she had learned. It wasn't much, but she felt like she had a bit more understanding of Isabella, the doctor, and delicate constitutions now.

SEVEN

The next day after breakfast, Maddie, Katrina, Ben, Helena, Sam and Felipe set out for a walk to collect holiday greenery in the drifting, sugar-like snow while David played cards in the sala with Al. Maddie paused to press her hand to the stitch in her side, trying to draw a deep breath. Obviously, she'd been spending too much time in those *heathen* speakeasies and not enough in good, wholesome exercise. And she decided she wasn't going to start engaging in the stuff, either, if it was this unpleasant.

Suddenly, she glimpsed a man looming in the distance, near the sledding slope. He wasn't just *any* man, but quite a dramatic sight, tall and lean as a scarecrow, and dressed like one in faded cords, a tattered wool hat with silvery hair sticking out every which way from beneath its brim, tall boots, and a long, patched brown coat. He cradled a rifle over his arm as he studied them, unmoving. He looked a bit familiar, as if she'd glimpsed him before, though not so close-up. Maybe when they were out yesterday?

'Something wrong, Maddie?' Katrina called. She looked much happier that morning, rosy and smiling as she stomped through the snow.

Maddie gestured toward the strange figure. 'That man over there, who is he? He rather gives me the shivers. I'm sure I've seen him before.'

'Oh, that's Harry McTeer,' Helena said, turning away from cuddling with Felipe to study the scene. Her eyes widened when she saw the madcap figure. 'He shouldn't be so close! Papa will shoot him if he sees him hanging about.'

'Or he'll shoot your father,' Felipe said. 'That rifle looks like it means business.'

'*Looks* is the operative word,' Ben said. 'Harry McTeer and his son Jim like to appear dangerous, but I bet that isn't even loaded. He just wants to try and intimidate us.'

As if he heard them, Harry McTeer turned and vanished between the skeletal winter trees. Like a ghost.

'I think I saw him before, maybe in the fields over there,' Maddie said. 'Perhaps while we were sledding yesterday.'

'Papa hates them. He shouldn't be there.'

Hardly a surprise, Maddie thought, since Victor Luhan seemed dedicated to hating everyone. She'd didn't realize she'd actually said the words aloud until Helena and Katrina burst into laughter.

'I think Mrs Upshaw rather likes Harry's son, Jim,' Ben said.

'No!' Helena gasped. 'Where did you hear that?'

'Just idle gossip,' Ben said. 'Why do you look so upset?'

Helena sniffed and turned away. 'I'm not upset, good heavens.'

'Is that why your father hates the McTeers? Because of Mrs Upshaw?' Maddie asked.

'I doubt he knows a thing about it, or that woman wouldn't still be here,' Helena said. 'He doesn't like them because he says they're interlopers. They didn't get that land from the King of Spain in 1650 or whenever. They bought it from the Candelarias a few years ago. They're *outsiders*.'

Maddie nodded. She knew about being an outsider. Most of her Santa Fe neighbors, except for her artist friends who had escaped the East as she had, had lived in New Mexico for centuries. It wasn't easy to gain their trust.

'And what do the McTeers think of your father?' Felipe asked.

'They hate him right back, of course,' Helena said. 'Especially since he killed some of their sheep.'

'Killed their sheep!' Maddie cried.

'Oh, yes,' Sam said, loading piles of the greenery they'd cut on to the sled. He moved the heavy loads effortlessly, his shoulders shifting under his coat. 'They run sheep herds on their land and sell the wool to some local tribes for weaving. Drives our father batty. Some of the poor creatures kept wandering past the fence, and one day Father shot a couple of them. Said he was hunting and it was an accident, but who can believe that? Harry McTeer has been a right nuisance ever since, along with his sons. Sneaking around here at night, digging stuff up, breaking into sheds, things like that.'

'You don't seem worried,' Maddie said, sure it was rather strange as Sam seemed to do all the work there.

He shrugged. 'Who can blame them? They're just trying to make a living from the land, just like we are.'

Who could blame him, indeed, Maddie thought, gazing thoughtfully at the spot where McTeer had disappeared. It seemed Victor Luhan had a real knack for making enemies right and left. If this was one of the detective novels she loved to read, Christie or Chesterton, he would surely bring himself to some sticky end.

She laughed at herself and was glad this was real life instead. She'd already found enough dead bodies to last her a lifetime. Soon she'd be away from the sinister countryside and back in Santa Fe, where the only quarrels were over art and music instead.

That night the snow came down even thicker, an impenetrable white blanket closing the house in silence. The pale flakes against the windows and the crackle of the fireplace seemed to wrap it all up apart from the rest of the world as Maddie played mahjong with David, Kate, Helena and Gunther while Buttercup snored on a settee.

Blessedly, Victor had retired right after dinner complaining of a headache, probably tired out after a long diatribe on how the French of all people were also ruining civilization along with flappers and jazz, and Mrs Upshaw soon followed him upstairs. Isabella took dinner in her room with her doctor. Al dozed through the meal and retired soon after, and now Ben and Sam were playing chess while Felipe refereed. It was a quiet night, but strangely taut and watchful. Maddie wondered if the old hacienda was really haunted.

For a while, the only sounds were the pop of the flames, the click of the mahjong tiles. After a while, Ben left his game and wandered to the phonograph. He shuffled through the records until he found one he liked. The strains of 'Rose Marie' filled the room.

'Careful,' Helena said. 'You might rouse Papa and stir him to come down here and shout at us again.'

'With the lovely Mrs Upshaw to distract him?' Ben said with a laugh. 'Not a chance.'

Maddie studied the decorations around the sala, the greenery they'd gathered tied up with red and gold ribbons into wreaths and swags, the tree in the corner waiting for lights. She thought of her family mansion in New York, all the elaborate arrangements brought in by florists, and her own simple sitting room at home where the twins would make paper garlands to drape everywhere. Their laughter and chatter seemed so far away right then, and she ached with missing them. 'What was Christmas usually like here?'

'Oh, it was wonderful,' Helena said. 'People would come from all over for Los Posadas around our chapel, and Mama would have dances. There would be bonfires, and games of snapdragon and charades. We'd find a Yule log for Christmas Eve, and when I was very small my grandfather would play Papa Noel and give us the loveliest presents. There'd be sledding, and ice skating on the pond when it froze up enough . . .'

'I couldn't do that,' Felipe declared. 'I can't swim! What if the ice broke?'

'And there'd be someone playing that piano all the time,' Ben said. 'It's such a waste it's so quiet now.'

'Well, it certainly doesn't have to be silent! I can't swim, but I can certainly play the piano,' Felipe declared. He sat down at the instrument and ran his long, elegant fingers over the keys. 'Yes, we have no bananas! We have no bananas today . . .'

Helena took her brother's hand, and she and Ben galloped recklessly from one end of the sala to the other, dodging furniture and cushions. Laughter rang out around them.

David stood and held out his hand to Maddie with a wide, enticing smile. 'May I have this dance?'

'Always!' She went into his arms and nestled there against his shoulder, as if she'd always been just exactly there, always where she should be. They twisted and spun, giggling along with the others.

Their laughter blended joyously with the music, making the strange, snowy night lighter and brighter – until the door flew open with a crash. Al stood there, his eyes wide in his gray-ish-pale face, his hair standing on end. He trembled like an autumn leaf in his sweat-soaked pajamas. Maddie shivered to see the fear and panic that clung around him in a dark cloud.

'Darling!' Katrina cried as she ran toward him.

'They're back,' Al said, eerily calm. 'They're always coming back. They know just where to find us.' His voice rose and cracked on those last words. 'It's too close, too close!'

'Darling, no one is coming,' Katrina said gently, clasping his shaking arm with both hands. 'We've talked about all this, remember? Come along, let's find your medicine . . .'

'No!' Al roughly shook off her touch and backed away from her, his expression frantic. 'You just want to drug me so I can't defend myself. You *want* me to die, to send me back to hell!'

His hand shot out and overturned a nearby table, sending glass crashing to the floor in a crystalline shower. David and Al's brothers rushed to him.

David put a strong, restraining but gentle arm around Al's heaving shoulders. 'Come along, I'll show you, you are quite safe here.' He led him out, Katrina trailing, wringing her hands.

Maddie found she was shivering at the scene, worried about Al and Katrina, trapped in that room. She wrapped her arms tightly around herself. Suddenly, all she wanted was to go home, to lock her own bedroom door behind her and crawl under the covers with her dogs, safe and warm in the haven she'd created for herself. Dear heavens, but had this raw fear and panic beset her Pete, too? Had he felt trapped and terrified? She couldn't stand the thought.

'I do promise we haven't always been such a mad house,' Helena said. She'd found a broom somewhere and was sweeping up the glass, as if she'd done that many times before. 'Christmas was once a lot of fun. But now it's all gone so dark.' She stared down at the shimmering pile of glass. 'I do wish I could get away,' she added, quietly, fiercely.

'Why can't you?' Maddie asked.

Helena gave her a twisted little smile and reached for a silver cigarette box on a side table. 'Money, of course. I don't have much of my own, so I have to do what my father says. So do we all. Ben has to be a lawyer or something when he finishes school, Sam has to run this place, and I have to find someone to marry, or else moulder here forever. And Al. Poor, darling Al. Oh, Maddie. You're so lucky to be free. I'd give anything to have that, too.'

Maddie's sleep that night was restless, plagued with vague and scary dreams, flaming images of wild dances, gunfire, blood dripping down walls, loud laughter, rough voices shouting of the death of morality. She struggled to wake up, to leave the drugging miasma of those nightmares behind her, but she seemed tangled, trapped.

Finally, she broke away and came awake with a gasp, sitting straight up in her bed. As she dragged in a deep, ragged breath, she saw that Buttercup still slept, snoring at Maddie's feet, curled up on a cashmere blanket like she hadn't a care in the doggie world. Maddie missed Juanita and the twins with a deep, painful ache.

She slid out of bed and went to open the window curtains. Snow fell in a steady sheet of silent white, broken by faint moonlight. It seemed to trap her inside, but it was real at least; *she* was real. There were no ghosts there.

Sort of. Beyond the bedroom door, out in the corridor, she heard a low rumble of voices. It sounded like a quarrel, a man's angry mutter, a woman's frantic whisper. Maddie couldn't make out the words, couldn't even tell who was talking. And she didn't really want to know. She'd had enough of drama for one night.

She crawled back under the blankets and closed her eyes tight as she tried to summon a peaceful sleep. The voices outside rose, shrill and sharp, a loud squeal – then a deep *thump*. Then silence. Maddie pulled the pillow over her ears and hoped whoever it was had left.

It took a very long time, but at last sleep caught her, and she fell back down into restless dreams again.

EIGHT

'In the bleak midwinter, frosty wind made moan . . .' Maddie sang softly as she marched along the snow-piled path, trying to raise her spirits. She'd woken up from those restless dreams very early and decided to take Buttercup outside before breakfast and gather her thoughts before she faced people again. It was really a magical-looking day, like some winter fairyland, snow and ice sparkling like diamonds, the sky the palest blue overhead. Silence stretched in every direction, echoing the song back to her. The only sign of any life was a whiff of woodsmoke on the wind, a puff of gray rising in the distance.

She paused under a white-shrouded tree to tighten the laces on her stout walking boots. She was glad she'd remembered to pack some sturdy clothes, and also very glad to be outside despite the cold wind. The crisp air smelled clean and bright-sharp after the stuffy house, and it made her remember the wonderful sense of freedom she'd felt on first coming to Santa Fe.

Here, with the mountains in the distance, the wide-open paths, she could just be Maddie, as she never could back in New York. Whoever *Maddie* really was – she was learning more about that every day. But she was deuced glad she wasn't a Luhan. Katrina's in-laws were one of the strangest bunches she'd ever seen, Victor and Isabella and their little entourage of doctors, 'secretaries' and secretive housekeepers. Voices at night in corridors, people running through the gardens at all hours, hostile neighbors. No wonder poor Al couldn't get better, living with such unpredictability and flaring tempers. How did Ben, Sam and Helena do it?

A bit of dampness touched her cheek, and she peered up into the sky, now turning the dove gray of a South Sea pearl, clouds sliding back in. More snow on the way. She felt as if she'd never get back to her comfy home.

'Come along, Buttercup, we'll miss breakfast if we don't hurry,' she called, and turned back toward the house. At least Marta Sanchez's cooking was fabulous.

They didn't meet anyone else on the path back through the trees, but it was all rather slow going with old snow and new covering the gravel, mud puddles forming to catch at her boots. She paused to lean against a weathered old statue of Cupid with his bow to adjust her boot. There was a sudden, startling noise of rustling from beyond the line of trees, making Buttercup jump, her hackles raised. Maddie spun around to look, but she could see nothing. The snow and the winter tree limbs were too thick. There was a cloud of smoke rising up above the trees, but other than that she saw nothing.

'Just the wind,' she murmured. 'I must still have the spooks from last night.'

She and Buttercup hurried onward, along the riverbanks where the water ran sluggish and clogged with ice as it meandered toward the pond and summerhouse, turning at the little wooden bridge that led on to the lawns and tennis court. She slowed as they came near what would be a rose bed in the summer, and she glimpsed something dark and bulky on a heap of snow. A bunch of rags, a bag of old leaves that had escaped burning? Why would someone leave such a thing out there? She remembered the McTeers, and feared maybe they had left a nasty dead animal or some such as a message to Victor.

Maddie scooped up Buttercup and veered off the path toward the snowbank, just to check on it. She would have to warn Katrina at breakfast if it was something horrid, before Al could see it. She glanced around, hoping she could call for help from a gardener or something, but no one was in sight.

Within a few feet of the dark heap, Buttercup let out a sudden, piercing howl. Not just an ordinary 'I want dinner *now*' howl, but an ear-splitting shriek of rage. Or terror. She twisted hard in Maddie's arms, almost sending them both off-balance and tumbling to the snow.

'Do stop that, Buttercup!' Maddie cried. She wrapped her arms tighter around the shivering dog. 'Such fuss for a pile of rags . . .'

She tiptoed closer – and saw the red stain on the snow. A dark shoe sprawled out.

'Oh,' she gasped. It was certainly *not* a pile of rags. There was a coat, a trailing scarf, all overlaid with a dusting of snow. She forced herself to peer closer, and saw a head turned to one side, a jowly jaw gone slack, blue-gray skin.

It was Victor Luhan, dressed in a fine dark suit and black overcoat as if he was off to a business meeting. The back of his head was reduced to a bloody pulp.

This can't be happening, Maddie thought in a daze. Not after that body during Fiesta last autumn. It was a curse!

She breathed deeply of Buttercup's musky doggie smell, grasping her heaving, shaking, sturdy little terrier body close, but there was still that awful roaring in her head. That sick, sour roiling in her stomach. This had to be a dream, a very bad dream.

When she raised her head, though, the body was still there, the blood dark against the snow. The coppery tang of it hung in the air, contaminating the fresh winter wind.

Buttercup whimpered softly, cowering against Maddie's shoulder. 'It's OK, darling,' she murmured, patting her on the back like a fretful baby. She wondered fleetingly if she should check Victor's pulse, but she knew it would be utterly futile. He was *definitely* dead, and probably had been for several hours if she could judge by the amount of snow covering him, the way his limbs were sprawled at stiff angles.

And next to him – oh, no. *No*. Next to him was Al's cricket bat, the one Maddie last saw on the wall in the billiards room. The one with the initials AEL etched in the worn handle. It was covered with blood, a long crack running along its flat side.

So Maddie did the only thing she could think to do. She spun around and ran toward the house as fast as her feet could carry her, stifling screams all the way.

NINE

The whole house was in utter chaos.

As snow fell harder and thicker past the windows, blanketing the rooms in white, silent gloom, the people in the house were far from quiet.

Maddie stood in the corner of the sala, shivering despite the fur coat Rosa had wrapped around her shoulders. She could scarcely grasp that any of this was real. She'd stumbled on a dead – a *murdered!* – body. *Again*. She had the worst bally luck, and she brought bad luck with her. She dared not close her eyes, dared not think, or she would see it all again. The blood on the snow . . .

She blinked hard and made herself study the room in uproar around her. Isabella laid on her chaise, her thin, pale face puffy and red from weeping, her silvery-blonde hair flying around her shoulders as she sobbed into a large handkerchief. Dr Pierce hovered over her, frantically trying to soothe her with soft words and proffered bottles of pills, but she didn't even seem to see him as she wept on.

Sam strode from one end of the room to the other, roaring about how it must be those McTeers, someone should 'do something' about them; he would get revenge for this. Maddie wouldn't have thought quiet, stoic Sam much for blood and thunder melodrama, but grief certainly did strange things to people. Gunther watched him in wide-eyed fascination, as if taking notes for future writings.

Ben and Helena whispered together in a corner, quiet and frantic, while Felipe stood behind them, awkward and uncertain as to what to do now. Maddie was sure he hadn't been expecting this when his college buddy asked him home for the holidays.

Al was nowhere to be seen. He'd had a bad night, Katrina said, nightmares, hours of no sleep. When he was told the news of his father, he'd gone completely white, completely still. Katrina and David led him upstairs.

'Here, Miss Maddie, do sit down,' Rosa pleaded. She dragged a tapestry-cushioned chair closer and urged Maddie to take it. She stared at it for a minute, not quite remembering what a chair was possibly for, before she dropped down on to it, her knees trembling.

'It must have been such a shock. I would have fainted away,' Rosa said. She straightened the coat over Maddie's shoulders and reached for a cashmere blanket tossed over a settee to smooth it over her lap. Maddie felt quite swaddled, but she had to admit it was a comfort. Rosa was young, but she seemed to see just what people needed.

She nodded. 'I – yes, a shock. Where is Don Victor now?'

'Still outside! Strange,' Rosa whispered, her lovely caramel-brown eyes going even wider. 'Not that I would know what to do. Dr Cole got someone on the phone before the line went dead in this snow, some police inspector from Santa Fe. The policeman insisted we leave him – that is, it, Don Victor's body – there so he can examine it when he gets here. He told us to stay away from the spot. It seems so – so blasphemous somehow . . .'

Maddie patted her hand. 'It does seem barbaric, I know, but there can be lots of little clues left around the body that can be destroyed if it's moved.' A terrible thought struck her. 'Wait. Was this inspector named Sadler?'

'I think so. Yes, that sounds right.'

'Oh, no,' she groaned. Just what the Luhans needed! Sadler and his bowler hat crashing around on them.

'That is, if he could even get through. They say the roads are even worse than usual with the snow. We're all stuck here for now.'

Ugh. Stuck in a strange house with strange people, a murdered body – and surely a murderer, too. And now Sadler. Merry Christmas indeed.

She studied each face in the room carefully: Isabella, Marta, Helena, Sam, Ben, though Felipe was not there now. Where had he gone? She wondered what their motives were for possibly killing Victor, and if they had opportunity. Helena, Ben and Sam wanted to choose their own lives. Isabella's husband had been unfaithful to her, dismissive.

'How are you feeling now, Miss Maddie?' Rosa said quietly. She was such a kind girl, truly, and so pretty. Maddie wished she wasn't always buried out here at Los Pintores, not caught in this ugliness now. 'Should I find Dr Cole for you?'

'No, no. He's needed with Al right now. But thank you.'

Rosa shook her head. 'Poor Señor Alfonso. It's all been so awful for him. He used to be so funny. So full of jokes and pranks.'

'You've known him a long time, then, Rosa? You must know them all well.'

'Very long, yes. I always lived with Tia Marta. She never married, and always worked here, ever since she got a job as kitchen maid when she was younger than me. She has a cottage on the estate, just past the kitchen garden, and we live there. I went to school in Albuquerque for a while, and came back last year to help her in the house. Just until I can find an office job or something like that.' She glanced across the room at Ben and Helena.

'I knew Don Victor wasn't – well, he wasn't a very nice man,' Rosa whispered quickly, as if she was driven to confide something. Maddie was never averse to listening to any gossip, and she nodded for her to go on. 'Lots of people didn't like him, and I could see why. But he was good to my aunt and me when I came here. He gave us a bigger cottage, let me read the books in his office. He even helped Tia Marta send me to that school! I hated when he shouted, and he did hover around me so much, but – well, he didn't deserve to die like that.'

Maddie wondered what other different sides there could be to Victor Luhan. Bully, stern paterfamilias, considerate employer. Not so considerate as a father and husband, though. 'No one deserves that. I'm so sorry, Rosa.' She squeezed the girl's hand.

'Rosa!' Marta called as she swept into the room carrying a tea tray. 'Cease chattering like that; I'm sure Mrs Vaughn-Alwin has many things to attend to. I need your help in the kitchen.'

'Of course, Tia,' Rosa murmured, and scurried away. Maddie

was sorry to see her go. She had nothing at all to attend to, and it left her too much to think around in circles.

Marta handed her a cup of tea. 'That niece of mine. Smart as a whip, she always was, and curious, but it sometimes gets in the way of her work.'

'She does seem quite an intelligent young lady, Mrs Sanchez, and kind. You must be very proud of her. You've brought her up so well.'

'Harumph,' Marta said, and carefully sliced a cake on the tray. 'I have tried. Her dear mama, Angela, was my sister, and I have tried to do my best for her daughter. Angela was beautiful, you see, but flighty. Wild. I always feared she'd come to a sad end, and she did. But none of that is Rosa's fault. I have always tried to make sure she doesn't end up like her mother.'

Maddie wondered what exactly had happened to Rosa's mother. 'She does seem like a very good girl. Exactly what my own parents wished I had been! And she is very pretty.'

Marta gave a humorless bark of laughter. 'Angela did get all the beauty in my family, as you can see in me, Mrs Vaughn-Alwin. My sister could have gone on the stage, she was that pretty. She worked here as a maid, like I did, at first, but she could have done more with a bit of sense. Rosa is her image.'

'And Rosa's father?'

Marta shrugged. 'I never met him. Just some fella Angie met at one of her speakeasies in Santa Fe. She was always getting some rancho hand or other to drive her up there on her days off. One of those days she found herself in trouble by someone she found there. That sure wasn't in her plans! We had the idea I would look after the baby while Angie found work in town. But then she died, soon after Rosa was born.'

Maddie swallowed past the tight knot of tears that closed her throat at that story. 'I'm so sorry.'

Marta scowled. 'Angie was always like that. But it wasn't so terrible. I always thought I wouldn't marry or have children, and yet God gave me Rosa. She is a daughter to me, and a sweeter one you would never find, truly. But now she is growing up, she needs to be careful. I keep a close watch, but . . .' She glanced at Sam and Ben, the two of them now whispering by the window since Sam had finally quieted down. Marta frowned at them.

Maddie was struck by a terrible thought. 'But maybe you're afraid of the Luhan boys . . .'

'Not one of them. It would be too wicked.' Marta slammed the teapot down, spilling a few drops on the tray cloth. 'But you never know about men. I have seen too many things myself. Rosa is a pretty, vulnerable girl. I must always watch.'

Isabella called for tea, and Marta bustled away with a cup for her. Had one of the Luhan boys, or even Victor himself, pestered Rosa? Caused her trouble? Or maybe one of the boys was interested in Rosa in an honorable way, and Victor hadn't liked that? Wasn't that usually the motive for violence? Sex and money.

Gunther joined Maddie, pulling a chair close to her so they could whisper. He offered her a plate of cake as they watched Ben go to the piano and run his fingers softly over the keys, coaxing a flurry of music into the tense room.

'You should eat something, Mads darling,' Gunther said gently. 'Keep your strength up, especially if it's true that old Sadler is about to show up on the doorstep.'

Maddie sighed and reached for a scone to nibble. Sadler. Yes. If he could possibly snowshoe his way to Los Pintores, he would. A bloody murder amid a prominent family. He couldn't stand another scandal after the Montoya case. It all had such parallels to that tragedy – an old Santa Fe family, a scandal threatening to race through the streets. Sadler had a reputation as a strict law-and-order sort to maintain.

Marta brought Gunther another cup of tea, and he topped it off with a bit of Poquaque Lightning from his trusty flask. He added some to Maddie's cup, too. 'Drink up, darling.'

'Gunther, you are, as ever, a lifesaver.' Maddie took a gulp of the bracing brew and drew in a sharp breath. 'This is not quite the Christmas we envisioned.'

'Christmas is usually a fearfully boring time, as I'm sure you remember from New York, my dearest. I was hoping for bonfires and cider here, maybe some dancing and some pan dulce to eat, but I've certainly never had one nearly as dramatic as this. I am, as they say, shocked but not surprised.'

'How so? I'm pretty shocked *and* surprised.'

'Well, just think about our paterfamilias, Victor Luhan. Such anger from every corner of this fair rancho! So many reasons he's made himself disliked by nearly everyone. With us all trapped like this in the middle of nowhere, hemmed in by the also-dramatic snow and that howling wind, like something in a Poe story. Something is bound to snap. Human nature can only take so much.'

'*The Secret of Chimneys*,' Maddie murmured.

'Chimneys, darling?'

'Oh, it's the very newest Christie, a friend in New York just sent it to me. It hasn't even been published in America yet! Not her best at all, in my opinion. There's a stolen diamond, you see, and a deposed monarchy and something about a British oil syndicate, not like here. But they are all rather stuck at a house party where no one is what they really seem.'

'You think one of the Luhan sons is an imposter? Delicious!'

Maddie laughed. 'If only it was that easy. I think they're sons who had a complicated relationship with their parent. But I do think there is one person here who didn't hate Victor.'

'Mrs Upshaw, maybe? He's her bread and butter, I bet, but my dear, those utterly vile hats.'

'So bad hats correlate to psychosis? I hate to know what you might really think about my new green cloche.'

'The color could be better, Mads, but of course fashion can say much about a person! And Mrs Upshaw's is – interesting. So bad it almost tips back into good, at least in an eccentric way. But maybe she became overwhelmingly irritated at his pompous ways and could not take it a moment longer, even if he *is* her golden ticket at the moment. She might see herself as the future Mrs Luhan. Victor could have raised her hopes, and then refused to leave Isabella.'

Maddie considered this. 'The Luhans have been married forever, though, and have a position to uphold in society. And then there's the Church.' She gestured to the retablos in the wall niches, the silver cross on the wall. 'He didn't seem the sort to give all that up for a secretary, no matter how great her hats.'

'See. One reason for Mrs Upshaw to do the deed in a fit of fury.'

'Maybe.' Maddie had certainly heard that, besides the aforementioned sex and money, maintaining the status quo was the main motive to kill. It often was in Mrs Christie's better literary efforts. Love, passion, jealousy, all those played big parts, but losing one's reputation, a high position, a comfortable home, was the most fervent. 'Would she have the strength to wield a cricket bat like that? It was all cracked on one side, and his head was a mess.' She felt a rush of sour sickness in her throat at the memory of that terrible sight.

'I am sorry you had to see that, darling,' Gunther said gently, pouring more of his num-num flask into her tea. 'Whatever were you doing wandering around so early?'

'I . . . I just couldn't sleep.' Maddie sniffled, afraid she would start weeping. Gunther, always full of useful practicalities, handed her a lavender-scented handkerchief. She dabbed at her damp eyes. If only she could wipe the memory away, too. 'I had such strange dreams, and I thought I heard someone arguing in the corridor.'

'Arguing? Who was it?'

Maddie closed her eyes and tried to remember. It felt like eons ago now. 'I'm not sure. A man and a woman. They were talking too quietly, drat them, for a really good snoop. They did sound angry. When I woke up so early, everything did seem wonderfully quiet, the cold wind so bracing. I thought I'd just walk a bit, think about the paintings I want to work on back home. Just be alone for a while.'

'It does seem one can never be alone in houses like this. So much noise and distraction everywhere.'

'Then why did you come here? You said your new book is far behind where it should be.'

He shrugged, his vivid blue eyes shadowed and tired. 'It's true I am a teensy bit stuck in my current tome, and my publisher is making squeals about when it might cross their desks. Isabella offered me a casita for the holiday, a place away from town and all our lovely parties where I could concentrate, and it sounded rather the thing. I've told you Isabella loves to be seen as a patron of the arts! I didn't know they were playing out a Jacobean drama here. They've all been quarreling ever since I arrived, and someone is always knocking at my casita door. I've written hardly a chapter. But maybe, once things are solved and settled, some of this *sturm und drang* might be useful for the next story.'

'I don't ever want to paint that ghastly scene I came across today,' Maddie whispered. Gunther put his arm around her shoulders and held her close, the two of them like a wall against the horror.

Everyone, even Sam and his temper tantrum, had settled into silence when David appeared in the sala again, Katrina beside him. She looked even more windblown than usual, her cheeks puffy and pink with tears, her hair piled atop her head in a bird's nest, her gaze shadowed and distant.

Maddie rushed to her, taking her arm to lead her to the tapestry chair. 'Katrina, darling, do sit here with me. Gunther will make you one of his special cups of tea; it will do you such good.'

David seemed to read her mind. He drew more chairs to their little corner, and they huddled around together. Katrina seemed frozen, her eyes blank, but a few warming sips of Gunther's tea seemed to help. She shook, and sucked in a deep, ragged breath as she slumped back against the cushions.

'How are you feeling?' Maddie said gently. She touched Katrina's hand, and it was as cold as the snow outside.

'Well enough now,' Katrina said, her hearty voice dismayingly faint. 'Your dishy doctor here gave me a draught, and now I feel a bit more like myself. I don't feel like ants are crawling over me any more.'

'Quite a normal reaction to a shock,' David said. 'Your color does look much better now, and your pulse is steady.'

'And Al?' Maddie asked.

A small frown flickered over David's lips, and he rubbed wearily at his jaw. 'I gave him a stronger sedative. He's asleep now. Marta sent a lad up from the kitchen to stay by his door and keep watch so he can call me at a second's notice. He was very agitated at the news, of course.'

'He kept shouting that *he* should have been the one to do

it, it was his duty. You could all hear it, I know!' Katrina said. 'And something about demons. Demons he could see floating in through the windows, following us all in the house.' She broke off on a raw sob. She gulped down the last of her tea and buried her face in her hands. Her wedding ring gleamed in the snowy light. 'I thought, hoped, he was doing better, becoming himself again. Now this will send him back, make him even more depressed!'

'I have told you, Katrina, he should go to an asylum,' Isabella called across the room. She sat on the edge of her chaise, brushing back Dr Pierce when he tried to make her lie down. 'It won't be safe for any of us for him to stay here. Look what happened! He needs to be properly looked after, for everyone's safety. People will talk once they hear of all this. To think – a *Luhan* displaying their dirty linen for everyone to see!'

She broke into wild, stormy sobs, and collapsed on to her cushions again, taking a bottle of smelling salts from Dr Pierce. Helena glared at her, arms crossed, and Sam stared out the window. It seemed only one of them could rave at once.

'Dirty linen,' Katrina scoffed to Maddie. 'She's one to talk, with the ever-so-devoted doctor always hovering over her, and Victor and his secretaries and actresses. Helena sneaking out whenever she can. Al's illness isn't shameful!'

'Of course it is not,' Maddie assured her. But everyone else – yes, so many secrets in the manor house. Mrs Christie had been right about that.

'Shell shock is quite a much-seen, if not much understood, reaction to horrible sights no human has the power to endure unchanged,' David said. 'Al merely needs some help to find a new way of moving through the world. I would definitely recommend a peaceful place after all this is over.'

'Not a lunatic asylum!' Katrina cried.

David shook his head. 'Not an asylum. A spa town, maybe. Then a small, quiet home, a place where physicians can call on you, you can follow a proper regime. I can help you find such a situation.'

Maddie smiled at him, her heart bursting as she looked at this gorgeous, caring man she'd found. A man she could count on. 'And don't worry a jot about any money, Katrina, we'll sort it all out.'

Katrina flashed them a grateful smile and twisted a handkerchief between her fingers. 'You are such good eggs. It helps to know we have friends nearby. But I don't know how we'll get out of this all right. Surely when this inspector gets here, he'll think it's my Al who did it. It was his cricket bat, after all, and if his own mother thinks . . .'

'Anyone could have taken that bat! It's hardly Fort Knox here,' Maddie protested. But, after working with Inspector Sadler and his tendency to make quick judgments before, she was secretly worried. Al did seem an obvious suspect. Why look further into a houseful of them?

'Plenty of others have motive, too, and surely we all had opportunity,' Gunther said, a story-plotting gleam in his eyes. 'Where was everyone last night, anyway?'

'We will just have to find out who had the *most* motive,' Maddie said. 'Hopefully before Sadler gets here.'

Katrina glanced wide-eyed around their little circle. 'Are you *detectives*? Like Hercule Poirot?'

Maddie and Gunther laughed. 'Not quite like Poirot, of course. My little gray cells are very little indeed,' Maddie said. 'But we've been able to help out in a sticky situation or two, and I think we've learned some stuff along the way. We want to help you if we can, Katrina darling.'

'Well, I do know Al didn't do it,' Katrina insisted. 'He couldn't have!'

'I'm quite sure he couldn't,' Maddie said. 'But someone here did it. I fear we are not especially safe, sitting here in the snow. Your mother-in-law is right about that, anyway. We'll have to be discreet.'

Katrina nodded solemnly. 'I can be quiet, Mads, you remember.'

Maddie thought of those school hockey fields, Katrina hollering exhortations, and realized she knew no such thing. But Katrina would certainly do anything to protect her husband.

'I think the first thing we should do is get out of this room for a while, get some fresh air,' Gunther said. He shuddered.

'The atmosphere in here is too, too ghastly. Let's go for a walk. See if we find anything out there.'

Maddie nodded. Getting out of that stuffy, shadowed sala sounded necessary. Katrina glanced at the doorway, uncertain, but David persuaded her Al would sleep peacefully for quite some time, and it would certainly be a long while before the inspector could make it over the roads. They stood up and hurried to fetch coats and gloves.

'Oh, can I please come with you?' Helena cried. 'I will start screaming if I stay here another second!'

'Helena, you must be careful!' Isabella cried, but Helena ignored her mother.

'Of course, do come,' Maddie said, and Helena hurried out with them to find her own fur coat and mufflers.

Ignoring Isabella's screams that they would all be killed, and Marta's warnings about pneumonia, they plunged out the front door into the snowy, bitingly cold day. Even a storm seemed safer than staying in that house.

'It's really a beautiful house,' Maddie told Helena as they reached the top of a slope that led back down to the thick line of trees hiding the terrible scene. They both turned to look around them at the house and gardens, at Katrina walking with Gunther and David at the foot of the slope.

Los Pintores seemed so peaceful there in the drifts of snow, skidding clouds casting shadows over its pale beige walls, its portals and windows. It seemed silent, timeless, not at all like a place where violence had burst out so suddenly and passed away just as swiftly. It had all left a heavy air of unreality in its wake.

Helena tilted her head as she studied her family home, an unreadable expression on her pretty face. She didn't seem to be very grief-stricken or frantic now at her father's demise, or even frightened that a killer might be on the loose. She just seemed tired, thoughtful.

'Yes, I suppose it is. My great-whatever grandfather was granted it by the king of Spain in seventeen-something. I think the house had five rooms originally, with towers at each end to guard against raids, just like in a novel! But they had lots of kids, and the place grew to twenty rooms and a stable that's the casita now, plus the pond, the grist mill, the chapel. I don't really see it any more. I've just wanted to get away from it for so long.' She bent down and scooped up a bit of snow in her gloved hand, letting it drift away on the wind like a shining silver ribbon.

'I can understand that.'

Helena glanced at her, one penciled brow arched in surprise. 'Can you? But it sounds like you're so independent, with your own house and your work painting. And your gorgeous fiancé, who I'm sure you chose yourself.'

'I suppose I am, now. But before I came to New Mexico, my situation was much like yours. A family who always thought they knew what was best for me, that followed tradition and society's expectations and wouldn't allow me to do otherwise. I felt trapped in that house in New York, trapped by all the years of my family's life bound up in those walls.' Maddie wrapped her arms tight around herself as she thought of that Fifth Avenue house, the dark corridors and rooms stuffed with gilt-framed art and looming old furniture. The eyes always watching, ears always listening.

'Then how did you get out?' Helena asked eagerly.

'I was very lucky. I had some money from my grandmother that became my own to control once I married, and my first husband left me some when I lost him in the war. I loved him very much, and was pushed into what seemed like a deep, dark hole when I realized I would never see him again. Never laugh with him again. But Pete and I knew each other a long time; we came from the same world and understood each other, and I knew he would want me to find a brighter way forward. A way just for myself.'

'So you chose to come *here*?'

'I didn't set out to. I have a cousin who wanted to be an actress, so I headed on a trip to California with her, as I didn't know what else to do. The train stopped here, and I was just gobsmacked by what I saw. I never imagined light like this, so pure and clear and piercingly bright. Such a sky, so much open space, room to breathe. So I stayed. And it's been grand.'

Helena gave her head a disbelieving shake, her glossy dark

bob swinging under the brim of her fur-edged hat. 'Amazing. You are very brave, Maddie. I wouldn't even know where to start all by myself.'

'It's definitely not easy to take that first step,' Maddie agreed.

Helena kicked at a drift of snow, sending it sparkling up into the air. 'I thought I might want to go East when I was younger, try a school there. I loved reading stories about girls in their boarding schools, playing pranks and making friends. Learning new things. I do like fashion – everything about it, the fabric and color and movement – so I imagined maybe writing for a lady's magazine. Papa wouldn't hear of it, of course! Luhan ladies always marry, have children, keep a fine house, entertain other old families, go to church. That's what he always said, always banged on about. So, I was sent to Loretto.'

Maddie thought of the twins, skipping up the stone steps into their school past waiting sisters, bells ringing. 'It's not a bad school at all. My friend's daughters go there; they love their lessons.'

'It's true, it didn't turn out so dreadful. The nuns were strict, but I could get around them easy enough.' Helena's eyes sparkled with mischief, and Maddie was sure those were very true words. 'I liked the books of poetry we read, liked sketching and our French lessons. Best of all, I liked finally being in town after being locked up here forever. There was dancing and music, cocktails. Handsome boys.' She kicked out at a rock emerging from the snow. 'Then I was dragged back here. I'm too young to get stuck with some boring old husband. A house like this. No wonder Mama is always so ill.'

Maddie nodded. She thought of Helena dancing with Felipe, galloping across the floor in gales of laughter. It didn't look like such a prison in those moments. 'Felipe is handsome. Does his family have a place like Los Pintores?'

'Oh, sure! They're out toward Taos. He's dishy, isn't he? And young, not much older than me,' Helena said with a thoughtful frown. 'His family are the Martinez-Campbells, they have a large rancho. We didn't see much of them when I was growing up, but my mother's cousin married into them. That's why Ben is allowed to be such friends with him. He'd do well enough. But he's still at college. What would I do in the meantime?' She suddenly laughed and gave a little spin. 'Of course, Papa is gone now. Everything is different.'

Different indeed. 'Aren't you frightened a murderer is still lurking around? It gives me the shivers.'

Helena glanced back at Maddie in surprise. Maddie wondered if she hadn't thought of going onstage herself; she had a very expressive face. Fear, calculation, shock, joy. 'But surely that was some passing maniac, and they've vanished off into the snow again.'

'Is that who you think did this?'

Helena walked on, striding down the slope toward the trees. 'Who else could it be? Maybe some escaped convict from the penitentiary. I bet it was a burglar, and Papa surprised him. I don't think it could be anyone else. There's not much for miles and miles. I know that all too well.'

Maddie studied the McTeer place in the distance. 'There's your neighbors.'

'The McTeers?' Helena cried.

'They don't seem to have gotten along with your father.'

'How could they?' Helena laughed. 'Papa hated them. They weren't the family who sold them the estate; they haven't been here for hundreds of years. They aren't even Spanish, and they keep sheep and grow the wrong crops. It was too, too dreadful for them; they're just trying to make a living, a home for themselves, like everyone else. Papa could just never realize this is 1924, not 1824. But the McTeers mind their own business, they never wanted to pester my father or anyone else.'

Helena sounded quite fierce about that. Quite decided. 'So, you like the McTeers?'

'I – I don't know them very well.' Helena shrugged. 'I'm not allowed to be friends with them, am I? But I do know my father. Whatever happened, I'm sure they weren't the ones who started it! No one would bash someone over the head for being a bad neighbor; there'd be no one left. Not a *normal* person, anyway. Now, if it had been a McTeer killed – I'm sure it would have been Papa who did it.' Her eyes widened. 'Oh! I hope someone warned them a maniac is wandering around. They should be careful!'

Maddie thought Helena definitely seemed more worried about the neighbors than about her father, but really after years of being cooped up, limited, disregarded, who could blame her? 'Inspector Sadler will be here soon; I'm sure he's put out the word.'

'But who knows when that will be? News can move pretty slowly out here. Maybe I should go over there and talk to them?'

'I'm not your mother or anything, Helena, but surely I shouldn't let you walk around alone with an escaped convict on the loose,' Maddie said sternly. She felt like her old nanny, being stern, though surely she couldn't be much older than Helena.

'Hmph. Well, you're probably right,' Helena admitted grudgingly. She gave the snow one more kick, then turned back toward the house. David, Katrina and Gunther were already walking that way, as the wind was whipping closer again, catching at coats and mufflers with icy fingers. 'It's actually really nice of you to worry, Maddie. If you *were* my mother, I doubt you'd care at all, unless you thought I would cause some gossip.'

Maddie thought of Isabella Luhan, spending her days on her chaise, her doctor hovering close. 'Has your mother always been in delicate health? That must be so hard for everyone.'

'As long as I can remember. Lots of fainting spells, nerve pain, days in her room. Who could blame her? She has a nice suite all to herself, lovely and quiet. She doesn't have to listen to Papa, or even do much about running the house. Marta does that. She also brings up Mama's meals whenever she likes. Mama doesn't even have to sit through interminable dinners listening to how civilization is going to ruin thanks to bobbed hair and jazz.'

'And has Dr Pierce been helping her for long?'

'Hmm. A year or so? She always has some doctor or *curandera* or other out here. Poor Mama. I've been doing a lot of the chatelaine duties here for a while, ordering and menus and such, with Katrina's help, and I'm tired of it. They say Mama was the most beautiful girl in Santa Fe when she had her first ball.' Helena gave another little spin, her arms outstretched like a snow angel. 'Maybe we can all do something different now!'

They met up with the others and followed Helena around to the kitchen door at the back of the house, falling into the warm, flagstone-floored hallway on a blast of freezing wind. As they took off their wet boots and shook out their coats, Katrina hurried up to check on Al, and Marta appeared. She studied them disapprovingly, hands planted on her hips.

'Señorita Helena! You've been outside too long; you will catch a cold.'

'Good thing we have two handsome doctors here, then,' Helena said cheerfully as she kissed Marta's cheek and Marta patted her hand. They did seem affectionate, and Marta had been with the Luhans for a very long time. What did she know about all the secrets lurking in a house like Los Pintores? 'Is Mama upstairs?'

'No, there is someone in the sala now, and somehow he seems to think Señora Luhan is in charge now,' Marta said as she gathered up their scarves and hats.

'Mama in charge? What an odd notion. Who is it, then?'

'That policeman from Santa Fe, of course. Dr Cole called for him, and he did come out here quicker than I supposed. Tracked mud and melted snow all over my clean floors! And we'll have to put them up in the old maids' rooms behind the kitchen, too,' Marta tsked. 'Rosa just took in a cake, fresh from the oven, and some biscochitos. You'd best get in there. Your mother seemed all flustered; she can't be taken ill again. After all that's happened . . .'

'Of course she would be flustered! Good heavens, police at Los Pintores.' Helena seemed quite excited by the possibility. 'Maybe he can tell us about escaped convicts. Just like in *The Shock*. You know, that movie about the gang of blackmailers . . .'

Marta scowled suspiciously. 'Where would you see a film, Señorita Helena?'

Helena waved her hand as if to brush away such queries. 'Oh, you know. I read about it.'

Maddie took in a deep breath, hoping against hope someone besides the inspector had come. 'What was this policeman's name, then, Marta?'

'Siler? Simpson? Oh! Sadler. What sort of name is that, I ask you?' Marta said. 'And such an appetite! Already ate a plate of sandwiches while you were out in the snow. I had to send in a cake I just finished – it was meant for tea, to cheer everyone up after such a shock. If we can't get more supplies in, I will have nothing left for Christmas! Tomorrow is Christmas Eve, you know.'

Maddie sighed. Of course it was Sadler, despite her hopes they might send someone else last minute. She and David exchanged a long glance and wry grimaces. She could only hope the teensy bit of softening she'd detected during the Montoya case would move along. 'So, the holiday festivities are going ahead?'

'Of course! Christmas has *always* happened here at Los Pintores. Music, feasting, visitors. Why should it cease now?'

Maddie nodded. Why indeed? No one really seemed terribly cut up about Victor Luhan getting his head bashed in, Maddie thought. Maybe Sadler, if he had to be there, would have some useful thoughts about it all.

Maddie left her snow-wet coat at the side door and marched up the stairs toward the sala. Floating from behind that door was the rumble of a deep, flatly accented voice, going on about 'law and order,' 'get to the bottom of things,' and so on. A horribly *familiar* voice.

Maddie sighed as she marched resolutely into the room. She and Sadler were certainly old – could you call them *acquaintances* by then? After Juanita's husband, the movie murder, and the Montoya case, they'd gotten rather used to each other, if not terribly understanding. But she couldn't say she liked the man yet. He was still too officious and narrow-minded, though softening a bit. Santa Fe could do that to a person.

One wouldn't think there had been any 'softening' at all from the fierce scowl on his face now. His bulldog face was bright red from the cold outside, his red-gray beard in need of a good comb and dose of beard oil, his pale blue eyes beady and determined. Cake crumbs were scattered across the front of his old tweed jacket. Next to him sat his constable, Rickie

Archuleta, an old friend of Eddie Anaya's who had heroically managed to work with Sadler for a year now, a notebook open on his knee. He smiled and nodded at Maddie. Rosa offered him a cup of coffee, and he grinned up at her, the two of them whispering together.

'Hello, Inspector!' Maddie said in her cheeriest voice. 'It's been a while since we met. How maddening for you to have to get out in this dreadful weather.'

'Barely made it through with the storm coming this way. They just closed the road from Santa Fe,' Sadler muttered, in the middle of lifting a bite of cake to his mouth. 'We're going to have to stay here while we investigate.'

Oh, goodie, Maddie thought.

'Closed the road?' Isabella cried, her coffee cup clattering in its saucer. 'You mean we are *trapped* here with some homicidal maniac running free?' She'd obviously been talking to her daughter. Dr Pierce calmed her, urging her to sit back again, take more coffee. Settling that 'delicate constitution.'

'I thought you'd probably be here, Mrs Alwin, when it was Dr Cole who called me,' Sadler said. 'You're always billing and cooing at each other these days.'

'I object, Inspector! I never coo, and I'm not at all sure how to bill,' Maddie answered with a laugh. 'But we *are* engaged, so yes we are together for Christmas.' She sighed, thinking the Christmas she'd hoped for was quite tattered now, and David was always so busy on holidays.

'Well, I should have known you'd be here,' Sadler said. 'Wherever you are, there's trouble for my police department.'

Rickie left Rosa to fetch a chair for Maddie closer to the fire. 'Believe me, Inspector, I wish this trouble was far away. I only wanted a peaceful, old-fashioned sort of holiday.'

Isabella glanced between them, eyes narrowed suspiciously. 'You and this man know each other, Mrs Vaughn-Alwin?'

'Sadly, yes, Mrs Luhan.' Maddie sighed. She smiled up at Rosa as the girl handed her a cup of coffee and took a blessedly warm sip. It was quite sad that Gunther and his flask were seated so far away, as he had started noodling at the piano. The strains of Gershwin floated toward them, a funereal version of 'Fascinating Rhythm', if she wasn't mistaken. 'The Montoya business at Fiestas . . .'

'And the *Far Sunset* movie thing,' Rickie supplied.

'Poor Catalina Montoya,' Isabella said faintly. 'We were at school at Loretto together, you know. Shocking that she's engaged again already. But surely *you* could help us with this matter, Mrs Vaughn-Alwin, if you have some sort of . . . experience in this sort of thing. And discretion. We don't need more people trampling over our home right now! And we definitely don't need gossip.'

Sam turned from staring at the fire, much calmer than his earlier fury. Maddie wondered if Gunther's flask had got to him. 'Mama, if there's a deranged killer running around on the loose like you all seem to have decided, surely we can use all the security we can get right now.'

Sadler's pale blue eyes narrowed to pinpricks. Maddie had learned never to trust that look; it meant he was surely narrowing in on some notion of who did this, and once he decided it would be hard to shift him away from it. 'You think this was random, then? A wandering lunatic?'

'Or an escaped convict,' Helena cried. 'You do read about stuff like that all the time.'

Maddie didn't blame Sadler for looking doubtful. Lunatics and escaped convicts were not nearly as common as novels would have everyone believe, and where would such a person have gone in this weather?

Isabella glanced up uncertainly at Dr Pierce and set down her cup with a clatter. 'I – well, yes, of course. It must be. The . . . the shocking *violence* of it all! Not at all normal. And if it's not, then . . . then . . .' She broke off with a harried sob.

'Then it must be one of us,' Sam said. 'Or possibly one of the McTeers. No one else is close enough, are they?'

Helena turned on him with a furious glare. 'Surely not the McTeers! If anyone, Papa would have killed one of *them*. Yes, I'm sure it was a convict or something of the sort. Everyone reads about this sort of thing all the time.'

'Depends on what you read, I suppose,' Sadler said. He put down his empty cake plate, took a battered notebook from his coat pocket, and flipped through the blotched, closely written pages. Maddie was astonished he could read that jumble. 'There are no escaped convicts reported lately. And no patients with homicidal tendencies, am I right, Dr Cole?'

'Not to my knowledge, no,' David answered.

'Now, then. Who are these McTeers? And who is staying in this house right now?' Sadler asked, taking out a stubby pencil.

Isabella moaned and fluttered her hands. Her fingers were weighed down with flashing rubies and sapphires, an enormous pearl. Helena and Sam filled the gaps of information, listing the family and guests filling the rooms at Los Pintores, a bit about the fences-make-neighbors saga of the McTeers, as Sadler and Rickie took notes.

'We are, or were, expecting a few others tomorrow for Christmas Eve,' Helena said. 'Including Papa's friend Father Adrian, from Rosales. He usually says Mass for us in our chapel, and then there's dinner and dancing after, followed by Christmas games here in the sala. But I guess now he can see to the funeral rites.'

'As soon as we release the body, Miss Luhan. Procedures have to be followed,' Sadler snapped as he turned to David. 'Any ideas yet, Dr Cole?'

'It's very difficult to say; the body was out in the freezing weather for a while, and I haven't had a proper look at it yet,' David answered.

'Get him moved inside, then, as soon as we can get outside and take a look ourselves. I'm sure there's a shed or icehouse we can use until he can be moved to the morgue in town.' Sadler pointed his pencil at the window, where the snow was thicker now. 'And until we can get out of here ourselves.'

Maddie remembered the pretty chapel they'd walked past earlier. There were so many outbuildings, cottages and sheds and barns, where people and things could hide. She thought of the tales of the Los Pintores ghost, and imagined a chapel sounded like a perfect place for it.

'There is an icehouse, not far from the kitchen door,' Sam said. 'We can get him moved there when you're ready. Can't leave him out there heaped with snow, I suppose.'

Helena gave a bubble of wild laughter, like she couldn't stop herself in her shock. 'Like the most frightful snowman!'

Isabella snapped her fingers at them, those rings flashing in the firelight. 'Children! Such appalling manners. What a way to speak of your . . . your own father.' She gave a ragged sob, and turned her face away.

'Excuse me for a moment,' David murmured, and hurried from the room.

'And where is he going?' Sadler demanded.

Rosa paused in stacking the coffee tray to carry out. 'To see to Señor Alfonso, I think, Inspector.'

'Alfonso?' Sadler glanced at his notebook. 'Oh. The shell-shocked one.'

'He had a terrible war, Inspector,' Maddie said quietly. 'His wife, Katrina, was a school friend of mine in New York, and that's why I'm here. To try and help them if I can.'

'A terrible war, huh? Everyone had a terrible war, but they don't go to pieces over it all.' Sadler sniffed and turned a notebook page. 'But I can't say I'm unsympathetic. I was in Havana in 'ninety-eight. To see friends killed in that way . . .' He harumphed again, not looking up. 'So how does he behave when these spells come on him, then? Is he violent? Blackouts?'

Helena and Sam exchanged a long glance, and Maddie remembered it was Al's bat that had done the deed.

'Certainly not!' Isabella protested. 'Alfonso has always been my happiest child, so bright and sunny. Victor did have such high standards sometimes, of course, and liked them to be met quickly. He was not terribly flexible about life, and Alfonso could not always meet those standards these days. But surely . . .' Her voice trailed away.

'I see,' Sadler muttered. He wrote something rather long in that incomprehensible penmanship, and Maddie started to worry he might be focusing in on Al. 'Well, never fear, I'll get to the culprit. This is the 1920s now, and this place is a *state*, not some back-water, outlaw territory. American law and civilization rule here.'

That's what Maddie worried about. Families like the Luhans had been on their ranchos for generations, they all knew each other, and they were used to managing as they pleased.

Cooperation, 'civilization' of any other sort, would not impress them. And Sadler hadn't yet learned how to discover what he needed from all the New Mexico sorts.

He suddenly put away his notebook and pushed up from his chair. 'I'd like to see the house soon and meet everyone as quickly as possible.'

'Of course,' Isabella said. She reached for the embroidered velvet bell-pull next to the fireplace. 'I'll send for Marta – our housekeeper Mrs Sanchez – and she can show you.'

'I can show you to the kitchen, Inspector Sadler,' Maddie said. 'I am sure Mrs Luhan should rest.'

'Indeed she should,' Dr Pierce said in a very steely tone. 'Her health is most fragile. She really should be admitted to a clinic for a rest as soon as possible. I only hope it is not too late.'

Isabella reached out to clutch at his hand. 'Whatever would I do without you, my darling doctor? No one else understands what I suffer. The pain today! I can't bear it.'

'Please, Inspector,' Dr Pierce admonished. 'Do be careful of my patient's health. She has such weakness, and this makes it all dangerously worse.'

Helena muttered something to her brother, and Sam covered a hiccupping laugh. Maddie waved to Sadler and Rickie and led them from the sala and towards the stairs that went down to the kitchen.

'Crazy dame,' Sadler growled. 'One doctor trailing around after just one woman! Is she really that ill?'

'I couldn't say at all,' Maddie answered. 'She does seem quite exhausted – and is it any wonder? So much tension in this family. And I should know.' She thought of her own mother's icy, silent anger, her father's distance, and shuddered. All those emotions and furies rushing around under still waters, it couldn't be healthy.

'In what way?' Sadler asked. He examined a set of prints hanging along the staircase wall, views of the Alhambra. 'What's going on with these people?'

'I . . .' Maddie glanced back, unsure what she should, or could, say. What she could trust. 'Are you asking my advice?'

'Well . . . hmph, Mrs Vaughn-Alwin. Not *advice*. Per se.'

Sadler straightened one of the prints. 'But I guess you were a bit helpful with that Montoya business.'

'And with the film set,' Rickie said helpfully. 'And with Eddie's dad . . .'

'Sure,' Sadler snapped. 'That's all water under the bridge now, never mind. You just seem to know how to talk to people like this. Get through to them. All sorts of people, really.'

Maddie tilted her head to study his expression, the abashed way he stomped down the rest of the stairs, his face reddened. 'People like this?'

'Snooty sorts. And artsy sorts. I'm not good at all that round-about and fol-de-rol.'

Maddie wondered where he got such phrases. Dickens novels? 'Really, Inspector? I never would have noticed.'

'I'm an old-fashioned, straight-to-the-point man.'

'Hmm. And people like the Luhans are old-fashioned, too. Like, 1750-style old-fashioned. It's a special language. Everyone has one.'

Sadler frowned as they turned along the long flagstoned corridor that led to the kitchen. 'What do you mean?'

'I mean, I guess, that I'm an artist. We learn to see way below the surface, even when we don't seem to look at all. Even when no one *wants* us to see, and we don't even want to see it ourselves. People like the Luhans, like my own family, they aren't used to being questioned. To have anyone look beyond their surface, which they've spent decades, centuries, polishing. I'm really surprised they let me, an outsider, come here at all right now.'

Or let an outsider like Katrina marry into their locked confines. But then, Al and Katrina hadn't exactly asked permission, and now they were in trouble.

'Then maybe you could do me a tiny favor, Mrs Alwin,' Sadler said. He tried to smile, a strange stretching of the lips that was far more frightening than any of his scowls.

'What would that be?'

'Maybe you could tell me your impressions of the people here at Los Pintores. Just informal like.'

Maddie glanced out one of the high windows that looked out to the kitchen garden, which was now blanketed in snow.

No one was going anyplace soon. 'Do you think it could be a wandering maniac?'

'I think that's unlikely, don't you?'

'Yes, probably.' Maddie sighed. 'It just would have been so convenient. Right. What do you want to know?'

'Just anything you think might be helpful. Anyone with grudges or quarrels against Mr Luhan . . .'

Maddie shook her head. 'Oh, Inspector. I don't think anyone liked Victor Luhan. Except maybe Mrs Upshaw.'

'Mrs Upshaw?'

'His, um, secretary. You'll see when you meet her. Isabella Luhan is always with her doctor, and Helena says she's always been frail, living her own separate life, so I suspect Mrs Upshaw is not the first "secretary." Though it's odd he would bring her to his home. Ben is a college lad, not here often now, and Sam runs the place. Helena wishes she could live in town. And the neighbors, the McTeers, have a feud with Victor that sounds like it's been ongoing since they moved in.'

'People are loony wherever you go.'

'No truer words, Inspector.'

Sadler rushed ahead, but Rickie lingered behind to speak quietly with Maddie. 'Er – Mrs Alwin. Do you think Rosa – that is, Miss Sanchez – might be in any danger?'

He was blushing! Maddie thought that was utterly adorable, but she dared not coo over Rickie's little romance. He was a friend of Eddie's, the two of them working together at La Fonda before Rickie decided to join the police like his uncle, and she'd known him since she'd come to Santa Fe. Time had flown impossibly fast, and he was now a tall, solemn, hard-working grown-up, yet he still seemed like a rackety kid to her. 'Why, Rickie. How do you know Miss Sanchez?'

His blush deepened. 'Just from when we were kids. She knew one of my sisters, from school in Albuquerque. They were always running around our house in school breaks, stealing my ma's apple cakes. Ma felt sorry for her, since her parents were long gone and she only had her aunt.' Rickie's mother had eleven kids; Maddie was sure one couldn't matter. 'She was the prettiest of all, even then. I'd love to take her to dinner at La Fonda sometime.'

'I'm sure Eddie would love to see you soon if you go – he still works there, you know. But Inspector Sadler seems to keep you pretty busy.'

Rickie laughed. 'It's busy, all right, but I like it. Never the same day twice.'

'I'm just sorry you ended up with him as a boss.' When Sadler first came to Santa Fe, he'd been full of insults against people like Rickie's family. He'd calmed down since, but it still boiled Maddie's brain to hear it.

'Aw, he's not so bad now that he's been here for a while. I think he's getting more used to our ways.'

Maddie thought of his impatience at the pace of New Mexico life, and grinned. 'Still pretty impatient, though. I told him it wouldn't do any good to lose his temper; he won't make the clock tick faster.'

'I don't think he'll ever get over that! But the truth is, Mrs Alwin, I've learned more about *him*, too. There's ways to get around him. If I can do well working for him, just for a couple of years maybe, it'll be a lot easier to get ahead. Get really good at this job. He's *el fastidio*, as my abuela would say, but he sure knows a lot about the law. I might like to go to law school someday, even.'

Maddie nodded. She could see Rickie's ambition, his shining desire to make something good and useful of his life, just as Eddie did. 'You really like the job, I see.'

'Oh, I love it, Mrs Alwin. Well, gee, not *all* of it, true. That Montoya business was tough. I like how I can help my family, our whole neighborhood, this way. Really help them. I understand them; I can make sure they know how to stay safe.'

'And Rosa is your "neighborhood?"' she teased.

The blush turned positively scarlet. 'I guess she is, yeah. I'd love to be really worthy of a pretty, smart wife like her someday. She's got the sweetest heart. I need to learn how to be a good husband, a good dad, someone a lady like her and my kids could be proud of. My own dad wasn't around much, always hitting the bottle. I won't be that way.' Another reason he and Eddie were such friends. They both understood they did *not* want to be like their fathers.

Maddie completely understood, too. 'And I know you will!

Anyone who can work this hard with Sadler without knocking his block off can succeed anywhere. And Rosa *does* seem very nice.' She took Rickie's arm and they continued on down the corridor. 'Does Sadler have any thoughts on this sad business yet? For a country rancho, this place is crowded as Grand Central Station for Christmas. And I'm afraid they all seem to have reason to hate Victor Luhan. It's quite confusing.' She tried to imagine it like a painting, each element, each color, blending with the whole until a viewer could back up and see the entire image. She couldn't quite focus yet.

'I don't think he's seen enough of it all yet, to be honest. We weren't told much before we rushed out ahead of the weather. Just to wrap it up quick, because no one wants people like the Luhans to complain, or anyone high-muckety to say we're too slow, too careless, we let crime run wild.'

'Course not.' Sadler and his 'law and order.'

'To be *really* honest, Mrs Alwin – and don't tell anyone I said this,' Rickie whispered.

'Certainly not! A future lawyer would *never*.'

'I think he likes the sound of your friend's husband for it.'

'Al?' Maddie gasped. Just as she'd started to fear. Oh, poor Katrina.

'Everyone in Santa Fe knows his wife has been taking him around to doctors. Nightmares, wild behavior, all that war stuff. Sadler thinks it might be easy-peasy to wrap it all up, especially once he heard it was Al Luhan's cricket bat that did the deed. But you know why I'm telling you, Mrs Alwin?'

'You secretly want to be demoted?'

'Because I've learned enough in this job to think poor Senor Alfonso didn't do it. He is too sad, too lost in himself. We need to look around, yeah? The inspector is smart, like I said, and he thinks we all move too slow. When something is this serious, moving too fast is a big mistake.'

'You're pretty smart yourself, Rickie.'

He grinned, a wide, white, delighted smile, and Maddie smiled too, thinking that Rosa was a lucky young lady. 'So are you. Eddie always says you can be trusted. I know you'll figure more out than the inspector could, that you can really talk to people. I bet you already *have* talked to them.'

'Some of them. I might have seen a teensy thing or two since I got here. Let's just see what we can find, and share?'
Maddie felt a sharp, sad pang as she thought of Katrina's pale, worried face. 'Poor Katrina. I think you're right. Al didn't do it. He couldn't!'

Or was that merely wishful thinking?

'Ricardo!' Sadler's shout echoed from the kitchen at the end of the corridor. 'Get in here! What are you dawdling around there for? There's work to do!'

'Go on then,' Maddie whispered. 'I bet Rosa could use your comforting presence. I'll be down directly to show you where the body was found.'

He nodded and headed towards Sadler's shouts, while Maddie climbed the stairs into the shadows.

Maddie wished she was anywhere else at all – maybe even her mother's New York drawing room with all her dreadful relatives. Well, maybe not *that*, but close. She stomped her way through the snow with Sadler and Rickie, who had torn himself away from the lovely Rosa. They were headed toward the spot where she'd found the body. At least David was with her, holding her hand, quiet but supportive.

The snow landed on her lashes, fine and diamond-bright, making her cheeks sting. She knew she couldn't start crying, or she'd turn into a veritable icicle.

Up ahead, they glimpsed the terrible mound in the snow. It was covered in a blanket, and then more layers of white, so it wasn't nearly so gruesome, but she still shivered and longed with all her might to turn around and run.

'Over there, you see,' she said, gesturing to the spot.

Sadler had no qualms about getting closer. He strode ahead, snow flying off his battered hat, while Rickie followed, taking out a notebook and pencil. They knelt down to examine the frozen figure of Victor Luhan.

'Are you all right?' David whispered to her, squeezing her hand.

'Oh, yes. A bit tiddly on the tummy, maybe, but it will pass. After spending so much time with you in the hospital morgue, it's a walk in the park!' She swallowed hard and tried not to think about the cold, antiseptic-smelling hospital basement.

'I'm nothing if not romantic, it's true,' David said. 'I do know how to show my girl a good time.'

That made Maddie laugh. She sucked in a deep breath and tiptoed over to glance over Sadler's shoulder as he peeled back the icy blanket to reveal Don Victor and his bashed-in head.

'And he was just here, like this, when you found him?' Sadler asked, as Rickie drew quick, dark lines in his notebook to approximate the scene. Maddie imagined there would be no getting a photographer and his equipment out there in this weather.

'Yes. Lying just like this, his head turned that way. I didn't move anything at all.'

'And you didn't see anyone else?'

'Not a soul. The weather was quite dreadful, you see, and it was early.'

Sadler glanced up at her suspiciously. 'So why were *you* out?'

Maddie closed her eyes as she remembered how nice the fresh air was, the winter wind, the distant song of birds – until she saw the blood. 'I just wanted a minute alone, after being cooped up inside. The atmosphere in the house can be – well, rather claustrophobic, if you want the truth. I wasn't intending to stay out long. And I certainly didn't intend to find a body!'

Sadler looked back to the wounds. 'You're sure he hasn't been moved or changed at all?'

Maddie swallowed past that ridiculous lump in her throat again and peered closer. 'Nothing at all that I can tell.'

Sadler's bushy brows drew together as he poked at the frozen neck. 'Any tracks will be long covered. This weather, always getting in my way!' He reached for the shoulders. 'Help me turn him, then.'

Rickie and David assisted Sadler in shifting the body, which made a terrible cracking sound as it came free of the ice that had surrounded it.

'Bashed on the head but good,' Sadler muttered. 'Never stood a chance.' He glanced up at David. 'I don't suppose you can tell much in these conditions?'

'I'll have to get him to the icehouse and see. The Luhans say we can use it for a temporary morgue, but I don't have many tools with me. Time of death will be a bit tricky to decipher.' Yet Maddie could see the excitement of the challenge in his bright-blue eyes.

Sadler gave another grunt. Maddie supposed there wasn't much more to say about it at that point. 'And Alfonso Luhan's cricket bat was over there?'

Maddie bit her lip as she thought of that crack in the bat. 'Yes, about there, where there's that dip in the snow. Like it had been dropped on its side.' Or placed there.

Sadler slowly circled the horrible lump of the body as Rickie sketched in details, sometimes jotting down a note Sadler muttered to him. Maddie studied David, trying to decipher what he saw in it all. She also tried to listen to Sadler's asides, wishing he would speak up a bit.

'Who else here do you think might hate him, then?' he suddenly barked at Maddie. 'You met them, yes? Sure, but who knows with these old Santa Fe types? You, I know, will tell me the truth. As you see it, anyway.' His voice was rough, begrudging.

But Maddie still felt a little warm satisfaction at the compliment, slight as it was. Sadler was a tough nut to crack. 'Well, yes, if I can. I do want to help. Katrina is my old friend.'

'Help, mind you,' said Sadler, wagging his gloved finger. 'Not interfere.'

'I hardly want to go where I'm not wanted, Inspector! But let's see . . .' She told him what she knew about Isabella and her doctor, Helena, Ben and Sam, Felipe, Mrs Upshaw, the McTeers, even the theory of the passing lunatic.

Sadler shook his head at it all. 'I still say it must be Alfonso.'

Maddie flashed with anger. 'No! Believe me, Inspector, Al couldn't do such a thing. And so many people had reason to resent Don Victor . . .'

Sadler scowled at her. 'He couldn't do it because he's married to your friend?'

'No. Because he is too ill, he couldn't plan such a thing. If it had been a sudden impulse, a shove down the stairs or a stab of a dinner knife, maybe, but this . . .'

'Alfonso Luhan is indeed shellshocked, a bad case,' David said. 'I agree with Maddie – he wouldn't be able to calmly plan such an attack.'

'Hmph.' Sadler turned away. 'I'll be the judge of all that. Usually the obvious answer is the right one. I'd put my money on Alfonso and his bat.'

'No,' Maddie protested again, but she knew words wouldn't get her far at this point.

Sadler just marched away. Rickie gave Maddie a sympathetic grimace, and David took her hand again. She knew better than to argue with Sadler when he was stuck in an idea, but oh, it was sure tempting! But she had to help Katrina now, had to stay calm and watch everything around her.

'I think we're ready to move him now,' Sadler said.

'I'll get the stretcher from the car,' Rickie said.

David glanced down at Maddie. 'Why don't you go straight to Katrina and Al, darling? I'll join you as soon as I can. I'll get set up in the icehouse, and start – well, you know – first thing in the morning . . .'

'Got it,' Maddie said, thinking again of that basement morgue. 'I definitely don't need to be there for that.' She glanced once more at the body and turned away. If only she could shrug it all off so easily!

TEN

Maddie tried to push away worry about Inspector Sadler's premature suspicions from her mind as she approached Al and Katrina's door. She couldn't add to their troubles, not unless it was absolutely necessary. She put on a bright 'It's Christmas, never mind about murder!' smile, and knocked on the door.

Al lay in bed, silent and white-faced, while Katrina sat beside him with her own determined smile pasted on her lips. David was listening to Al's chest with a stethoscope, and then checked his pulse.

'Feeling homesick, are we, my darlings?' Maddie cried as she noticed that Gunther read to them from New York newspapers. She took David's hand, and tried to read from his expression how Al was really doing. He gave his head a little shake and pressed a reassuring kiss to her fingers.

'Feeling grateful not to be there any more,' Katrina said. There was a tense, try-hard edge to her usual enthusiasm, but Al seemed glad she was just there, holding his hand.

'But such lovely holiday windows this year, my ducks,' Gunther said from the window. He held up a photographic catalog spread of lights and tinsel. 'Just look at Macy's!'

Maddie sat down on the cushioned window seat, moving a pile of books as she glanced outside at the snow flying around the garden, hiding the fountain and statues, closing them all up inside. 'What were your English Christmases like, David dearest?'

'Plum puddings and carols, of course,' he said. 'And gray skies. There are always gray skies in an English winter. But the puddings were marvelous.'

'My old nanny was English,' Katrina said. 'She was a frightful old, no-fun stick until the twelve days came around, and then it was utterly curtains-up. She sang that song, too! The one *about* the twelve days of Christmas. At the top of her lungs, after unpacking a case of Graham's port wine that her sister would send over. I swear those bottles were gone in no time at all. But sometimes we could escape the house and her rendition of "Good King Wenceslas" and go off skating in Central Park, or maybe sledding if we were very lucky. That was absolutely topping!'

A wistful frown flickered over Al's face and his clasp tightened on his wife's hand, even though he didn't open his eyes. 'I'm afraid there's nothing jolly about *this* holiday, Katie. I'm sorry.'

Katrina smacked a kiss on his cheek. 'I'm spending it with you, that's all that matters. But we did promise Maddie a lovely Christmas for trekking out all this way. What a dreadful friend I've become.'

'It's still better than my old New York holidays,' Maddie declared. 'I didn't even have a tiddly port-sipping nanny to liven things up in my parents' house! It was so quiet. But one year my cousin Gwen *did* steal a bottle of my father's best champagne, and we consumed it all right before they took us to a pantomime at the old Metropolitan Opera house! We were frightfully sick all over the aisle carpet. We were in desperate trouble for months and months! But I suppose that isn't a very Christmassy tale. Gwen liked to steal champagne all year round.'

'How awful!' Katrina cried, even as she fell back laughing.

'I'll say. It put me off Bollinger for years. But besides that, there wasn't much music, no snowball fights, and very few cakes.' Maddie leaned back next to Katrina. 'I heard there's an actual chapel here at Los Pintores. That sounds like a real Christmas sort of thing.'

'Oh, yes. The Capilla de Nuestra Señora de Guadalupe. Built in 1750, with an altar painted by the Martinez Blue painter, no one knows his real name, just that he used that marvelous blue for the Madonna's cloak,' Al said drowsily. He tried to sit up, but David urged him back down, checking his pulse. 'We have Mass there sometimes, when Father Adrian visits. Even a christening there once, when everyone was stuck in snowstorm like this. I think the good Padre should be here soon, poor man. What if he hasn't heard the news yet?'

'He's good friends with your father?' Gunther asked.

'Yes, I think they went to school together as boys. A strange pair, eh? But then, maybe Papa wasn't always like what he became later in life. So angry all the time. Disappointments get to all of us,' Al said. 'When I was a kid, Christmas here could be . . . really magical. Special. Then I turned out so different from what he expected, what he wanted.' He turned beseeching eyes toward Katrina. 'This was all probably my fault!'

'No, darling! Never, ever,' Katrina cried. She leaped up and knelt beside him, clasping him close as he wept. 'You could never have been a disappointment. It's all just wretched *life*. Bad luck. None of this is your fault!'

'It is. I never should have lost my temper at him like that. I can't even remember what happened!' He turned away from his wife, burying his face in his hands. David took a medicine bottle from his valise and measured out a portion. 'I can never remember what happens after. Oh, Kate-kins. What if I really did it? Killed him?'

'No! You don't have that in you.' Katrina sobbed. 'It – it was a passing lunatic, just like Helena said.'

'Katrina.' Al's voice was fainter now, as the medicine took hold, but he clung to his wife's hand. 'This isn't one of those detective novels you like so much. It's us, our family! We hated him. All of us did. Mama, Helena, Sam, probably even Ben. But I'm the only one with such a fury inside of me, such a burning. It tears me up sometimes.'

Clearly he was not, Maddie thought, remembering the sight of that body in the snow, the blood. Someone else out there hated with a fire. But she couldn't bear to think it could be poor, wounded Al; that good-hearted Katrina could be hurt.

Katrina smoothed the blankets gently around him, like he was a sleepy child. 'You must not say things like that, my darling,' she whispered. 'There's a policeman here! What if he hears you?'

'You aren't listening! No one listens!' he cried, growing agitated again. David gave him a smaller second dose, and Maddie and Gunther stood up to discreetly tiptoe out. 'No, stay, please. Stay with us. We shouldn't be alone.'

'I think we can use a bit of air.' Maddie pushed open the window a couple of inches and drew in a deep breath of the cold, clear bracing air, touched with piñon and woodsmoke. She heard Ben shout as he caught a snowball in the face out there in the garden, and raced to knock Felipe down in a bank of snow. They laughed, a strangely joyful sound, a touch of life within death and fear.

A woman laughed, too, a silvery, bell-like sound, and clapped her hands. Maddie craned her neck to see who it was, and glimpsed a woman on the portal, slim and elegant in a fox-collared coat. At first she thought it must be Helena, but when she leaned over to call out to Ben, Maddie saw it was Isabella. Up from her chaise, no doctor close by.

'We can have a happy Christmas, Kate-kins, in our own way,' Al said, clearly drifting away into sleep. 'Don't worry, *querida*. There's still a few days until Christmas, isn't there? Anything can happen.'

A few days until Christmas, Maddie thought. A few days to find a real killer, and make sure her old friend was safe again. She glanced at David and saw in an instant he knew what she was thinking and agreed. None of them had to be alone this strange, scary holiday.

ELEVEN

The next day

'Do you think Al could be helped, David? Really helped?' Maddie asked as they walked hand in hand along the portal before tea, bundled up against the snow falling steadily just beyond. The fresh air was refreshing after the stuffy house, and after David's morning spent examining the body with Sadler in the icehouse.

David frowned in thought. 'I've seen cases like his improve sometimes, of course. Go from unable to rise from bed to even working a job again, with lots of care. But there have also been many cases where the patient becomes worse, falling into catatonia, hallucinations. I'm not an expert on these treatments, though I've read some interesting papers by Dr Myers with their theories. The use of electricity, anesthesia, talking cures . . .'

'Could Al consult an expert on those methods? Be helped by them?'

'I'd love to think so, Maddie. But I'm very concerned about these blackouts he described. And I'm sure you know how much successful treatments in such cases depends on the patient's surroundings. Peace and quiet, support, a good diet, lots of exercise. Katrina is obviously a wonderful wife, but this place . . .'

Maddie glanced up at the house rising behind them, the blank windows. 'Not much peace and support here, huh? More like Christmas at the House of Usher.'

David laughed and she squeezed his arm. 'Not quite *that* bad. But then we haven't had a look at the old chapel yet. Who knows what's in there.' They walked on, their boots crunching on the flakes of ice coating the flagstones. 'Once this is all over and we can go home, I'll see how quickly I can get Al into the right clinic. There's a good one outside Denver, I think.'

Maddie thought of Sadler's conviction that Al must have killed Don Victor. 'If he isn't arrested.'

'Indeed,' David answered solemnly. 'I don't want to think he could have done it any more than you do, darling.'

'But he does have those blackouts?'

'Yes.'

'What did you find with the body this morning?'

'Not a great deal. It's impossible to do a full autopsy here, yet I think I can make a fair guess as to cause of death.'

'Bashed with a cricket bat.'

'Just so. The first blow would have stunned him, driven him down, the next two done him in. Otherwise, he seemed quite healthy, strong heart and lungs, a bit of liver damage. I'd say he was examining something out there, and someone came behind him and hit him before he even realized. Once would have stunned him, like I said, and twice killed him, but they made sure. Then the assailant dropped the bat and left. The snowfall would have covered any tracks.'

'I guess you couldn't say how long he'd been dead when I found him?'

'Not with the cold like it is. I would guess roughly eight to ten hours, maybe, because of the state of rigor, the temperature that night, but I wouldn't swear to it.'

'I wonder where everyone was then,' Maddie mused. She thought of the night before, the dancing and noise. 'What did Sadler say?'

'He did insist on staying in the icehouse during the exam. I hate people hovering while I work.'

'Especially Sadler.' Maddie imagined his beady, pale eyes boring into someone's back while they tried to concentrate. She shivered. 'Does he still think it was poor Al?'

'That was his theory, I'm afraid. The cricket bat, the blackouts.'

'Al did say he felt fury toward his father, even rage. I don't think the state of the body says "sudden rage," though, does it? Up close and personal, sure; bloody, but a frenzy of anger?'

David's head tilted thoughtfully as he studied her. 'I'd say you're probably right about that. It seems planned out, like someone lured him outside, away from the rest of us, to a place where he probably wouldn't be found for a while. He would have been there even longer, covered with even more snow, if you hadn't gone for a walk.'

'You mentioned he might have stopped to look at something. I guess they could have put whatever it was there to make him go outside. A double switch, like in *The Murder on the Links*! Sadler told Rickie to check out the household laundry. I'll ask him what he found there. If it *was* Al, surely his clothes would be spattered with blood.'

'Definitely so.'

'And yet . . .' Maddie remembered something she'd forgotten in her panic: that cloud of smoke above the trees as she fled. She knew she would have to tell Sadler about it. 'Unless whoever it was sensibly got rid of what they were wearing. Do you suppose it definitely would have been a man?'

'It wouldn't have to be. Coming up behind him, with the first surprise blow a stunner – a woman *could* do it, and the first wounds did look angled upward, though Don Victor was a tall man.' The snow was coming down thicker, and Maddie trembled. David steered them back toward the door. 'I have to say, though, all the ladies here seem like rather dainty flowers. Like my New York rose,' he teased.

Maddie laughed and nudged at his side. '*This* dainty rose is tougher than she looks.'

'Don't I know it. I'm a very lucky man.'

'Aren't you just, Dr Cole? And if I killed every bossy man who irritated me, I'd have a string of prison sentences. Katrina would be strong enough, or she certainly was back at school, and maybe she'd do anything to protect Al, yet she's also got one of the biggest, softest hearts I've ever met. I don't think her nerve would hold. Helena is very petite, and Isabella an invalid. Although . . .' Maddie thought of Isabella laughing and dashing about earlier.

'Although?'

'I saw her out here, when we were upstairs with Al and Katrina. She seemed much more energetic and livelier than when she drapes herself over her chaise in the sala. What do you know about Dr Pierce? Could he be some sort of charlatan who drugs lady patients into submission?'

'Now we *are* in a Poe story. But you might be on to something.'

'He really could be drugging Isabella?'

'I doubt that. She doesn't behave like someone on a strong substance, her conversation is too sharp. More like she is someone who *wishes* to be ill. I can't say I blame her a bit, it must be an easier way to keep out of her husband's path as much as possible.'

'You're quite right there. Rosa and her aunt say Isabella usually takes her meals in her own suite of rooms, and Helena and Katrina do a lot of the chatelaine duties like ordering and menu planning. So, you think she's shamming?'

'Not shamming exactly. I don't doubt she feels ill. She's been told that she is for so long, by Dr Pierce and no doubt by others. She seems to get little exercise or diversion. I've certainly seen physicians take advantage of situations like this, mostly in England. It can be lucrative to have such regular patients.'

'Does Dr Pierce have such a reputation?'

'I don't know him well at all. He doesn't practice in Santa Fe, though I know he takes on mostly private patients. Our cases have never overlapped. It would be interesting to know who most of his patients are. Will Isabella be wealthy now, as a widow? More independent?'

'Now *that* would be a good bit of information to have. I wonder who knows the contents of Don Victor's will? I know the Luhans are wealthy, lots of land, rental properties in Santa Fe, things like that. I would imagine Sam would get this rancho – he's the oldest and already runs most of it – and Helena might have a dowry of sorts. Don Victor seemed old-fashioned like that, insisting Helena marry only someone "suitable" while she just wants to Charleston the night away. But I have no idea what Isabella's portion would be, or Ben and Al's.' A thought suddenly struck Maddie. 'If the doctor isn't drugging Isabella, could he be courting her and just got impatient?'

'I did once hear a rumor going around the hospital that Dr

Pierce owed a large debt to another doctor. Gambling, maybe, or a property? I wish now I had listened closer!'

Maddie laughed. 'You really are shockingly uninterested in gossip, darling.'

'Too busy with all that surgery nonsense,' he agreed with a grin. 'But if Isabella really is going to be a rich widow . . .'

'Then the doctor could be our man!' Maddie cried. 'That would be just too convenient. There's just something about him I can't warm to. Could you try to get him away for a little chat, doctor to doctor, sometime? Or I could do it!'

David held on to her arm just before they went in the house, his expression quite worried. 'Maddie. Please, please be careful. This isn't exactly Santa Fe, where everyone is always watching. We're pretty isolated out here, and if someone is a murderer who believed they were about to be found out . . . Well, I could never bear it if you were hurt. Not now I've finally found you.'

'Oh, David. My darlingest darling.' Maddie was afraid she might start to sob, the look in his beautiful eyes was so tender. She went up on tiptoe and kissed his cheek, holding him close. 'I'm not such a dumb dora as all that. I wouldn't be alone with the man. If you're worried, you're most welcome to stay in my room tonight. As my, y'know, bodyguard.'

He laughed. 'Don't tempt me, when I'm trying so hard to be an old-fashioned gentleman! And you are never a dumb dora. That's just the problem. You're too curious and kind, you rush to the defense of anyone you care about. It's why I love you so much. And why I worry.'

'You mustn't worry. I can't lose you now, either. I want us to have lots and lots of Christmases together. Much jollier than this one. I'll be ever so careful.'

She held on to David, feeling the reassuring beat of his heart next to hers. But as she glanced over his shoulder, down the slope of the snowy garden and into the icy circle of the trees, she felt a shiver of something besides hope. This was a beautiful place, a postcard of 'Christmas' with its green and white, sparkling landscape.

But a man had been killed there, amid all that beauty, seemingly in a cold-blooded plan by someone in the house where Maddie was trapped now. Not to mention David, Gunther, and Buttercup! David was right. If the killer thought they would be found out, who would be next on the list?

TWELVE

They retreated to the warmth of the sala to find that everyone was gathered there, except Mrs Upshaw and Sam. Isabella was reading, while Helena and Felipe played cards, and Ben doodled at the piano. Marta had laid out another splendid tea. Scones, petit fours, tiny salmon paste sandwiches, even a beautiful Christmas fruit cake with white icing that looked like the snow outside.

'Just like when I was a boy in England.' David sighed happily as he took an ecstatic bite of the cake. 'You are a wonder, Mrs Sanchez, truly.'

The usually taciturn housekeeper beamed at him and offered yet more cake. 'Well, when they said a real Englishman would be visiting, Dr Cole, I did look up a fine Christmas pudding recipe in *The Lady's Home*. I've never tried it before.'

'It's absolutely perfect. And your scones – I could vow I'm back in Brighton at the Mock Turtle tearoom. My grandmother took me there every month for a great treat.'

'I *have* thought, every now and again, of opening a little tea place in Santa Fe. Just cakes and pastries, maybe, my mother's old recipes for empanadas and pan dulce,' Marta said. 'Try something new. I've been here for so long.' She looked wistful to leave. Maddie wondered what was driving her away now.

'You would have lines out the door,' David said, taking another scone.

'So, you would leave Los Pintores, Mrs Sanchez?' Maddie asked.

Marta glanced at her niece, who was chatting with Rickie across the sala as she offered him a platter of sandwiches. 'There isn't anything for a young lady like my Rosa out here. I need to help her settle her future. A business in town would be good for us both.' She called out to Rosa to help her, and bustled away to fetch more tea, as if she'd said too much.

Rickie came to join Maddie as David went to look over the card game.

'And where is our dear inspector today, Rickie?' Maddie asked, offering to refill his teacup.

'Taking a look at the perimeter of the rancho with Sam Luhan, checking for breaches in the fences or spots where anyone could have camped out, stuff like that,' Rickie said with a laugh. 'You should have seen him, riding off on a borrowed horse, Mrs Alwin! I never saw such a terrified expression. Not that I would have loved riding in such weather, either, but he acted like the poor old mare was a dragon.'

Maddie laughed too, imagining such a sight. 'I can see why no one would care for a gallop today.'

'I'm supposed to look through the cupboards.' He grinned. 'Truthfully, there's not much more left to do in here. We've interviewed everyone in the house, searched the place.'

Maddie had the distinct feeling Sadler hadn't done quite *everything* he could, or talked to everyone in any depth. 'So does he still think Al did it?' she whispered.

Rickie's expression turned solemn. 'He says he can't see who else it would be. But between you and me, Mrs Vaughn-Alwin . . .'

'Yes?'

'I don't really see how it *could* be him. Rosa says he's so quiet most of the time, off in his own world. Unless he snapped. I think it could be just about anyone, really.'

'That's exactly what I've been thinking, Rickie. And maybe whoever did it planned to make a getaway but got caught by the snow.' Maddie examined the faces of everyone gathered for tea, trying to read signs of panic or impatience. Everyone just looked a bit bored.

'Rosa says Victor Luhan sometimes gave her the shivers, though he was kind to her,' Rickie said.

'Did she?' Maddie remembered how Victor had paid for Rosa's school. Was there something less than avuncular in it? 'Did he try to proposition her?'

'Nothing like that, I think. She says this place is actually a nice one in that the menfolk don't come after her like that.

"Gentlemanly," she called them. But since she came back from Albuquerque to live here with her aunt again, Don Victor has been paying her a lot more attention. Finding her in the kitchen or the garden, asking her questions.'

'What sort of questions?'

'Oh, just stuff about the future, if she might like to marry soon or go to college. What she likes about Los Pintores; if she prefers the town.'

'And this interest was something new? It made her uncomfortable?'

'She hardly ever saw him except from a distance when she was younger. She didn't understand why he's talking to her so much now.' He lowered his voice to a whisper. 'She was afraid maybe he and Señora Luhan were going to part, and he wanted a younger wife. Maybe more kids.'

'Ugh!' Maddie felt quite sorry for poor Rosa, who had felt afraid she would have to marry a rich man almost old enough to be her grandfather.

'He never said anything like that, though, so she wasn't sure. She just started hiding if she saw him coming.'

'That poor girl. Her aunt just said she's been thinking about moving to Santa Fe, opening a teashop, getting away from Los Pintores. Maybe she just wanted to get Rosa away.'

Rickie's face brightened. 'That would sure be swell if they were in Santa Fe!'

Maddie laughed. 'Swell for you!'

He blushed and scuffed his toe over the floor. 'She is awfully nice. And pretty.'

'Very pretty. Such lovely eyes! I would enjoy painting her portrait.' She thought of Rosa's pale, blue-gray eyes and thought they seemed rather familiar, though she couldn't quite remember how. 'Rickie, how did you get on with the laundry?'

He grimaced. 'One time, I had to sort through old garbage pails behind the fruit shop to look for a knife a thief threw away.'

'This was that bad?'

'Not as bad, no. Marta is a good housekeeper; she wouldn't let such a stink grow. But just like that "needle in a haystack" feeling. The laundry house is on the other side of the kitchen garden, and it was really full. Clothes, sheets, towels from all over the estate. I was there all afternoon and into the evening.'

'I'd bet Rosa brought you some cocoa,' Maddie teased.

'And a sandwich! It did make it all go a lot faster. I didn't see anything bloodstained, though. Just an apron of Marta's she used while preparing a roast lamb. I put that away for testing, just in case, but I know that can't be what we're looking for.'

'No. Disappointing, but not surprising, is it? It would be a dumb killer indeed who put his bloodstained clothes into the laundry house.' She thought of a news story she'd read in the summer, about a would-be thief who got tired and decided to take a nap in his would-be victims' house. 'Then again, most criminals aren't exactly evil geniuses, are they?'

'I haven't met many geniuses, that's for sure. Greedy for money or jealous over a romance gone bad, that's what it always comes out to.'

'Do you think that's what's going on here?'

'Maybe. There's a lot of money, for sure, and a lot of unhappy relationships.'

'I do think you're right, though I don't know exactly who or what yet.' She glanced around. 'Speaking of romances gone bad, I haven't seen Mrs Upshaw, Don Victor's secretary, in a while.'

'She says she's "prostrated" by all the horrors. She's been making Mrs Sanchez bring all her meals up to her room, and Rosa says it's a right mess up there. When the inspector tried to interview her, she kept breaking down in sobs and yelling about her "poor old Vicky." Couldn't get anything out of her, not even how she came to work for him.'

'Maybe I'll try to talk to her. Get Gunther to mix up some of his famous Pink Ladies – you didn't hear that, Rickie, no booze here, no sir. That would get her talking.'

Rickie smiled in relief. 'That would sure be a big help, Mrs Vaughn-Alwin. And I never saw any booze here, of course. Even if the Prohibition agents are hundreds of miles away.'

'I did mean to mention something to Sadler, which escaped me until now in all the confusion,' Maddie said. 'When I was walking that day, just before I found Don Victor, I thought I saw some smoke in the air, beyond the trees. I thought maybe it was the McTeers burning some trash, but now I wonder if it wasn't more. Maybe those lost bloody clothes?'

Rickie nodded solemnly. 'I'll sure tell him right away.' He went in search of the inspector, or maybe Rosa again, and Maddie fetched a cup of tea and made her way toward the fireplace.

'How are you feeling now, Mrs Luhan?' Maddie asked as she sat down in an armchair beside the invalid chaise and handed Isabella the tea.

'So very kind of you, Mrs Vaughn-Alwin. I am trying to bear up for my poor children, but I do have such pains all over! Like lightning all down my legs. I haven't slept a wink.' She took a long sip of the tea and sighed. 'Dr Pierce insists I must go away for a rest cure once this is all settled, of course. If I stay here, my health is sure to shatter completely.'

'A rest cure does sound exactly the thing,' Maddie agreed. 'You deserve it.'

'I've never done well in the winter here. Perhaps you know a good clinic in New York?'

'There are many very reputable facilities there, to be sure, but just as cold as here, I'm afraid.'

Isabella's lips pursed in disappointment. 'Well, the really important thing is to get away from here as soon as possible. But I would so enjoy a real city.'

'Perhaps Europe? Lots of people go to Switzerland, or France.'

'I did visit France once as a girl. Some of the nuns took us. Such music and lights! So wonderful. Then I was pulled back here, to *this*. Perhaps I could return there soon.' She smoothed the floaty skirt of her ivory lace tea gown and gave her satin slippers a little kick under its rolled hem. 'In Paris, they said I had the tiniest, most elegant feet. I was famous for them. So admired.'

Dr Pierce came into the sala just then, and hurried over to them, studying his patient with a frown. 'I hope you are not tiring yourself, my dear Mrs Luhan. You really should be resting.'

Isabella put on a 'brave and gallant' face and reached for his hand. 'I can rest here as well as in my room. I must be here for my children now.'

'We were speaking of France and Switzerland, all the wonderful spas and clinics that offer rest cures there,' Maddie said. She studied Dr Pierce carefully, remembering the gossip about his debts, but he looked nothing other than grave and professional, the trustworthy, graying physician.

'I certainly do recommend a long voyage, as soon as possible,' he said earnestly. 'A complete change of scene is imperative after all these dreadful strains.'

'I quite agree,' Maddie said. 'And I have heard so much of your fine reputation, Dr Pierce. I am sure your words carry great weight.'

His eyes narrowed as he stared at her. 'Who have you been speaking to, Mrs Vaughn-Alwin? I am always most grateful to hear of my satisfied patients. To make lives better and happier, in any small way – it is all I could wish; all I have striven for in my career.'

'To tell the truth, I have had some troubles of my own lately,' Maddie said, quickly improvising so she wouldn't have to tell him her 'sources.' 'Nerve pain, especially in my – my face and shoulders. Quite unbearable at times.'

'Oh, Mrs Vaughn-Alwin! You poor, dear thing,' Isabella cried. 'I do so sympathize with those who suffer as I do. Dr Pierce, you must help her, at least until she can get to her relations in New York. She is an Astor, you know.'

Dr Pierce's expression grew more interested as he studied Maddie. 'I should certainly do my best for you.'

'Perhaps I could visit your office after we return home?' Maddie said.

'Well . . . er,' he stammered. 'I do mostly make house calls these days. So much more convenient for my sort of patients, so much more . . . discreet.' He took a card case from his jacket pocket and handed her a pasteboard square. It had only his name and a post office box number printed on it, along with a telephone extension. 'If you call this, they will leave me a message most expeditiously.'

'I certainly shall, thank you.'

'Oh, I can't stand this a minute longer!' Helena suddenly cried and threw down her cards.

Isabella pressed trembling fingertips to her temples. 'Helena! Such noise. My nerves!'

Helena ignored her. 'Let's go out and build a snowman. I need some air.'

Everyone seemed to agree with her, eager to escape the hacienda and pretend it was a normal holiday, nothing amiss. They all bundled up, while Marta sent carrots from the kitchen for the snowman's face, and they rushed out into the snowy garden. The sky was gray but clear, the air icy and sharp as Maddie took in a deep breath.

Ben found a spot where the snowdrifts were the highest, on the edge of the trees beyond the garden wall, and the powdery weight of it was drier. Laughing and shoving, he and Felipe rolled the snow over and over, making the lower part of the snowman larger and larger until he was a veritable yeti. Helena set about making the head, a bit lopsided but she declared it would surely suffice. Sam came along with stones for the eyes and an old knitted hat to add to the carrot nose and ears.

'Remember the snowmen we used to make when we were kids?' Helena asked her brothers.

'They were wonderful! We even rigged the twiggy arms of that one to move,' Ben said. 'Until there was the one tutor. What was his name? The one who was constantly in a sour mood.'

'That would be all of them, thanks to you,' Sam said. 'They never started out that way until you got hold of them. That's why we got sent to St Michael's for school.'

'You should have seen the relief of the Sisters once I left Loretto,' Helena said merrily. 'What trials we were to the poor monks and nuns!'

'I know the tutor you mean, though. He got smacked in the face with one of those twiggy arms,' Sam said. 'Papa gave you such a hiding for that.'

'He was good at that sort of thing,' Ben agreed.

'Here, Maddie, why don't you finish the face?' Helena said.

'You're the artist. The poor snowman does deserve a bit of dignity, even though he'll surely melt tomorrow.'

'Heaven knows dignity is in short supply around here,' Sam said.

Maddie nodded, happy for the distraction of the task. She created bushy eyebrows from sticks and a distinctly aquiline carrot nose. 'There. Now I think it looks like my own old governess.'

'Very nice, all of you!' Katrina shouted in her old head-girl voice from the shelter of the portal where she sat with Al and Gunther. 'Now, do come for some cocoa!'

'In a minute; we need to finish his arms,' Helena shouted back, but Maddie went to sit with them, glad of the comparative warmth under the overhang. They sipped at their cocoa and watched the snowman take his complete form, emerging from the winter shadows, as Al snoozed in his wrappings of blankets.

'It could almost be like any other Christmas,' Katrina said wistfully. 'Snowmen and cocoa. But why can't I just enjoy it and forget things?'

Maddie reached out and squeezed her hand, and they smiled at each other as if recalling schoolgirl holidays for just a moment.

'Christmas is never easy at all,' Gunther said. 'Everyone expects it to be. Singing jolly carols, the perfect gifts, hugs and reconciliations. All we ever really seem to get are arguments and slights, and dry turkey.'

'And murder, I guess,' Maddie said. 'Don't forget that part.'

Katrina hiccupped with a guilty little laugh. 'True. But really, nothing has ever felt right since we came here. I feel something I can't quite define lurking underneath this house, as pretty as it is on the outside. Something that's never been right. Helena and Sam have always tried to be kind, though I can see they don't quite know how to treat Al now that he's not exactly the brother they once knew. And Helena seems so unhappy, despite her gaiety. I was hoping Felipe would really cheer her up.'

Maddie nodded. She'd felt just the same, ever since they drove up to Los Pintores. Something being not quite right. 'It must be lonely here, for a young woman like her.'

'Lonely for everyone,' Gunther said with a shudder. 'I'm definitely a city mouse myself; I can't write with all this silence, even though I've tried. How can anyone think straight here at all?'

'I miss towns, too,' Katrina said, giving her sleeping husband a tender little smile. 'Al needs quiet, though; that's what all the doctors said. Not that he gets it here. And even though Dr Pierce is always around lately, he pays no attention to Al, doesn't help him at all. Just Isabella. He's always listening to her talk about the parties of her youth, her gowns and jewels, and he gives her those pills. I don't know what to do any more.'

The snowman suddenly toppled over, among loud shrieks and cries that startled Al awake. Katrina shot him a worried glance, but he smiled.

'Good to hear some laughter again, isn't it, my Katie?' he said. 'It happens too seldom these days.'

The sound of a car motor chuffing along the drive beyond the portal broke on the winter breeze, and everyone came running to take an avid look. Maddie hoped it was what everyone wished for, a new guest, a new diversion, or at least a sign that roads were opening again. But she feared it might be more police, come to arrest Al.

A little Citroën stopped by the empty fountain, wheezing and gasping as if it had struggled on its last legs over the snow-clogged roads. A tall, lean man unfolded himself out, a white priest's collar peeking out from beneath a black overcoat, a glimpse of dark hair beneath a squashed felt hat.

'Father Adrian!' Helena cried and ran to give him a quick hug. 'You *are* a darling, daring the roads these days. You've come to say Mass, I'm sure.'

He gave her a hug in return and shook Sam and Ben's hands with a wide smile. 'Yes, of course. And just to see if I can help in any way, since I heard your terrible news. A priest visiting from Santa Fe told us; he heard it from a friend in the police department there. Don Victor was a great friend to the Church, of course.'

'A great contributor to the Church coffers, more like,' Al muttered to Maddie. 'But Father Adrian is a good man in spite of that.'

'An old friend of your family?' Maddie asked.

'As long as I can remember. He was at Helena's christening, though he was very young then, new to the priesthood,' Al said. 'He got us into St Michael's, when Ben was such a handful.'

Maddie studied the man as he came closer, Helena holding on to his arm. 'He looks a bit familiar, something about that lean face. Maybe Father Malone knows him?' Father Malone was Juanita's priest, and a fellow lover of detective fiction. He'd helped Maddie out once or twice on real-life puzzles. She wished he was there now.

Katrina poured out more cocoa. 'Father Adrian comes to the chapel here to say Mass and take confessions once in a while, isn't that right, Al darling? I'm not Catholic, but he does always seem jolly nice.'

'Yes, he is nice,' Al agreed. 'A good listener.'

'I'm surprised he made it through the snow in that wheezy little car,' Gunther said with a wondering tone. His Duesenberg was his own sweet baby; he would never have risked it in the snow.

Katrina went to the edge of the portal, Maddie following. 'Father Adrian, how nice to see you again,' she said.

'Mrs Luhan – Katrina,' the priest said with a sad smile, a touch to her hand. 'I'm so sorry for what's happened here.'

'Well, we are all very glad to see you. I'm sure it will be an enormous comfort,' Katrina said. 'However did you get through, though?'

He laughed. 'The Lord has mysterious ways, and new tires. I had to see if I could offer a bit of solace, and also deliver some of Don Victor's important papers to Dona Isabella. He left them in the Church office's care.' Father Adrian glanced at Maddie.

'Oh, this is my very dear friend Maddie Vaughn-Alwin, Father,' Katrina said. 'She lives in Santa Fe, and kindly agreed to come keep me company for Christmas. I bet she's jolly well sorry now!'

'I'm not sorry at all that I can be here with you now, Katrina, really,' Maddie assured her. 'How do you do, Father Adrian.'

He smiled as he shook her hand. 'I believe we have met

before, Mrs Vaughn-Alwin, at a church bazaar at the cathedral, and I know you know my colleague, Father Malone.'

Maddie nodded and wondered if, like dear Father Malone, Father Adrian might be of help. 'That's why you looked familiar! Father Malone is such a dear man. But I think he owes me a book I loaned him months ago!'

Father Adrian laughed. 'I'll be sure and remind him.'

'Shall we go in?' Katrina asked. 'I know Isabella will be eager to see you.'

'And there's Marta's wonderful Christmas cake,' Helena added.

'I am always eager to sample Marta's baking,' Father Adrian said.

Maddie turned to follow them, eager to leave the freezing wind behind and feel the heat of the fireplace tingle on her toes again, but she paused to glance back at the garden and the fallen snowman. To her shock, she saw a real man at the edge of the trees, a tall, golden-haired man in a shabby brown coat. Jim McTeer. He seemed to see her watching, and he turned to vanish into the cover of the woods, making her wonder again about the possible fire smoke the day she found Don Victor. What did the McTeers have to do with it all?

It was an hour later, when everyone else had retreated to their chambers to rest for dinner, by the time Maddie could slip outside for a little lookie-loo. She headed away from the hacienda, toward the trees, but all too soon got turned around on the narrow paths, the skeletal branches blocking her view. She could find no sign of a fire pit or any clues – though she wasn't sure what she expected – a note saying: 'I did it, coppers, take me now!' She eventually glimpsed the roof of the little summerhouse in the distance and headed toward that, only to stumble on a hidden branch near the steep banks of the pond. Her ankle gave a wrenching twist and she reached down to clutch it with a gasp. Just what she needed now, a bum ankle holding her down!

'Can I help you?' asked a whiskey-deep voice, filled with suspicion.

Heart pounding in fear, skin gone clammy-cold despite her

heavy tweed coat, Maddie glanced around, feeling like the greatest fool ever for letting her guard down.

It was the younger McTeer, Jim, the man she had seen earlier. He was tall and lean in his caped brown coat, hat pulled low over his brow, golden beard gleaming in the snow light. A gun rested over his arm, and he watched her warily, but not with fury.

'I . . . yes,' she answered, with her brightest 'I'm a harmless girly' smile. She hated that smile, but sometimes it was necessary. 'I must have taken a wrong turn somewhere, and now I've hurt my ankle. I'm Maddie Vaughn-Alwin, I'm staying just there at . . .'

'Los Pintores. Yeah, I know.'

She studied him carefully. Was he a spy, like the bartenders at La Fonda, knowing where everyone was all the time? 'How did you know? I only met your father once, very briefly.' And glimpsed him for a few seconds, watching them as they sledded.

'Not much goes on in these parts. A Christmas party is big news.' He nodded at her foot, which she had slipped out of her boot and held on to gingerly. It seemed to keep growing every second in aching swelling. 'You're hurt?'

'Just tripped on some branches I didn't see in the snow. I'll be fine, if you could just point me in the right direction?' And she would *not* ask what he was doing wandering around the Luhan summerhouse.

'You're bleeding.'

Maddie glanced down, surprised to see blood had seeped through her stocking. Suddenly the pain felt much worse. 'Oh, nertz!'

Jim McTeer smiled, a real smile, and he suddenly looked very different. Like a golden teddy bear on a toy store shelf, not a fearsome wilderness grizzly. He laid the gun aside. 'Come along, then, Mrs Vaughn-Alwin, let me help you out. We can go to our place, it's not far. We can get you patched up and then I'll see you home.'

'I . . .' She glanced around uncertainly.

She must have looked awful, with her cold red face and hurt ankle, because he smiled at her even wider, more reassuringly. 'You shouldn't be out here alone right now. Our maid, Hildie, is there, and I'll let you carry my gun yourself, if you like.' He frowned at her doubtfully. 'You *can* shoot?'

Maddie thought of her grandfather's duck camp on Long Island. It had been long ago, but who could forget? 'I can shoot well enough. Yes, you're right, I wouldn't get far on foot right now. Thank you.'

He braced her arm over his shoulder and carried her forward, as if she was a feather. He *was* handsome, she realized again as she studied him close up. Sharply etched, thin features, golden hair, cheekbones to cut glass. She wanted to paint his portrait as a Renaissance prince or something.

'What brought you to New Mexico, then, Mr McTeer?' she asked.

He helped her hop over a rotten log. 'Land, really, at a good price. We, my dad and me, came from Iowa originally, and before that Ireland. He'd heard the Candelarias were selling up from some passing friends, that they were in a hurry to leave. We thought it was kinda strange, they'd lived here so long, but it was a bargain. A place to live away from Iowa and all those memories.' He laughed. 'Guess we should have asked more about the neighbors. No wonder they were so eager to leave.'

'You don't much like the Luhans, I gather.'

He laughed again, that dark-whiskey sound. 'You could say that. Mostly because they don't like *us*. We just want to do our work in peace, but they keep harassing us, making it all harder. Then the sheep . . .'

Maddie remembered the story of Victor shooting some McTeer sheep. 'That is awful. I wouldn't want to live near Don Victor, either.'

'Well, none of us have to now, do we?' He paused to help Maddie climb down a low slope, toward a tan adobe ranch house with peeling blue-painted windowsills and doors, smoke spiraling from the chimneys. 'Can't say I'm sorry he's gone, but it must have taken a really dark heart to do a thing like that. Well, here we are, then.' He helped her over a stone threshold and into a small foyer, along a corridor to a sitting room.

Maddie wasn't sure what she was expecting from the McTeer house. After tales of family feuds turned deadly to sheep, maybe even to humans, she'd thought maybe cobwebs and poison bottles. But it was a cozy space, smaller than Los Pintores, but with polished wood floors covered with bright rag rugs, deeply cushioned chairs, herbs hanging from the vigas to scent the warm air, framed photographs lining the fireplace mantel. Not a lair of killers at all.

'Dad'll be upstairs; it's his resting time.' Jim helped her sit down on a velvet-covered settee nearing the crackling fire and fetched a footstool for her ankle.

Maddie gratefully stretched her freezing fingers toward the radiant heat. 'What a pretty house. Have you lived here long, then?'

Jim took a kettle that had been warming on the hearth and poured out a pottery mug of tea he handed to her. 'A while. We came here from Iowa like I said. My dad wanted a fresh start, and he liked the weather here in New Mexico. The blue skies, the space, the quiet.' He glanced around the sitting room thoughtfully before he took a basket down off the shelf and pulled out a roll of bandages. He was very prepared. 'Most of this stuff was my mother's, her furniture, those paintings over there. This quilt, she sewed it herself. We just set it up as she would have. Any prettiness is down to her.'

'She had fine taste. I do love this quilt, the way she paired the colors, the lines. She was surely an artist!' Maddie ran her fingertips over the blanket, its tiny stitches. 'I would imagine there isn't much time for decorating. Running a rancho out here seems like such hard work.'

His eyes narrowed. 'True enough. The last owners hadn't done much with the land for years. It's been working dawn to dusk to try and restore it, but it's coming along well enough. There's good profit in sheep, lots of potential. We'd be doing even better by this point, if . . .' He paused, a quick cloud of anger passing over his sculpted face.

'If it wasn't for hostile neighbors, maybe?' Maddie ventured, hoping for any scrap of information on his true feelings toward the Luhans.

He didn't look at her, just knelt beside her settee to reach for her foot. He slid off her boot and examined it, shaking his head before he bandaged it tightly. He was very competent at nursing, she thought, just as he was at sheep herding and keeping house. Maybe also organizing an ambush on a pesky neighbor? 'You're friends of the Luhans. Maybe you think we shouldn't be here, either? I think you're a newcomer, too, though.'

Maddie shrugged. 'I'm friends with Katrina Luhan. We went to school together in New York yonks ago. I've never really met any of the others until now. And yes, I did just come to Santa Fe a few years ago, looking for a new start – like you. I'm an artist, it's a good place to work. Lots of inspiration.' She winced a bit as he tightened the bandage, but then realized it felt much better. 'I imagine it's not so easy, living so close to a family like that.'

He laughed, and it sounded rusty, as if he didn't use it much. 'You could say that again. How's that ankle now?'

Maddie rolled it carefully. 'Much better.'

'That support should hold it for a while.' He fetched a bottle of brandy and two glasses from a cupboard. 'Have some with your tea? It'll warm you up before I get you home. It's not really a day for a stroll.'

'Yes, I know, but I was rather desperate for a bit of fresh air. And I will have a sip or two, thanks.'

He poured out two measures and sat down beside her in a rocking chair. He stared into the fire as he took a contemplative sip. 'Cheers.'

'Cheers. Thanks for being there to rescue me.'

He laughed again. 'Rescuing maidens from the snow makes a change from mending walls.'

Maddie was sure plenty of 'maidens' would clamor for rescue from him, with that golden hair and rugged Viking thing about him. 'I do feel silly for venturing out far.' But she had to search sometimes, didn't she? 'Helena did once mention ice skating on the pond if it froze enough, but I don't think that will happen any time soon.'

His expression shifted again, and he frowned into his glass. 'So, what do you think of Señorita Helena, and the others?'

Maddie hesitated for a moment. The McTeers were the

Luhans' rivals, weren't they? But maybe he could give her information on them, and his real feelings toward his troublesome neighbors. 'She seems nice. Smarter than she gets credit for, I think. And Sam does seem solid. He works hard.'

'Sam is OK. He's given us a tip or two on farming here in this climate.' He poured a splash more into his glass. 'I don't know the younger son all that well, just saw him in Espanola once. He's never at Los Pintores.'

'Ben. He's at university. He brought home a friend, Felipe. I think he's courting Helena.'

'Is he now? Well, those old families do stick together, don't they?'

'Sometimes. I don't think Ben is much interested in working the land. I suppose it will be easier to deal with his brother than his father, for you – for everyone.'

Jim glanced at her from the corner of his eye. 'I'm sure you get an earful over there about our little drama with Don Victor.'

'A bit, yes.'

'Well, I don't like drama. I like quiet, calm, getting on with work. We're just trying to make a living here. I don't appreciate the trouble he caused us, just because we're newcomers. My dad has had a hard time since my mother died; he needs peace. Sure, things'll be quieter now. I can't imagine a lady like Isabella will want to trouble us much, and Sam just wants to work, same as us. But I wouldn't kill anyone over it all.'

Maddie studied him carefully. He was certainly strong enough to bash someone over the head, but there was a stillness about him, a peace that seemed incongruous with such violence. But what would people do when they were desperate? Would he go to such lengths to protect his father, his land? 'Because killing would be drama?'

He smiled, a quick quirk of his lips. 'And all the mess. The animals get spooked by the smell of blood. I wouldn't have had the chance, anyway. I think I was in the barn with an injured sheep when it happened. Can't afford to lose any more.'

'You didn't see or hear anything that day? No one sneaking around?'

He shook his head. 'The barn is on the opposite side of the

field. But I tell you – there are people around here who certainly didn't trust Don Victor as far as they could throw him. We sure aren't the only ones whose lives will be a little easier now.'

Maddie nodded, wondering who all those people could be. 'Anyone in particular, would you say?'

He shrugged again and swallowed the last of his brandy. 'I couldn't say. I'm just a farmer, yeah? Not a detective. You just be careful over there, you and your friend Katrina.' He stood and held out his hand to her. 'You all right to walk now? I can help you get back to Luhan land.'

She rolled her ankle again and nodded. 'Yes, it's much better. I must have just strained it a bit. Thanks for the hooch. And the warning.' It wasn't as much information as she'd like, but it seemed like he'd used up all his allotment of words for the day.

She wrapped up in her coat, which he'd left by the fire to dry a bit, and as she turned she glimpsed his father on the stairs, a quick, shadowy figure with wild hair who fled and vanished again. Another wounded soul, like Al, who needed protecting?

Jim led her across the fields holding her arm as he helped her over boulders. The snow had slowed down, leaving the day diamond-clear, cold and sharp. He pointed out the chimneys of Los Pintores in the near distance. 'Can you get back from here?'

Maddie nodded. She was sure there would be more trouble than it was worth for him to show his face at Luhans' doorstep. He tipped his hat to her and melted back into the trees. Only once she had limped her way to the garden gate did she really wonder why he had been there in the first place.

THIRTEEN

Maddie carefully limped into the dining room that evening to find that Mrs Luhan – or, more probably, Marta and the rest of the household – had gone out of their way to make everything even more elegant despite the heavy, dark cloud that hovered over all their heads as the time ticked past after the murder. Al was resting upstairs, but everyone else was in place, with the damask tablecloth gleaming white in the glow of candles, elaborate silver candelabras lining the buffet and Christmas greenery in bronze vases.

Maddie found herself seated next to Father Adrian. She smiled at him as the first course, a mushroom soup, was served in elegant gilt-edged china.

'It is good to see you, Mrs Vaughn-Alwin, though the circumstances are sad,' he said. 'Father Malone speaks so highly of you.'

'Only because I lend him all my new detective novels,' Maddie answered. She took a sip of the wine. 'He is such a good friend. Do you work with him often?'

'Not as often as I'd like. Our parishes are not very near, though we share many charitable concerns.'

'And you come here to say Mass for the Luhans?'

'From time to time, yes. Victor, rest his soul, is an old friend to my family.' He leaned closer as the fish, a salmon in dill sauce, was brought in and more wine poured. 'Father Malone tells me you don't just read detective novels, but use their lessons in real life.'

Intrigued by the suggestion, Maddie nodded. 'Once in a while, yes.'

'I went to check over the chapel when I arrived, and I suspect someone has been using it for very irreligious purposes.'

'Using it?' she whispered, fascinated.

'I mean staying there. Mrs Sanchez told me it's been locked

up, except for a bit of dusting and some family prayers once in a while, since I was last here, but I found blankets and a basket in a cupboard, along with some old clothes. Mrs Sanchez didn't know what they could be used for there.'

Maddie thought of the laundry, of blood and missing garments and woodsmoke. 'Helena did say she thinks her father was killed by a passing lunatic. An escaped convict or something of the sort.'

'I don't sense the police think so, though.'

Maddie studied him closely, his kind, intelligent brown eyes, and something made her sense she could trust him. At least to an extent. 'I do think Inspector Sadler believes it's someone here in the house. Probably Alfonso. But I think he couldn't have done it.'

Father Adrian frowned. 'Is that because of your friendship with Katrina?'

'I certainly would wish it for her sake, yes. She's the kindest soul, she deserves some happiness. But also because it doesn't seem his – well, his style, I guess. Too calm and measured for a man with so many troubles in his mind.' She glanced over the candlelit table. Helena chattered with Felipe as if nothing was at all amiss, and David smiled at Maddie as she gave him a little wave before he went back to talking to Ben. 'Though I have no idea yet who it could have been. And if someone has been hiding out in the chapel . . .'

'I'm not sure if it was a hideout so much as some sort of secret, romantic rendezvous.'

Maddie's eyes widened. 'A love nest? How would you . . .?'

Father Adrian laughed. 'I wasn't always a priest. The blankets, the remains of wine in the basket. Other . . . er . . . signs.'

Maddie looked closer at the women – Isabella and Dr Pierce, Helena and Felipe. 'And no sign as to who?'

'I'm afraid not.' The fish plates were whisked away and lemon sorbet served before the entree, more translucent French china sparkling with gold. Maddie thought of what Rickie said – money or love. There seemed to be plenty of both floating around. 'I can say, though, Mrs Vaughn-Alwin, that though Don Victor was much respected in charitable circles, he was not universally loved. Perhaps especially, sadly, in his own household.'

'I confess I've noticed there's not very many people torn up with grief here.' Except maybe for the secretary who wouldn't leave her room, though she was there at dinner that evening – more subdued, perhaps, but still brightly dressed in crimson satin and diamond clips in her marcel-waved hair. Isabella did not glance at Mrs Upshaw once, though Gunther chatted with her, being his usual charming, twinkling self. Maddie wondered what they talked about.

'Don Victor entrusted me with some of his paperwork, which I'm to deliver to the attorneys in case of something happening to him suddenly. I will visit their offices as soon as we can leave through the snow. I was lucky my car got here today.'

Maddie was intrigued, though she feared getting her hopes up for a glimpse at Don Victor's legal affairs. 'Such as a will, perhaps?'

Father Adrian nodded. He glanced about as if to make sure no one was listening to them, but they were all now laughing at some tale of university hijinks Ben and Felipe were sharing. 'He did make a few versions. He was quick to anger, as I'm sure you guessed, Mrs Vaughn-Alwin.'

'I had an inkling.'

'So sometimes people would be in and out of the will. This last version was sent to me in the summer, and appears properly witnessed and notarized, so I am sure it will stand.'

'Would everyone know the contents?'

'If he chose to share them, or maybe threaten with them. But I'm not sure.'

'Can you tell me any of the provisions? Maybe I could share some observations.'

He seemed to think this over, fiddling thoughtfully with his heavy silver fork, before he nodded. 'I'd certainly like to help find who committed this terrible act, if I can. Don Victor was not the most amiable of men, but no one deserves such a vile death.' He waited while the roast was served, then continued, 'It actually was much as you might expect, considering his large family and his changeable attitudes toward some of them. Sam inherits this estate.'

'That makes sense. He appears to be running it already.'

'But does he *want* to be?'

'What do you mean? Has he expressed resentment at the responsibility?'

'Once, he confided he might wish to join the priesthood.'

'What?' Maddie cried, surprised. But then she realized she shouldn't be. Sam did seem quiet, stoical, inward-looking. More monk-like than priest, maybe, but it made sense. Had his father thwarted his vocation, and it turned bitter?

'That was a long time ago. For now, he is the main legatee. Isabella receives the portion she was guaranteed when her marriage contract was drawn up, plus a small house on Luisa Street in Santa Fe.'

Maddie glanced at Isabella, who was chatting with Dr Pierce, positively animated in the flickering, golden light. 'Could she have been expecting more?' Enough to live in France, maybe?

'Perhaps. Yet it's no paltry sum. Her father was an Otero, very wealthy and powerful. He was careful with his daughter's welfare in the contract. She can live very comfortably in Santa Fe.'

'Dr Pierce says she needs a rest cure in a spa town, probably in Europe.'

'With his company?'

'Maybe. Or maybe *he* expects more from this will. I did hear he owes rather a large debt. What of the other children?'

'Helena has a sum left in trust, for a dowry when she marries or to be paid in installments starting when she's thirty. Which is some years away.'

Poor Helena, who wanted her freedom so much, Maddie thought. 'And that's it?'

'Yes. Don Victor didn't think highly of female intellect, though Helena has always seemed very smart to me. Shrewder than she wishes to appear.'

Maddie studied Helena, who laughed with Felipe. Maybe she would get that dowry soon, if she knew the provisions of her inheritance.

As if he read her thoughts, Father Adrian said, 'Though perhaps she'll marry and have her inheritance soon enough.

Ben was also left a trust, to pay for the remainder of his education and to help set him up in business after. Provided he goes into an approved career, of course.'

Maddie laughed. 'Was Don Victor afraid Ben might run off to be a poet in Mallorca or something?' She feared she couldn't quite read the seemingly light-hearted Ben; she didn't know what he wanted deep down inside.

'We don't really know with young Ben, do we? He tends to, shall I say, dabble. I think that's what worried Victor.' He smiled as the dessert, a wonderfully dark chocolate and dried cherry confection, was brought in. 'And there is a sum for his secretary.' The smile turned to a disapproving moue.

'Mrs Upshaw?' Maddie was surprised. That didn't seem the usual sort of mistress thing.

'Odd, yes. To set up a typist's office, I think he said. And a small pension for Mrs Sanchez, and a couple of other staff members. A larger pension for Rosa Sanchez.'

'For Rosa?' Maddie thought of what Rickie had said, of Victor's questions and conversations with Rosa, which had made the girl uneasy. Perhaps now Marta and Rosa could set up their teashop, their new life. But why leave Rosa, a housekeeper's niece, a sizeable legacy?

'Yes. That's about all, except for some bequests to a few charities. Provisions for a funeral Mass here in his chapel.'

'And what about Al?'

'An allowance, to be paid under supervision of Katrina and a few other trustees. It should keep him comfortably enough, if they're careful. Your friend Katrina does seem very sensible.'

'She is.' Yet Katrina needed more money than a small 'careful' sum if she was to help Al and find him the right treatment. Maddie studied the gathering again, which seemed more relaxed after the fine food and copious wine. No one would be made wildly rich, but did they all know that? Were they expecting something very different?

'Shall we return to the sala for coffee, ladies?' Isabella asked as she stood up from the table, her dove-gray silk and silver lace gown gleaming, diamond necklace and hair ornaments sparkling. 'We can leave the gentlemen to brandy and cigars, and be terribly old-fashioned.'

Dr Pierce reached out to tenderly touch her hand. 'Remember, my dear, you should rest.'

She waved him away, laughing. 'I am very well, my dear doctor, don't worry!' She wafted out of the dining room, trailing her hand over the men's chairs. Helena and Katrina followed, and Maddie rose from her seat.

'Thank you, Father, for a most interesting conversation,' she said as she gathered up her shawl. 'You've given me a lot to think about.'

'I do hope you can help in this sad matter, Mrs Vaughn-Alwin. Father Malone does speak so highly of you.'

'I'm not sure what to make of it yet. But I'll certainly try.'

When she reached the warm, firelit sala, with the silver coffee service laid out near the piano, she found Isabella settling herself on her chaise, with Helena and Katrina nearby and Rosa preparing the coffee.

'I'm afraid poor Mrs Upshaw is ill with a headache,' Isabella said brightly. 'My mother always did say that cheap scent was hazardous to the sinuses. Mrs Vaughn-Alwin, would you like some coffee?'

'Yes, please,' Maddie answered. They sipped at the delightfully strong brew and chatted about fashion mags until the men joined them. Gunther set about mixing some of his famous cocktails, while everyone chatted lazily, and tried to ignore the heavy clouds that always hung over everything.

'Now, what shall we do?' Isabella said, clapping her hands as her diamonds sparkled and shimmered. 'When I was a girl, we spent the twelve days playing games like charades and piggy squeak. Quite old-fashioned now, probably.'

'We could play "kiss the four corners of the room,"' Ben suggested with a teasing grin.

'Oh, really, Benito, you are shocking,' his mother chided, but she giggled.

'In England, we like to tell ghost stories around the holiday fire,' David said.

'It sounds more like Día de los Muertos than Christmas,' Helena exclaimed. 'I love it!'

'What sort of ghosts?' Felipe asked.

'Well, let me see,' David said. 'Gray ladies, lots of houses have those, drifting up and down staircases and crying. Beasts in medieval dungeons. Spirit carriages. They often seem to portend curses or tragedies. Guides at castles love to tell such things, and my grandmother loved to tour them when I was a child, so I heard many.'

'I remember one!' Gunther said enthusiastically. He always loved creepy tales. 'There was a young couple, much in love, but the husband lost most of their fortune in some bad business deal with an old friend he had once slighted.'

'This sounds too prosaic by half,' Helena sighed. 'It happens all the time!'

'Just listen,' Gunther said. 'The husband became more and more withdrawn, isolated and in despair. Nightly, he would climb an old, hidden staircase to the roof of their house. Once, his wife went with him and thought she glimpsed the friend below, but he then vanished. Word came that the friend had died, but the husband still went to the roof, still refused to speak to his wife, to eat, to sleep. Then one night, he vanished. A servant said he saw the husband walking away with the dead friend.'

'Ghostly revenge,' Ben moaned, and tickled his sister to make her shriek.

'I remember a story,' Felipe said. 'A true one; it happened to the family on the rancho neighboring ours. They had several children, but the youngest, the prettiest little daughter, drowned in a well. For years after, they would hear moaning and singing from near the covered-up well, hear someone calling for their mother. They would also see a pale figure outside the windows on moonlit nights, saw little hands pounding on the glass, but there was no sound at all. A maid tried to open the window one night, and had to be forcibly stopped, for everyone knew if they let the phantom in, they would all be doomed.'

'I see it!' Helena screamed, and she certainly did look pale and shadow-eyed enough to have seen a spirit. She pointed a trembling hand at the window.

'Helena, don't be so silly,' Isabella said, her voice shaking. 'We are on the second floor! How would a ghost climb up here?'

'Ghosts can go anywhere, Mama,' Helena said, and gulped

down another drink. 'That's why they're so frightening. We're never alone. And anyway, it wasn't in the window. It was in the garden. I'm sure of it.'

They all sat in the sala a little longer, talking of things that were not ghosts, but everyone seemed rather subdued. They all agreed to turn in soon after.

'That's the last time I listen to ghost stories after Gunther's drinkies,' Maddie said as she and David climbed the (haunted) stairs into the shadows. There was a weird howl past the windows that made her jump, until she told herself it must be the wind knocking a tree branch.

'I should never have started it,' David said ruefully, holding tight to her hand. 'I just remember my grandfather talking of Anne Boleyn drifting around as she carries her head under her arm and such nonsense!'

'Oh, no, I absolutely love ghost stories. We shall tell them every Christmas from now on! But safe in town by our own fire.'

'I can't wait.' They paused at the top of the stairs for a long, sweet, lingering kiss that wiped Maddie's spooky jitters away – and gave her new, delicious ones in their place. 'Will you be all right, darling? I can look in on you after I've made sure Al is settled.'

'I'd like that so very much! But I guess we shouldn't – we've been so good so far. I'll be fine. I'm just being silly. I know there are no ghosts here.' She kissed him again, and he turned to go towards Al and Katrina's room. Maddie went up the last short flight to her own chamber, a bit dizzy from the cocktails.

Something pale flashed and shimmered at the end of the corridor, lit by the snow glow from the window. Maddie almost shrieked – *'It's a ghost! Look out!'* – before she clapped her hand to her mouth.

Then she dared to peek closer, and saw it was all too human. Or rather, *humans*. Two people, entwined under the garland of mistletoe that was hung by the window at the end of the corridor.

At first, Maddie turned away, eager to give them a bit of privacy. Then a flash of bright hair in the moonlight caught her attention. It was Mrs Upshaw! Not such a headache, after all. But the man had his back to her, and all she could see was that he was tall and clad in a dark dinner jacket, as all the men had been that evening. It could be any of them.

Mrs Upshaw moaned and sighed, and Maddie tiptoed into her room, quietly sliding the door shut behind her. Another illicit romance stalking the halls of Los Pintores. Her brain was spinning from drinkies and scandal.

FOURTEEN

Christmas Eve morning

A pinkish light, tinged with bright white, pierced past Maddie's closed eyes into her aching head. She groaned and rolled over, knocking over a fort of pillows stacked around her. She frowned as she wondered what on earth those silly pillows were doing so out of place.

Then she remembered. She'd piled them up herself, in hopes of fending off – what? Ghosts?

She forced her gritty eyes to open, and blinked as she took in her room. Curtains were half-open, letting in the morning light. Sun rays fell on the carafe of water and bottle of aspirin she remembered David bringing to her and insisting she take before she fell asleep. She also remembered, with a great, hot blush, clinging to him and begging him to stay there and keep the ghosts away. Sweetie that he was, he must have sat with her until she fell asleep.

She sat up carefully. Buttercup, who'd been just as scared as Maddie was – some watchdog! – was burrowed under the blankets, snoring softly, the only sound except for the slow tick-tick of the clock on the fireplace mantel. Maddie glanced at the time. It was earlier than any right-thinking person should be awake. She knew she'd never be able to get back to sleep, though.

She pushed herself reluctantly out of the warm nest of her bed and wrapped herself up in her quilted satin dressing gown. The fire had died out in the grate, and the air had a distinctly icy edge. She thought longingly of her warm cozy house, her deep bathtub and thick old walls. Next Christmas, she was definitely staying put in her own sitting room!

She went and eased back a little further the edge of the curtain to peer outside. She wondered if she'd imagined all the ghostly frights and illicit romances beyond every corner. Everything looked so pristine, so idyllic out there, a veritable winter wonderland oil painting of white and dark green.

Maddie watched the landscape for a long moment, entranced by the way the dawn light played over the glittering snow. She wished she could forget everything else and paint it all, lose herself in her work. Wished that she was locked in the sanctuary of her little studio, lost in her easel and brushes, making her own world again. But she couldn't leave everything half-finished, not when Katrina and Al needed her help. And she didn't know how to snowshoe her way out, anyway.

She turned away from the peaceful winter morning and dug through the wardrobe to find her warmest outfit, a blue tweed skirt and long, cream-colored cardigan to wrap over a silk blouse. As she dressed and tidied her hair, she thought about what Father Adrian had told her about Don Victor's will, and how the bequests were smaller and more restricted than might have been imagined. Did everyone know what they would really be bequeathed, and were they angry? Or bitterly disappointed? Father Adrian had mentioned there were other wills before this one, maybe someone thought one of those older ones was still in force. A more generous one.

Mrs Upshaw was left some money – yet it seemed Victor hadn't been her only romance. But who was her man under the mistletoe? 'Nertz,' Maddie muttered, wishing she hadn't been quite so tiddly and thus more observant last night. Sam? Ben? Felipe? Someone else? For all Maddie knew, the colorful Mrs Upshaw could have had him stashed in her wardrobe all the time. Maddie would just have to pay her a wee visit.

And speaking of cupboards . . . she remembered Father Adrian saying he thought the chapel closet had been used for trysts. By whom? When? Maybe it was the mysterious couple under the mistletoe?

Buttercup peeked out from under her blankets, blinking her big brown doggie eyes. She let out a low whine. Not her hungry or I-want-to-go-out whine, but a questioning, uncertain whimper.

'I know, darling,' Maddie told her. 'I want to crawl back

under there myself, preferably until after Christmas. But there's work to be done. We just have to pull up our socks.'

Buttercup clearly did not agree. She burrowed back into her pillow fort.

Maddie laughed and glanced again in the mirror, horrified at her pale cheeks and dark-circled eyes. 'Ugh, I look like a ghost myself.' She reached for her tube of trusty Elizabeth Arden. As she picked it up, she noticed her blue silk scarf drifting over the edge of the dressing table. Rosa had liked it; it matched her pretty, distinctive blue-gray eyes. And Rosa had been left money in the will. Maddie decided she would give her the scarf, and hopefully find out a little more about what Rosa had feared with Don Victor. What she hoped for the future.

Those eyes . . .

No. It couldn't be! Could it?

Of course it could. Maddie smacked her palm to her forehead. 'What a fool you've been! Not thinking of it sooner.' She berated herself. She spun around and hurried out of the room, leaving Buttercup on guard duty.

The house was silent and still as Maddie made her way down the backstairs. It all *did* feel a bit eerie, isolated, but nothing like the phantoms she'd imagined in the night. It just felt like a house where secrets crowded all around.

In the corridor to the kitchen, she finally heard some signs of life. The metallic clatter of pans, low mutters. She wrapped her cardigan closer around her and hurried toward the promised warmth.

Marta was baking, pots and pans covered with batter piled around her, and the smell of vanilla, sweet dried fruit and cinnamon hung delightfully in the air. For a moment, Marta didn't see her, as she was busily digging about behind the open door of the icebox, and Maddie studied her. She remembered how it was in her parents' New York house and Newport cottage – the staff were always there, quiet, watching, noticing. Marta had been at Los Pintores for a long time. What all had she seen? How was her life really entwined with the Luhans?

'Good morning, Marta,' Maddie said.

Marta spun around, clutching a covered bowl. 'Mrs Vaughn-Alwin! You're awake early.'

'I couldn't go back to sleep. I'm sorry if I'm disturbing you. It just seems so warm in here, and such delicious smells.'

Marta nodded with a pleased smile. 'There's coffee and toast, but I haven't finished breakfast for the dining room yet.'

'Coffee sounds perfect.' Maddie helped herself from the pot on the stove and sat down at the little table tucked by the wall, which was covered with more bowls of enticing-smelling goodies. 'You're up early yourself.'

Marta busily stirred at something on the stove. 'I can't sit still. I'm just thinking, thinking all the time now. Who would have thought this house would see such horrible days? At *Christmas.*' She held up the bowl. 'I thought I would make a plum pudding for your Dr Cole. Just like in English stories.'

'How kind you are! He did love your Christmas cake so much. He doesn't say so, but I wonder if he doesn't get a weensy bit homesick sometimes, especially at the holiday.' She remembered that Marta wanted a teashop, a place to sell her baked goods. How *much* did she want it?

'It is hard to be far from your roots for Christmas,' Marta said.

'Can I help?' Maddie asked, nodding at all the bowls.

'Of course. These dried apples need to be chopped. I harvested them myself from the orchard here, in the autumn. For apple empanadas.' She handed Maddie a paring knife and a plate of yellowed, shriveled apple slices.

Maddie felt a sense of calm come over her as she started the careful, methodical task, almost a comfort. It made her think of Juanita, and their own kitchen at home. 'Where is *your* home, Marta? Before you came here?'

'A little village, not far from here. San Pedro, it's called. My family lived there for many generations; my father was a miller, as his father was. It was a nice place, even though it was tiny. You knew everyone nearby, and we all helped each other whenever it was needed. There was a beautiful old church . . .' Her voice trailed away, and she shook her head.

Maddie nodded. She could picture it, like so many little villages dotted through the mountains; the old, adobe church with its square towers and tin roof, the cottages with flowers outside the blue doors, a little shop on the corner of the dirt lane. 'Why did you leave?'

Marta frowned. 'My mother died when I was very young, and my sister Angie was even smaller.'

'Rosa's mother?'

Marta nodded and stirred even faster. 'My father couldn't manage. He sent me to stay with my aunt; she was housekeeper at the estate next door, before the McTeers bought it, when the Candelarias owned it. She and her husband had a little cottage there. She worked very long hours, but she did her best for us, teaching us to read and write, cipher and keep accounts, kept us fed and clothed. I took care of Angie. She was like my own little baby.'

Marta sounded so dreamy, so far away, as if she was back in those Christmases with her dear sister. 'She was pretty? Like Rosa?' Maddie asked.

'She was like the summer itself. Slim and quick, and with golden streaks in her hair that shimmered like sunlight. Always dancing and laughing, twirling through the days.' Marta laughed wryly. 'I never could believe she was related to *me*! But she read so much, dreamed so much. She wanted so much, so many impossible things. I knew how everything really had to be. When I was old enough, I came to work here, and I helped Angie pay for a typing course in Espanola. I hoped she'd find a job there, or in Santa Fe.'

'How was it working here at Los Pintores then?'

Marta shrugged. 'Different than now, that's for sure. Señora Isabella was young when she married, and even though she was pregnant a lot, had so many kids to look after, she always loved fun. Lots of house parties then, dancing in the sala, concerts, summer parties in the garden. There was a big staff then, even a butler to watch over it all, so the work wasn't very heavy. I enjoyed it.'

Maddie thought of music and dancing and fun ringing through the now-quiet, haunted halls. She popped a bit of apple into her mouth and thought she could taste the summer-time sweetness there must have once been at Los Pintores. 'What happened?'

Marta shrugged and reached for another bowl. 'Señora Isabella became unwell after Ben was born, her youngest, and she couldn't manage so many parties. Don Victor never liked them anyway; he always preferred to have his house to himself. Hated noise. I think he was glad of the excuse to bar the doors. And as the children went off to school, one after the other, they didn't need such a large staff.'

'Did it become lonely?'

'A bit. Then Angie came to work here with me.'

'She didn't want to be a typist?'

Marta shook her head, not looking up from the batter she was mixing. 'She was so quiet when she got here. I tried to look after her, as I always had.'

'To be her mother?'

'I owed that to my own mother, to take care of her baby. I finally found out that Angie herself was going to have a baby.'

Maddie gasped. 'It was Rosa?'

Marta nodded. 'Yes.' That was all she said. She covered the bowl and went back to the icebox to fetch eggs for the dining room breakfast.

'Speaking of Rosa . . .' Maddie began cautiously. She took the carefully folded blue scarf from her cardigan pocket. 'Could you ask her if she might like this? She admired it when I arrived, and I'm afraid the color doesn't suit me. It would look the bee's knees on her.'

Marta's eyes widened as she examined the length of silk. 'Oh, Mrs Vaughn-Alwin! It's very pretty, but it looks too expensive.'

'It wasn't at all, really, but it is a lovely color and deserves just the right wearer. She's been so kind to me since I arrived.'

'That's most generous of you, Mrs Vaughn-Alwin. Rosa does love pretty things, as her mother did, and I can't indulge her as I'd like.' She took the scarf and carefully tucked it away in a drawer.

'Maybe that will all change now. With Don Victor's will.'

Marta glanced at Maddie with a suspicious expression. 'Wh–what do you mean?'

'I heard a whisper that when the will is read, she'll inherit a tidy sum.'

Marta's fists curled on the edge of the counter. 'Are you saying – do you think . . .?'

'I'm very sorry, Marta,' Maddie said gently. Marta and Rosa had certainly suffered and struggled enough in their lives, but it had to be known before Sadler dug it up himself. 'Is Rosa perhaps Don Victor's own child? I noticed her lovely eyes when we first met. Very distinctive.'

Marta crumpled, covering her face with her apron for a moment. 'No one can know! It would hurt Señora Isabella and the children, and we could lose our jobs here after all these years. I'm trying to save enough for my teashop.'

'Does Rosa know?'

Marta shook her head. 'I told her that her mother was briefly married, and her father died before she was born. I'm not sure she ever really believed it – she's a smart girl, is my Rosa – but it's what we always told each other.'

'Did you know about the bequest?'

'No! Oh, he always tried to press things on us. Maybe he felt guilty. I did let him pay Rosa's school fees. She deserves to have some choices in life, though I hated being beholden to him for it.' She sounded a bit bitter, and Maddie couldn't help but wonder if she'd had enough at last, if owing him for the school fees and keeping the great secret for so long had suddenly snapped inside of her. 'But maybe with a little money, she could start again far from this place. It used to be such a lovely house, and now it feels almost cursed. Rosa seems to like that handsome young policeman . . .'

'Rickie? Well, he likes her, too, certainly.'

'She could have a good, honest life with a man like that, away from here.' Marta turned and gave Maddie an imploring stare. 'You won't tell her what I told you, will you, Mrs Vaughn-Alwin? I want her to find some free, happy days after all this.'

Maddie studied her for a long moment, thinking of what David once said – that people liked to confide in her. She sometimes wished they didn't, that she didn't have to keep their secrets. And she desperately hoped Marta and Rosa had nothing to do with the murder. 'She won't hear it from me, I promise. But do be very careful, both of you! Watch where you step.'

Marta's eyes widened. 'Are you saying that if someone knew who Rosa was, knew she would get some of the Luhan money – she could be in danger?'

'I'm afraid I don't know what this is all about yet. Crime usually concerns love or money, so it wouldn't be unusual if Don Victor's will was part of it all. Perhaps stay as close as you can to Rickie until we can leave.' Maddie gave her a reassuring smile. 'Not that he would mind one jot!'

Marta gave a distracted nod. 'Thank you again, Mrs Vaughn-Alwin, I will certainly be careful. And I'm glad I told you. I've been holding it so close, so secret, like a stone all this time.'

Maddie nodded in return, though she wasn't sure how very secret it could really be. 'I'll leave you to finish up breakfast. I'm sorry I sat here taking up your time so long.' She handed Marta the bowl of apple slices.

She hurried toward the stairs again to make sure she was tidy for breakfast, but met Sadler and Rickie in the front foyer, the two of them bundled up against the cold.

'We're going to see if we can find the location of that smoke you told us about from the day of the murder, Mrs Vaughn-Alwin,' Sadler growled as he double-wrapped a knitted muffler up to his ragged beard. 'Though if there's a firepit, it's probably covered with snow by now, and I didn't see anything like that when I rode out with Sam Luhan.'

'I'm sure we'll find it if we just look closer, sir!' Rickie said, far too eager-beaver for the early hour. Sadler shot him a glare and Maddie bit her lip to keep from laughing.

'I think the smoke came from the direction of the McTeer fence line,' she said. She wished she could go out with them, but then everyone at breakfast would wonder where she was, and no one would let their guard drop with her if they thought she was buddies with the police.

They opened the door and Sadler plunged out into the cold wind, but Maddie stopped Rickie before he could follow. 'Rickie, could you be a darling and keep an eye on Rosa and her aunt? I have a strange feeling something is about to happen, and I wouldn't want them to get in the way.'

Rickie looked quite alarmed. 'Something will happen with Rosa?'

'I'm not sure, but I worry about her. She's so young and sweet. I know you wouldn't mind helping her when you can.'

He smiled widely, but there was still worry lurking in his eyes. 'I can definitely do that, Mrs Vaughn-Alwin, don't worry.'

He followed Sadler outside, and Maddie rushed upstairs. She could hear people stirring behind their doors, the day coming to life. She did wish she knew what it might hold. Who else was a secret couple? Who wanted who out of the way? She knew of one person who was definitely having a little romance. But she knew she needed some reinforcements, and she knew just where to find them since Gunther had moved out of his writing casita and into the main house. She stopped at Gunther's door to tell him that more of his Gunther Specials were needed, despite the early hour, and went on to the end of the corridor.

'Mrs Upshaw,' Maddie called as she knocked at the secretary's door. 'It's Maddie Vaughn-Alwin. Are you ill? Can I help?'

The door cracked open, and Mrs Upshaw peeked out. Her make-up was smudged, her bright hair tangled. 'Help?'

'I can fetch Dr Cole, or . . .'

'I'm not sick! Just – oh! This *crumb* of a house. I hate it! I gotta get out.'

'I do understand. It's all so awful. Maybe a little chat would help us both? Get our minds off these awful days.'

Mrs Upshaw paused and glanced behind her. Maddie wondered if she had a gentleman caller, her mysterious mistletoe man. Finally, she opened the door wider and let Maddie slip inside. It looked like a winter wind had swept through the chamber, leaving open trunks spilling bright satins and velvets, feather boas, bejeweled hats, heeled shoes and silk stockings everywhere in its wake. Papers teetered in an unsteady pile on the bedside table, next to paperback romantic novels.

'Packing?' Maddie asked.

'I gotta be ready to get away as soon as I can. This place gives me the willies. Doesn't it you?' She pushed a stack of lace and charmeuse lingerie off a tapestry sofa and plopped down with a sob. 'And this family! I can't stand the bunch of them, these snooty old so-and-sos. I – oh! Love is just the *pits*.'

Maddie took a handkerchief from her pocket and handed it to the sobbing woman. Mrs Upshaw loudly blew her nose. Maddie was a bit startled to see the woman so upset over Don Victor. 'I'm so sorry. Did you work for Don Victor long?'

Mrs Upshaw blew her nose again and shook her head. 'A couple months, maybe. He was OK when we were at his office. Generous, y'know. Seemed like an old pussycat. But here . . .' Her voice crawled toward a wail again. 'I knew I shouldn't have come here. It's not natural to be so far from civilization. I'm from Pittsburgh, y'know.'

Maddie sat down beside her and smiled sympathetically. 'And you loved him very much?' she asked gently.

Mrs Upshaw looked up, her mascara-smeared eyes shocked. 'Love Vicky? Of course not! I'm no chump. Who could love him? Sure, he gave some real nice presents, but he was so *grumpy*. I hope I've got better taste than that. I like a man who can have some fun.'

Maddie was a bit confused. 'Fun' was what Mrs Upshaw looked for in a man? She couldn't think who here would be fun enough to meet under the mistletoe. 'But you said love was the pits. I thought . . . well, the grief.'

'Oh, I'm sorry enough he's gone. I've got rent due, and really no one deserves to get cheesed off like that, no matter how stick-in-the-mud they are. Bashed over the head! Ugh. But *love* . . .'

'So you are in love with someone else?'

Mrs Upshaw shrugged and looked away, twisting the handkerchief between her fingers. A large pearl and diamond ring gleamed there. 'I didn't mean to. Sometimes a girl can't help herself.'

Maddie remembered how David had quite bowled her over, the first time she saw him on that train. 'I have never heard truer words, Mrs Upshaw. Love won't be denied. I do hope you weren't crying because this fella let you down? That would be too awful on top of everything else.'

Mrs Upshaw sniffled and gave her a watery smile. 'You're sure nicer than the others here, aren't you, Mrs Vaughn-Alwin?'

'Maddie, please.'

'Maddie. You seem swell.'

'I just know what it's like to lose someone. To be run over by romance.' She carefully folded a silver-fringed shawl and tucked it around Mrs Upshaw's shaking shoulders. 'To find someone rich and young and handsome, and discover they weren't what you thought at all.'

She laughed hoarsely. 'Young and handsome? Your fella really is a sight to see, Maddie, but a man's looks never helped a girl like me. I hope I'm smarter than to be fooled by all that.'

Maddie thought of the men at Los Pintores, most of them young. Sam, Ben, Felipe, all young and handsome, if not yet quite rich. Then who? It seemed Mrs Upshaw was not quite grief-stricken for Victor, after all. 'Then do you think . . .'

A knock sounded at the door, and Mrs Upshaw quickly wiped her eyes. Maddie opened it to Gunther, who bustled in bearing a tray of martini glasses and a gleaming silver shaker, his instruments to magic-making.

'I heard comfort was needed, pronto,' he announced. 'And nothing says comfort like a Gunther Gin Special before breakfast.'

Mrs Upshaw turned an astonished face toward Maddie, lips and eyes round just like in a movie. 'Mrs Vaughn-Alwin! Maddie. Did you ask for this just for me? You *are* the berries.'

'I'm afraid I did. I heard you crying, and it's true that nothing soothes quite like one of Gunther's cocktails. He's a wizard at it all.'

She burst into fresh tears. 'You two really are the bee's knees! Who would have ever thought I'd find such swell folks in an old dump like this?'

Gunther poured together the ingredients in his shaker, adding chunks of ice that looked suspiciously like he'd chipped them off his window ledge. 'Compliments like that will get you everywhere, my dear. Now let me just give this a nice shake, and you drink up and tell me where you got that heavenly hat over there.'

Maddie and Gunther exchanged a long, speaking glance over the martini glasses, and she knew she had an ally in finding out who Mr Mistletoe might be.

FIFTEEN

Maddie was making her way downstairs for lunch, only slightly unsteady on her feet after Gunther's comfort cocktails, though they had missed breakfast hours ago. They hadn't quite discovered who Mrs Upshaw's mystery man was, but they *had* heard tales of many past boyfriends (the sailor who turned out to be a rat, the printer who turned out to be a rat, the stockbroker who was definitely a rat from the start, and a teacher who was just a mouse but awfully cute). Maddie was sure the new fella's identity couldn't be long in discovery.

Through the window on the landing, she glimpsed Rickie and Sadler returning from their snowy errand. Rickie carried a brown paper-wrapped parcel, so she assumed they must have found something out there, despite the snow and wind. They disappeared under the portal and through the front door, and Maddie hurried down to meet them. They were knocking clouds of white from their boots and coats, Sadler cursing the New Mexico winter weather.

'Any luck, then?' she asked.

Sadler glowered at her from beneath his ice-crusted mustache. 'Come in here.'

'Say please.' She laughed, but she followed them down the service stairs and into a pantry lined with shelves of jars and cans, fragrant bunches of dried herbs hung overhead. They could hear Marta and Rosa talking in the kitchen, but it was muffled, indistinct. The light was faint from a bulb high overhead, and the space smelled of cinnamon.

Sadler unwrapped the parcel to reveal a charred little pile. 'I guess we know now why there were no bloody clothes in the laundry or anywhere else. You were right to think something was burning that day.'

Maddie studied the mess more closely. Underneath the sodden, blackened state, she made out shreds of fibers and a zipper. She brushed them off a bit and saw it had once been a dull blue color, maybe canvas of some sort. She thought there might indeed be some rusty stains, but it was very hard to tell.

'Drat it all! If we only had one of David's microscopes from the hospital,' she muttered. 'Are they work trousers, maybe?'

'Rickie here thinks maybe coveralls, like a factory worker might wear,' Sadler said.

'It's the zip pull, see?' Rickie said. 'This little bit of triangle here. My uncle wore one all the time when he was – well, doing some illicit stuff at a still. He doesn't do that any more!' he added quickly when Sadler shot him a sour look. 'It's a Goodrich brand zipper. And there was this.'

He unwrapped what looked like a charcoal lump. Maddie examined it and could make out some stitching. 'Part of a shoe? But it doesn't look like a work boot.'

'Too fine by half, though most of it's gone,' Sadler said. 'We thought maybe someone covered their ordinary shoes with gaiters or even rubber boots to go out in the snow, but messed up this one anyway and so on the fire it went.'

'*I* thought that,' Rickie grumbled softly.

Sadler ignored him. 'Do you have an idea of what sort of shoe it might be, Mrs Vaughn-Alwin? Man or woman? You seem to know fashion fol-de-rols.'

'Well, it's true, Inspector, I have a great fondness for fols and rols,' Maddie said as she carefully went over the lump. A bit of it crumbled against her finger. 'But I often don't see them in quite such a state. Let me take it to my room to look in clearer light. Maybe I can find a label or something.'

Sadler nodded. 'We don't think we can decipher much more from the coveralls. They're used so much in farm work as well as factories, and it seems speakeasies, so maybe Sam Luhan? Or a gardener here?'

'It could just have been stashed in a shed and anyone could pick it up,' Maddie said, thinking of all the outbuildings at Los Pintores. 'The McTeers next door probably use them, too. If we could tell the size . . .'

That seemed hopeless, though, given the condition. Burned and buried in snow.

'So, there wasn't anything else on the firepit?' she asked.

Sadler shook his head, looking even more grumpy-dumpy than usual. 'Too much to ask for in this weather. No footprints, surely no fingerprints, set up in a place that's not easy to see. It was a very small pit, stone-ringed, safely set for someone in a hurry. Pine wood, probably, catches fire fast, maybe brought from a wood pile somewhere. Lots of smoke, though, as you saw.'

'We raked it over several times, turning it all over, and didn't see anything else. They must have dumped the clothes right after they felled Don Victor, made sure it caught the flames, and got out of there, letting the snow put it out,' Rickie said.

'But the snow put it out before it was all completely gone,' Maddie said. 'Sounds like they knew what they were doing. They planned to steal Al's bat, planned to lure Victor outside, planned a spot to dump the evidence.'

Sadler nodded grimly. 'Definitely sounds pre-meditated to me.'

'Yet how could Al have been so cunning? He can hardly leave his room, let alone plan something so clearly,' Maddie said.

Sadler scowled. 'I've met plenty of people shamming to be sick or insane before. He was definitely strong enough to do it! His father provoked him over and over again. You saw it yourself. He needs money to get away from here.'

'Al is not shamming! I saw lots of poor boys like this during and after the war while I worked with the Red Cross in New York,' Maddie argued, desperate for Al and Katrina. 'He's too ill to plan any of this.'

'What about his wife, then? Surely she'd want to get her husband away from all this, have their own home.' Sadler smiled widely, as if he'd hit on a great solution that would have him off the case sooner rather than later.

Maddie was shocked. 'Katrina could never! She's very protective of Al, true – she loves him, tries to shelter him. But she would never kill; she has the kindest heart I've ever met.'

Yet *could* she do something so extreme, if would help her darling Al? Love could make people do wild things, just like hate could. And for the promise of freedom, the hope of better health . . .

Maddie shook her head. She had to put aside affection for a moment and try to see things exactly as they were – or could be. *Maybe* Katrina and/or Al could have been pushed too far. Maybe each would do anything for the other. Katrina might be physically strong enough, but would she have the cool, iron nerve to strike? Could she and Al somehow have done it together?

Maddie had the terrible feeling, though, that if Al had indeed done such a violent act, he would be catatonic now, destroyed by it. If Victor had died being shoved downstairs or pushed down to hit his head on the fireplace tiles, maybe then Al would make sense as a suspect. But not the premeditated way this murder was looking.

'We don't have a shortage of people who might have wanted Don Victor out of the way,' Maddie said. 'I was talking to Mrs Upshaw this morning . . .'

'The floozy secretary! Not a thought in her peroxide head,' Sadler scoffed.

'Indeed. Not the brightest bulb, maybe, but I think she's much shrewder than she wants to appear. And I saw her kissing a man under the mistletoe last night.' Maddie stamped her foot in a tiny fit of frustration. 'But, drat it all, I couldn't see his face! He was tall, though all the men here are tall. Gunther and I had a little chat with her earlier today. She's definitely in love with someone who is not Victor Luhan.'

'Who?' Sadler asked.

'That's the difficult thing. It was too dark for me to see when I caught them together. Just a tall man, his face shadowed as they kissed. And she wasn't tiddly enough this morning to tell quite all. I may have to try and sketch the scene, try to rebuild missed details. But I do know she was left some money in Victor's will.'

'The will?' Sadler exclaimed. 'How do you know about that?'

'You need to speak to Father Adrian, I think. He seems to be an executor of some sort to Don Victor's estate. And he said Mrs Upshaw is getting a legacy.'

'So she wanted to get rid of the old albatross and start again?' Sadler mused.

'Maybe. I should have looked over her shoes more closely – they were scattered all over the floor – and see if any were missing or singed. I may have to sneak back in later.'

'So, what else do we know about the will?' asked Sadler.

'What do you mean *we*?' Maddie teased. But she told him what Father Adrian said about the bequests. 'It does seem everyone wanted to be free of Victor and forge their own paths in life. No one seems to have liked him all that much. We just need to unknot all these strands.'

'This is all interesting, but I'm afraid the simplest explanations are usually the right ones, Mrs Vaughn-Alwin,' Sadler said. 'You can't be too upset when it comes out your friend's husband did it.'

'I won't be upset, Inspector. Because it didn't happen that way. You'll see.' She tucked away the wrapped bits of shoe and turned to leave. 'Oh, by the way, Father Adrian mentioned he thinks someone was using a cupboard in the chapel for some kind of assignation. He found blankets and bits of clothes there, I think.'

'Mrs Upshaw and her new fancy man?' Sadler said.

'Who knows? Los Pintores seems a hotsy-totsy place for romance these days. We should take a look at what's there, see if anything corresponds to this shoe and the coveralls.'

'*We?*' Sadler growled.

Maddie smiled sweetly. 'Of course. We're partners now, aren't we? I'm practically your deputy!'

'I'd say she's probably right, sir,' Rickie said with a grin.

As Sadler spluttered, Maddie spun back around and ducked out of the pantry and up the stairs, carefully tucking the delicate packet of evidence in her pocket. She glimpsed Helena coming down, bundled in her fur coat and wool beret.

'Going out, Helena?' she asked. 'Just before lunch? It's still beastly cold out there.'

Helena flashed a bright smile. 'Oh, I'm not hungry for lunch! I just need a bit of fresh air. I'm going stir-crazy in here.' She held up a blanket and a small basket. 'I'll eat a snack while I'm out. Won't be long.'

'Isn't Christmas Eve dinner and Mass tonight?'

'Won't miss it!' She opened the door and peered out at the snow beyond, the bright-white light streaming into the foyer. 'I wouldn't miss looking for the Yule log later this afternoon, either. It's always jolly fun. See you then!'

Maddie watched her leave, the door swinging behind her. Where was she really going? To the chapel, maybe, to meet someone on the down-low? Maybe Felipe? Maddie could have stomped her foot in a little fit of frustration she couldn't follow. She wasn't dressed at all for a plunge in the snow, and she would be missed at lunch after skipping breakfast. She'd just have to circle back to Helena later, along with Mrs Upshaw and her mystery man.

She turned toward her chamber to hide the grisly package, but found her door cracked open, which was strange. She was very sure she'd closed and locked it behind her, and it was a bit early for Rosa to come and clean.

She carefully pushed the door all the way open and peeked inside. Everything was as she'd left it, the blankets smoothed and pillow fort stacked up, nightclothes folded over a chair, detective novels stacked on the bedside table. Yet there was no Buttercup to greet her.

Maddie felt a sour bubble of panic rise in her throat. 'Buttercup?' she called. Silence.

She rushed into the room to find a quilt heaped on the floor on the other side of the bed, the quilt Buttercup had been burrowed beneath. Pinned in the middle of a pillow was a crudely lettered note.

> *I see you snooping around where you don't belong. If you care about your health – and your dog's life – keep to yourself.*

Maddie felt a cold wave of fear wash over her, and she was paralyzed for an instant. Someone had seen her asking questions and had snatched her precious pup!

She grabbed up the note and ran back into the corridor. She found David and Gunther coming up the stairs, chatting. David saw her and turned solemn in an instant. 'Maddie? What's happened? Are you ill?'

She frantically shook her head. 'It's Buttercup! Someone dog-napped her. Look.' She held out the note and David quickly read it. A nerve tensed in his jaw, and his eyes narrowed.

'They couldn't have taken her far,' he said.

'Not with Buttercup biting and snarling all the way, as I'm sure she would,' Gunther added. 'She has a keen sense of stranger-danger. Remember the speakeasy?'

Maddie nodded. Buttercup had followed and saved her that night; she had to do the same for Buttercup now.

'We just have to search,' David said.

Gunther nodded. 'I'll find Katrina and Sam; we'll get a search party together.'

As he went to find the others, David said, 'Come on, Mads, we'll start at the attics. I doubt they would have gone outside at this point.' They joined hands and rushed up a narrow flight of rickety steps to the top floor of the hacienda, going systematically door to door on the way. Sitting rooms, empty bedchambers, box rooms – no dogs.

Upstairs, Marta had said there was only storage, there being no need for so many staff rooms now. The space was piled with boxes and crates, old furniture, a dressmaker's dummy that made Maddie jump. At the most shadowy end of the long, narrow room she finally heard a low whine behind a paint-peeled, half-hidden doorway. It was locked.

'Buttercup!' she cried. 'Darling, is that you? David, I think she's in here!'

He tested the wood panels. It was indeed locked, but old and flimsy, and he splintered it open with one well-aimed kick. Maddie peered inside to find a dusty cupboard filled with moth-eaten coats – and Buttercup perched precariously on top of a crate. She let out a deep howl when she saw Maddie.

'Oh, my poor baby,' she cooed. She lifted the dog into her arms and held her close as Buttercup shivered and whined. 'You're safe now, it's OK. Who did this to you? The old meanies!'

David checked her over, as if she was a patient in his

hospital, and proclaimed her unhurt. 'But what about you, Maddie? What's this all about?'

She cradled Buttercup even closer. He frowned as he hugged her and the dog against him.

'I don't like this at all, Maddie,' he said. 'We have to get out of here as soon as possible.'

'I'd like nothing more,' she answered. 'No more rural idylls for me! Town from now on. But I can't give up, not now, not when Katrina and Al need my help. I'll keep Buttercup locked up tight going forward, but I can't be scared. Not when I'm sure we're so close.'

David sighed and kissed the top of her head. 'I was afraid you would say just that.'

SIXTEEN

Still Christmas Eve

Maddie tried to forget all her worries and puzzlement after a short nap curled up with Buttercup. She got up from bed, bundled up in her fur-collared coat and warmest wool cloche, and fortified herself with some hot cocoa that Rosa brought before joining the others on their Yule log search. She made sure Buttercup was tucked up safely with Gunther, as he tried to write his latest chapter, and her favorite chew toy, recovering from her ordeal. Maddie carefully locked her chamber door behind her and made her way down to the sala.

David waited with Al and Katrina, who was fussing that he shouldn't go out while he insisted he had to do *something* Christmassy. Helena teased and laughed with Felipe and Ben, all of them bundled up against the cold.

Out of the sala window, the afternoon light, bright and sharp, jonquil-yellow in a chalky blue sky, shimmered on the undulating snow. Maddie longed to catch it in paint, that perfect, peaceful winter moment, the blend of whites and creams and blues. She took the small sketchbook she always carried from her coat pocket and scratched a few lines and notes about color to attempt later. Once life returned to normal. But there was no time for art just yet.

Sam clapped his hands as he came into the room. 'OK, everyone! Our mission is to find the perfect Yule log, to burn in the sala fireplace until New Year's Eve. First we'll search the east quadrant of the estate, where the trees are thickest, and if nothing's there we'll head south. Deer are fallow in the west area where they over-winter, so we'll leave them be. Move along the river, we can't get lost. Hopefully we can find something dry enough to be useful.'

They divided up into groups to start the search, equipped with whistles to summon the others. They divided into two small groups, with Ben in charge of dragging the sled that would hold the Yule log. Helena insisted they sing carols as they stomped through the snow.

'*Oh, blanca Navidad, vuelve con tu mensaje celestial, Anunciar al mundo la paz,* ' they sang, a peaceful, sweet song that belied the strange holiday they were all experiencing.

They left the sheltered gardens near the hacienda, the paths dotted with snow-dusted statues and stone benches. The small, frozen pond they skirted around was clogged at the edges with ice and sludge, and Sam warned them not to get too close to the slippery banks. Maddie noticed it was finally growing a bit warmer, thanks to that pale sunlight peeking through the clouds, and the snow seemed softer, wetter, her boots sliding on it. Her ankle seemed to have suffered no ill effects after her fall there.

'*Anunciar al mundo la paz,*' they sang as they processed into the trees, like carolers in a book. Maddie glimpsed the McTeer estate in the distance, beyond a tall wire fence, and then they disappeared into the thick stands of woods and went around the edge of the pond, with its empty summerhouse. The light grew dimmer under the bare, waving branches.

'I thought this one might do,' Sam said, patting a thick, fallen log half-lodged in a snowbank. 'What do you all think?'

Everyone gathered around in a circle to examine it. It was indeed huge, a vast fallen god of a tree, as wide around as a man. Maddie wondered if it would fit in the sala fireplace, but then she had never looked for a Yule log before. It seemed delightfully Elizabethan.

Helena echoed those doubts. 'Will it actually fit, Sam?'

'Where there's a will, there's a way, right?' Katrina said, with an echo of her old hearty enthusiasm. 'We will *make* it work! It'll be splendid. Come on, everyone, let's dig together to get it out of there and on the sled.'

They all coordinated under Sam's shouted directions, and it did slowly, painfully, heft up on to the sled at last. It was frightfully heavy, and Maddie's shoulders ached as they heaved and shoved. Art was a mere summer's breeze compared to

Yule jollity, but she liked the distraction of it, the cooperation. She just wished it didn't look like almost any of them could be strong enough to commit the murder, wield the bat. She glanced about and noticed Helena wasn't there, but there was no time to call for her as Sam was shouting instructions to move to the house.

Finally, the log was secured for the trip back to the house, and they all turned gratefully toward the promised tea.

'We'll light it after dinner, with a great ceremony,' Ben said, hardly out of breath even dragging the sled. 'Mama will love it; she missed parties so much! Then it will burn until the new year, and bring us all luck.'

Maddie fell back a bit as the others sang and marched toward the house. She longed for a quiet moment to organize her thoughts. It had been long nights lately, and she feared she wouldn't sleep that night, either, not with worrying about Buttercup on top of everything else.

At the edge of the little pond, with its slippery, sloped banks and elegant, tiny summerhouse at one end, she was surprised to catch a glimpse of Helena's fur coat and bright beret, just inside the open-sided summerhouse. Maddie started to raise her hand to wave, then she saw Helena wasn't alone. A man had stepped out to meet her. Jim McTeer.

She rushed to him and into his waiting arms, going up on tiptoe to kiss him. No family quarrel there, obviously. Maddie watched them in astonishment for a moment. No – more like Romeo and Juliet families. Defying their elders for the sake of love? She couldn't help but cheer them on a bit – and also worry for them. She wondered if she should creep away, or tiptoe closer. Such love could definitely be the motive to get a disapproving father out of the way, after all.

But Helena saw Maddie before she could sneak off, and she jumped back from Jim. She wiped at her eyes and straightened her hat, and Maddie saw her pasting on a bright, careless smile. As she moved closer to the couple, walking gingerly along the slippery edge of the pond, she saw the taut lines of worry around Helena's eyes.

'Maddie,' she said, her chin tilted defiantly. 'I didn't see you out there.'

'I can tell, yes. But you don't have to worry a bit about me, Helena. I've read *Love Everlasting*, and I'm a complete sucker for forbidden romance.' She took a step closer, and Jim put a protective arm around Helena and drew her closer. 'That's what this is, yes? True love?'

Helena and Jim gave each other a long, silent glance, as if they were an old married couple with their own hieroglyphic language. Helena finally nodded. 'She's all right, Jim, I promise. A good friend. Yes, Maddie, we are in love. We have been for quite a while.'

'I've loved Helena since the moment I saw her, swimming in this very pond last summer,' Jim McTeer said in a new meltingly tender voice.

'And I him. So strong, but so kind! Different from the other guys I know,' Helena said. 'We meet whenever we can, and I'm afraid this Christmas we might have gotten a little reckless. But we never have enough time together! We can't go on like this much longer, or I'll utterly burst!'

'I've asked her, begged her, to marry me, forget all this nonsense,' Jim said. 'We can go away somewhere else, start again.'

'But I've been scared,' Helena said, caressing his cheek with her gloved fingers. 'Scared for your livelihood and family! Your land is right there, and my father so powerful. If he found out . . .'

Yet Victor wasn't there now. Helena seemed to realize that at the same second Maddie did, and she let out a ragged sob, her knees buckling. Jim caught her and held her close.

'So you were never interested in Felipe, not really?' Maddie asked.

Helena shook her head. 'He's nice enough, and surely handsome. Sorry, Jim, sweetie. Felipe's from a good family; Papa liked him. He seemed like a good distraction, so no one would realize what's really going on.'

Maddie studied the ice-choked waters of the pond. 'And Felipe didn't mind?'

'I told you, we're friends. He was happy to help me out. It also gave him a cover.'

'A cover?' Maddie asked, puzzled. 'So, he has a secret romance, too? Or just doesn't want to marry yet?'

Helena laughed and took Jim's arm between her hands to hold him close. He looked startled, as if she hadn't really reached out to him in public before this encounter, but then a brilliant smile lit his face, and he hugged her so tight Maddie wondered if he would lift her off her feet. 'Everyone always loves who they shouldn't, don't they? It's such fun, until it isn't. I'm going to marry Jim, and stay by him forever now.'

Maddie was sure Helena was quite right. Don Victor and Mrs Upshaw; Mrs Upshaw and someone else; Isabella and Dr Pierce; Isabella and someone else? Maddie remembered seeing what seemed to be Isabella running outside that first night. Helena and Jim McTeer. Felipe and someone? Rosa and Rickie. Who else? It was like a puzzle of bright pieces constantly moving about.

'Who is Felipe in love with, then?' she asked.

Helena shrugged. 'He never said. I do hope it's someone nice, he's a swell fella and a good friend. He just says we'll all find out when the time is right. Just like with me and Jimmy.'

She nodded at Maddie, and then she and Jim left the edge of the summerhouse and strolled away, arm in arm, laughing as if some burden was suddenly taken away from them. Pensive, Maddie walked away in the other direction, listening to the laughter of the Yule log party drifting on the wind as they neared the house. She thought about those puzzle pieces, trying to slot each couple in properly with each other, but the pattern kept changing in her mind.

She noticed Sam breaking away from the sled as it neared its destination and head off alone, and wondered if he, as the brand-new head of the family, knew about his sister's secret engagement. What would he think about it? Was *he* in love with someone, too? Mrs Upshaw maybe? He could have been the mistletoe kisser.

He noticed her, and waved at her, so she hurried to join him. 'Mrs Vaughn-Alwin,' Sam said. 'Just thought I'd find some good kindling for the Yule log. Be a shame if it was a dud after all this.'

'I'll help you.' They searched out and gathered sticks in companionable silence for a while, the only sound the wind whistling and singing through the bare trees. 'I suppose you'll be taking full charge of the rancho and family now. Such a large task.'

He shrugged and examined a pile of sticks. 'I've already been taking care of the land here for as long as I can remember. That won't be any different, except decisions will be made a lot faster if I don't need to consult Papa. As for the family . . .' He laughed ruefully, and Maddie realized she hadn't heard him laugh before. He seemed like a man carrying heavy burdens with him all the time, serious and solemn. 'Not even the Archangel Gabriel could control *them.* Papa tried, bless him, but I don't even dare attempt it. I can run the land or run them, not both.'

'So now everyone could marry as they wanted? Go where they want?'

'Sure. Why would I care, unless they turn to bank robbing or something?' He gave her a narrow-eyed glance. 'You mean Helena and Jim McTeer?'

'You know?'

'Of course. They could fool Mama and Papa with that Felipe smokescreen, but I see a lot. It pays to just be quiet and watch.'

'It sure does,' Maddie murmured, and vowed not to underestimate Sam.

'They can get married, if McTeer is brave enough. I don't know what Helena will think of being a farm wife, but at least she's nearby. As for Ben – I can't even see what he does out there in the East, let alone control it. I just hope he finds himself a good career he can enjoy.'

'And you? Do you enjoy your work here?' Maddie tossed her sticks in the large canvas basket Sam had put on the ground.

He tilted back his hat, and she saw he was really quite handsome, just like his father and brothers. But no blue-gray eyes. They were brown. 'I'll stay here OK, I guess. I don't know how to do anything else, and it's home, despite everything. I know I can raise the yields, hire more hands. Make it what it used to be.'

'Marry someone?'

'Sure. I have to. But I tell you this, Mrs Vaughn-Alwin – I won't rely on my mother's taste in brides. She can't be trusted.'

Maddie laughed, wondering about Isabella's past match-making efforts. Maybe if Isabella could get back to town, back to some of her old party-loving self, she wouldn't need the distraction of meddling. 'You'll need help with the house, then, if your mother moves away.'

'That'll be my wife's job, to run the house, find staff.' He bundled up all the sticks they'd gathered and tied up the basket. 'I can't imagine poor little Rosa will want to stick around long. She's had enough embarrassment, thanks to Papa. We all have.'

'You know?' Maddie asked in surprise, then thought of how she'd vowed not to underestimate him.

'Sure. No other maid's ever been trusted like she was around here, and just look at her face. She has Papa's eyes, doesn't she? She's a really nice girl; she doesn't deserve any of this.' He frowned and added quietly, 'None of us deserved it.'

'Her aunt was talking about opening a teashop in Santa Fe with Rosa.'

'I hope they do. I'll do whatever I can to help them. And I'll walk Helena down the aisle.' He hefted the basket on to his shoulder and turned toward the house. 'Really, Mrs Vaughn-Alwin, you'll think we're a wicked family, but everything is going to be much easier now.'

Maddie nodded and followed his tracks in the snow, studying the footprint to see if it would match the burned shoe. She could see that things at Los Pintores *would* be easier now. Everyone could look for their happiness without a fight. Would Sam, stalwart Sam, have done such a terrible thing to protect his family?

The wind picked up, a biting chill that nipped at Maddie's cheeks, and she hurried faster toward the house. She and Sam found most of the others were already gathered in the sala for tea and the other holiday task for that day – decorating the tree that was propped in the corner by the piano, majestic in its brass pot.

Ben and Felipe were making sure the evergreen was steady,

laughing and shoving and joking together. Maddie watched them, and wondered if maybe *they* were the romance? If so, Victor definitely wouldn't have approved of that.

Marta, Rosa and Helena, *sans* her new fiancé, were digging through boxes of ornaments as Isabella held up a skein of tiny red and green bulbs. 'Ooh, I forgot we had lights! I do hope they work. How are the ornaments, girls? Do be careful, some of them are so old! My great-grandmother brought those from Seville. And here are some boxes of tinsel. At least some of the supplies I ordered before Christmas did get through ahead of the snow.'

Ben and Felipe commenced tossing strands of tinsel over each other's heads, much to the scolding of Marta, and Helena and Rosa's giggles. Like nothing terrible had ever happened at the house, nothing had marred their holiday.

Dr Pierce and Mrs Upshaw weren't there, but David, Katrina and Al were at work at the long table near the windows, making garlands of greenery and red satin bows. Maddie hurried to join them.

'Tell me, Mads darling, when is the wedding to be?' Katrina cried happily as Maddie sat down beside her and reached for some ribbon. 'I just want to forget all of this and think of lace and cake and flowers.'

'You just want to manage poor Maddie's wedding and make it fancy, since our own was so plain,' Al teased. His voice was rough and hoarse, and a thick blanket was closely wrapped around his thin shoulders, but his complexion was pinker now, his eyes clearer. It looked like David was helping Al a bit, and Maddie was overjoyed to see it.

'It's true our wedding was tiny,' Katrina said, twisting a garland into a braided length to go over the fireplace. 'At a grubby city hall, before Al had to leave for France. But I *did* have a rather nice hat. What are you thinking for your big day, Maddie?'

Maddie glanced at David. 'We're not sure yet. A ceremony at Holy Faith, I guess, that pretty church down the street, then a reception at home. Juanita is already planning the menu! And the twins are clamoring to be bridesmaids. They're obsessed with the movies, and think it'll be like something in a Gloria Swanson movie.'

'Any dress yet?'

'Not yet. My cousin Gwen, the actress, is sending me something, she says. But who knows what it'll end up being, knowing Gwennie's taste!' Maddie laughed to picture what would happen between Gwen and the twins. A gold brocade gown with a ten-foot train and a feathered turban, arrivals by horse-drawn chariot, a ten-tier cake. 'I may just have to pull something out of my wardrobe last-minute.'

'In which you will look utterly gorgeous,' David said gallantly.

'Maddie always looked gorgeous in anything, even our appalling school uniforms,' Katrina said wistfully. 'But no date yet?'

'Not yet. After New Year, before springtime, when David gets even busier at Sunmount. You and Al will be there?'

If Al wasn't in jail. The unspoken words hovered in the air, and Katrina worked twice as fast on her garland, laughed twice as loud. 'With bells on, Mads!' She jingled a length of silver sleigh bells to make them all giggle.

They all chatted about Christmases past as they finished the work, and Maddie surreptitiously studied everyone's shoes. All matched pairs, none with just the distinctive sort of stitching along the soles that she could see.

'All right then, everyone, the moment of Christmas tree truth!' Ben announced. 'Gather round!'

They all rushed to the tree, covered now in shimmering gold and silver tinsel, dainty glass ornaments, and some of Marta's biscochitos dried and hung with bits of ribbon. Helena was stacking brightly wrapped parcels around its base. Felipe flipped a switch, amid a scatter of sparks, a whiff of smoke – and the tree blazed and glimmered, a beacon in a dark winter. A hope of future peace and happiness. Everyone applauded and laughed.

David slipped his arm around Maddie's shoulder, and she leaned into his reassuring warmth and strength. Everything felt so uncertain, so strange. Murder and holiday merriment all wrapped into one. But in that moment, she was overwhelmed with happiness and gratitude for the love she had found, the future they could make together. She had to stay safe to see it all, and she wasn't alone any more. Never alone again.

SEVENTEEN

Christmas Eve at night

Maddie's booted foot slipped and slid on the crunching snow, and she caught at Gunther's arm as her feet windmilled.

'Are we insane to venture out of the house like this?' she said with a breathless laugh.

'I'm very sure we are, darling, but what's new about that?' he answered, leading her onward, their arms tightly linked. 'That's why you are my best friend! Life would be so dull without you.'

'And mine without you. I'm afraid I do drag you into so much trouble.'

'I love it, and you know it.' They walked on, the night growing darker around them, the thick skeins of stars overhead sparkling and glowing like the lights of the tree. 'Though I admit this isn't *quite* my ideal Christmas. At least it will give me ideas for my next book. And wouldn't you just love to paint this night sky? It's so glorious.'

Maddie studied the stars, dizzy with the glory of them. 'I would. No murders in the scene, though.'

'All right. Let's agree. Next holiday – no murders.'

'Agree.'

'I'm glad you asked me to go with you tonight, though. I shudder to think about you wandering around alone.'

'I hope I'm not so dizzy-dumb as all that, though I do have my moments. Katrina wants to take Al to the chapel later, and David is helping them get ready. They're also looking after Buttercup, making sure she doesn't get snatched up again. I just wanted to talk to Father Adrian before he gets terribly busy.'

'What more do you think he'll know? Stuff about Victor's will?'

'I suppose it's more what he can show us. He thought someone was using a chapel cupboard for a meeting place, and he found some things there. Clothes and such. With all this illicit romance flying around, I thought we might recognize something.'

'You see, my dear? I could get several novels out of all this forbidden passion! Also all this greed. I had a little chat with Isabella after the tree was lit, and I fear the trusty Dr Pierce was nowhere around. She was rather peeved.'

'Oh, yes, Isabella is your mentor of sorts here, isn't she?'

'She offered me that casita as a cozy place to write for a while, yes, until I moved into the house because of the snow. She likes to be seen as a patron of the arts, and she told me today she hopes she can do much, much more now. Move to town, have a salon like the Hendersons, discover new painters and poets.'

'The Hendersons have a lot of dollars for stuff like that.' Alice Henderson, a good friend of Maddie's, was a poet, while her husband William was an architect and painter, both of them heirs to Chicago fortunes. 'Is Isabella expecting that sort of dosh from the will?'

'It sounds like she is. She asked if I'd like a research trip to London. On her dime.'

'No!' Maddie gasped.

'First class all the way. She thinks I should write an epic romance about Henry VIII's sister. Or was it his mother? Anyway, she sure has lots of ideas. It sounds like Ben does, too; she says he wants to go to Europe, maybe move there, take up playwrighting or something like that. She wants me to help him.'

'But it doesn't sound like either of them would have unlimited funds for a life like that.'

'They don't seem to realize that. I guess we'll know more once the lawyers can talk to them.'

They were almost to the chapel, the Capilla de Nuestra Señora de Guadelupe. It was a long, low, brown adobe building with a peaked tin roof and a pretty steeple holding a brass bell. The rows of stained-glass windows set in the deep walls glowed a mellow welcome. They brushed the snow off their boots and coats and pushed open the heavy, carved doors. A Bach organ fugue drifted through the chilly, incense-scented air.

It had a hushed, still sort of elegance, Maddie thought as she studied the scene. The long flagstone aisle was lined with short pews beautifully carved with roses and angels, cushioned in red velvet. It led to an elaborate, five-tiered altar, the frame carved with more roses, while side aisles led to candlelit niches. Silver altar goods gleamed on an embroidered cloth, and above their heads rose a balcony, reached by a narrow, twisting staircase. Despite everything, there was a sense of peace there.

'I'm always a bit afraid I'll burst into flames when I step into a church, aren't you, darling?' Gunther whispered.

'Old pagans like us? Certainly,' Maddie whispered back. 'But it's really beautiful in here. It must be nice to have your own private sanctuary like this, for all these years.'

'Mrs Vaughn-Alwin, Mr Ryder,' Father Adrian called. He emerged from a side room in white and gold vestments and hurried along the aisle toward them. 'How can I help you?'

'We don't want to keep you from your duties, Father,' Maddie answered. 'We just wanted a glimpse of where you think people have been hiding here.'

'Of course. The sooner we solve this terrible business, the better.' He gestured toward the small choir's balcony overhead. 'Felipe is here playing the organ, as you can hear. He's quite good. He came in here after dinner, rather upset, poor boy, and he thought music might distract him.'

Maddie listened to the otherworldly notes drifting into the chapel, and thought Felipe really was very talented. She'd seldom heard better in concert halls, his was such a sensitive, emotional reading of the Bach. It seemed Felipe had hidden depths.

'The others will be coming soon, but I'm happy to show you.' Father Adrian led them down a small side aisle and through a door to an antechamber where vestments and books were stored, piled up in every available space. He opened the door to a little closet tucked in a corner. 'It was in here. No one comes in here often when I'm not here; it's really just for storage. I almost didn't notice in the general disarray, but the door was a bit ajar. And there were blankets and empty wine bottles. You'd think they could have at least cleaned up after themselves!'

'Maybe they were interrupted, got in a hurry,' Maddie said.

A voice called out from the chapel. 'Father? Are you here?'

'Excuse me for a moment, please,' Father Adrian said.

'Of course.' Once he was gone, Maddie shut the antechamber door and she and Gunther got to work. They examined the blankets, the bottles and stained wine glasses. One had a smudge of lipstick on it, but it was a stylish rosy-pink, one she knew every lady there except Mrs Upshaw and Marta wore. But there was something . . .

'Gunther, look!' she whispered in excitement.

'What is it?'

She held up a shoe, lost in a tangle of blankets. A fine, flat-soled shoe, brown and white spectator style, beautifully cut of soft leather, though a bit warped as if it had gotten wet and dried without being stretched. A lady's shoe, in a small size. Just one.

'Very elegant,' Gunther said. 'Where's the other?'

'Not here. But I think I know.' She took the wrapped-up, burned lump from her coat pocket and they compared the stitching and cut. A match.

Gunther's eyes widened. 'You mean . . .'

'One was destroyed in that firepit of bloodied clothes; one seems to be here. But why? Did they lose this one, and wore some mismatched pair to do the deed? How? Why didn't they just throw this one away somewhere?' She held up the shoe to examine it closer. Dainty, stylish, not suited to the countryside. Small, like Helena, Isabella, Mrs Upshaw, Rosa. Even Maddie herself, who had to admit she'd love to have a pair of shoes like that.

'It looks too elegantly restrained to be Mrs Upshaw's; not a sequin in sight,' Gunther said. 'Though I can see her losing a shoe among that mess in her room.'

'Maybe a good bit of disguise?'

'Too flat for Isabella, but sporty enough for Helena? I heard she's a fine tennis player when the court here is cleared. Might be Katrina's style, too, but not her size.'

'Which of them would have an assignation here, and then go out to knock someone over the head with a cricket bat?' Maddie mused. Helena might have the assignation with Jim McTeer, sure, but the bat part? And she couldn't see Katrina running around on Al, but her head was whirling with all kinds of lurid, improbable images. She tucked the whole shoe away with the burned sole and looked through the rest of the heaped-up blankets and bits of clothes. Nothing very distinctive appeared, just the lingering scent of some stale cologne and spilled wine.

She took out her little book and quickly sketched what they'd found, then tucked it back, except for the shoe, which she tucked into her large handbag.

The voices and music outside grew louder, and she knew they didn't have much time. 'Come on,' she whispered to Gunther, and he nodded.

Most of the seats were filled when they emerged. Maddie and Gunther slipped into the back pew next to David, just behind Katrina and Al, who seemed peaceful, at ease, rosary beads clasped between his battered hands as he stared up at a window of Saint Sebastian and his arrows.

Everything seemed blessedly normal and peaceful there, even if it was only for a few moments. Maddie leaned her shoulder against David's as they joined in the singing. He smelled wonderful, of lemon soap and clean snow, so lovely after the stuffy anteroom, that whiff of stale cologne. Perfect and honest and lovely.

'Were you a churchgoer in England?' she whispered to him.

'As a boy, yes. It's just what my family did then. Trek down to St Frideswide's, then a Sunday roast in the good dining room. What most Brighton families did. I admit, I took a lot of comfort from that church, the music and ritual, that feeling of continuity, all the people who'd been there before. That feeling of never being alone.' His eyes narrowed suddenly and he shrugged. 'When my wife died, I lost all that. I felt completely adrift in the world.'

Maddie squeezed his hand tightly and suddenly felt terrible at the old memories this murder must have brought up in him. 'I can understand that. I couldn't go back to Grace Church after Pete died. But now I think I'm slowly finding some peace again. Living here in New Mexico, a person can hardly fail to see the spiritual all around.'

David nodded in understanding. 'The endless sky, the purity of it all.'

'Which is why I won't let it be stolen by these terrible events! This is my place, my home. I'll always defend it.'

He flashed her a tender smile. 'My Valkyrie.'

She held his hand even closer and smiled back. 'And my Sir Galahad. I'm ever so glad I found you.' She glanced around at the chapel, the stained glass and elaborate altar, the shimmering silver and embroidery. 'Wouldn't it be nice if we could get married someplace a bit like this? Someplace so very *New Mexico*, so unique.'

'It would be wonderful. Just one problem, darling.'

'We're not Catholic?'

'There's that. We'll find someplace equally perfect. Once this murder is behind us.'

They didn't have time to talk more, as the final hymn was playing from the organ, the service winding to a close. Soon they would have to leave that peaceful little sanctuary.

'*Jesus refulsit omnium, Pius redemptor gentium . . .*'

Everyone bundled up and tumbled back out into the star-bright, sharp-cold night. Maddie walked with David, Gunther, Katrina and Al. She and Gunther quietly filled in the others as to what they'd found.

'Well, I'm sure the shoe's not mine,' Katrina declared. 'It sounds like I couldn't even fit my big toe in it!'

'My Cinderella,' Al teased her. Katrina cuffed his shoulder and they laughed together, holding on to each other's arms. It was nice to see them happy together for a moment, despite everything going on around them.

'Have you noticed anyone else sneaking away often?' Maddie asked.

Katrina thought it over for a moment. 'Everyone does at one time or another. You'd go bonkers if you didn't. Poor Helena is always so restless, and Sam likes to work at all hours. Before the weather turned snowy, Ben was often leaving for town after he arrived here from college. Maybe there are those ghosts who walk, too?'

Ghosts who kissed under the mistletoe, Maddie thought wryly. Yet she had been affected by the spooky atmosphere of the hacienda, too, by the tales of spooks and haunts.

'Oh!' she cried as they reached the garden gate. 'I forgot my gloves, and my hands are freezing now. I'll be right back.'

David walked with her back to the chapel, and waited outside as she hurried in to find her gloves in their pew. They lay in a crumpled bit of kid on the cushion.

She glanced up at the balcony when she heard the notes of the organ, Felipe playing again. *Lacrimosa.* Hardly merry for Christmas. She climbed up the narrow, winding wooden staircase to check on him. His glossy, dark head was bent over the keys, and he seemed lost in his own world of music and thoughts. The cool air smelled of Christmas pine and woodsy cologne.

She hovered at the top of the stairs as the last notes faded away. To her shock, she saw the glimmer of tears on Felipe's handsome face as he closed his eyes and let the last strands of music flow over him.

'You do play so beautifully,' she said softly.

His head shot up, and he ran his hands roughly over his cheeks. When he faced her, it was with a careless grin on his lips that didn't quite fool her. 'My misspent youth as a choir boy, Mrs Vaughn-Alwin.'

'Not so misspent as all that. Your music has such wonderful texture and emotion to it. I nearly cried myself to hear it. So many don't realize Christmas can be such a sad holiday, a bittersweet one, but it certainly is at times.'

'Especially when the new year ahead doesn't look much brighter,' he muttered as he shuffled away his sheet music.

Maddie sat down on the bench beside him. 'Is it not? But you're young, handsome, at a fine university . . .'

'None of that matters when the one you love is beyond you!' Felipe burst out, his fists curling around the music, crushing it. 'You're a widow, Mrs Vaughn-Alwin, I know you must understand.'

'Yes, of course. I always think so much of Pete this time of year.' She studied him with pity, wondering if someone he loved had died. Or broken up with him. 'But surely Helena is right here. If you could convince her to marry you . . .'

He swung around to face her, and his pained expression told her she was quite right to know that, just as Helena didn't love him, it wasn't her he thought of now. As Helena wanted Jim McTeer, Felipe must want . . . who? What?

She felt a sharp pang of pity for him, for all of them. She gently touched his arm and smiled. 'Come on. It's cold in here, and listening to sad songs won't mend lost love. Let's go back to the house for some warm brandy punch, yes?'

He nodded and gave her a weak smile. 'Yes, you're right. I can't stay here forever.'

The tall clock in the sala struck two when everyone was gathered around the hearth, watching the Yule log crackle and blaze to life. A rousing game of charades had just ended, leaving everyone giggling.

'Well, then, *chicas*,' Isabella said, uncharacteristically cheerful and lively. Even her milk-pale cheeks were now rosy-pink, to match her embroidered silk, fur-edged shawl. Maddie could see what she must have been like during the days of parties at Los Pintores. 'What do you all wish for the new year?'

'A car,' Helena sighed. 'To drive away from here, far, far, far!'

'You would only get to the end of the drive with these roads,' Ben teased. He took another glass of punch from Marta, who pinched his cheek indulgently.

'Then what do *you* want, brother?' Helena asked.

'He wants to take Los Pintores off my hands,' Sam said.

'Ha!' Ben scoffed. 'Fat chance. Like Helena, I'm going to run away. Maybe I'll write plays in New York or London. It's what I've really always wanted, but Papa insisted I study business. Blech.'

'You won't leave me alone at university?' Felipe said. He looked quite recovered from his melancholy moment in the church, lounging on a sofa and lazily kicking his foot toward the floor. 'It would be way too dull there all by myself.'

'Oh, I'll stay to graduate. Might come in useful someday. But after that . . .' He trailed off, staring into the flames as if he saw visions of European spires there. 'So sorry, Sam old man. You're stuck with Los Pintores.'

'Not so stuck as all that, I hope,' Sam muttered.

Isabella glanced at him sharply. 'What do you mean, dear?'

'I don't *have* to stay here. The soil here is good: orchards, meadows for sheep, a steady water supply. This hacienda, the outbuildings. It could all fetch a fair price. Maybe even the McTeers might want to expand.'

Ben and Helena looked shocked, then rather delighted. Helena clapped her hands. Isabella just looked appalled.

'Samuel! Whatever can you be thinking of?' she cried. 'This is your legacy.'

'Some legacy,' Sam said. 'When did it ever give anyone a particle of happiness? I do well enough here, and can carry on, but what about everyone else? Look at you, Mama! Sick and lost. Now you can go away to a spa town with your Dr Pierce. Where is he tonight, by the way? Helena can move to town, Al can get the help he needs, Ben can finish school. And I . . .'

'And you, Samuel? What about you?' his mother demanded.

'I can do whatever I bloody like.' And with that he strode out of the sala, leaving Isabella spluttering and everyone else open-mouthed with astonishment, as if they were at a play.

Helena and Ben even applauded. 'Who knew old Sam had it in him?' Ben said.

'God bless us, every one,' Gunther said, and gulped down the last of his punch.

EIGHTEEN

Christmas

The sky was still gray-lavender with dawn outside Maddie's window when a soft knock sounded at her door, making Buttercup whine. It didn't startle Maddie, though; she'd been up reading for hours, unable to fall back asleep after dreams of organ music, snow and ringing quarrels. She wrapped her dressing gown around her shoulders and tiptoed to the door, telling herself a murderer wouldn't knock.

She peeked out into the shadowed corridor, and her heart melted when she saw David there. He wore his own dark-blue dressing gown, his gold-tinged hair rumpled over his forehead, a sweet smile on his lips as he held out a wrapped package.

'Happy Christmas day, my love,' he said, offering the package as his smile widened. 'I know it's early, but I couldn't quite sleep, and I wanted to give you your gifts before everything gets noisy here.'

She pulled him into the room and went up on tiptoe to give him a long, lingering holiday kiss. 'And happy Christmas to you, too! Not quite what I pictured for our first holiday as an engaged couple, but I'm so happy you're here with me.'

'And I've never been happier than when you're with me. I've never been happier at all, Maddie, not once in my life. Despite the murderers running loose.' He kissed her back, and for one sweet moment she forgot everything else entirely.

'Just imagine. Next year, we'll be an old married couple! In our own home.' She paused to lean her cheek on his shoulder. 'If we get out of this place first, that is.'

He kissed the top of her head and drew her over to sit down on a chaise by the window, where the dawn light could reach them. 'Are you so frightened here? Has something else happened? Not that what's already happened isn't enough to give anyone to the willies . . .'

She shook her head, and talked about Buttercup being locked in, the sensation of someone watching her outside, the fear that whoever had killed Victor hadn't moved on but was trapped inside just as they were. 'What's going to happen next?'

He held her hand tightly. 'I'll stay in here with you from now on.'

'David . . .'

'I insist! I thought my life was nothing before I found you, just marking time; it would certainly be nothing if I lost you. We have a long, happy life ahead of us here in Santa Fe. I'm not going to let anyone take that from us.'

'Oh, David darling. Neither will I! You've made my life so bright and wonderful; I don't intend to miss a single day.' She glanced at the enticing packages he'd put on her dressing table, wrapped in red paper and tied with curled ribbons. 'Are my gifts an instructional manual on self-defense? A guide for modern housewifery?'

David laughed, a low, rumbling, sweet-dark sound that always made Maddie think of rich hot chocolate, so delicious. 'I do hope I'm not so unromantic as all that. Nor do I really need a housewife.'

'Especially when Juanita is so wonderful at it! May she never, ever leave us. She would never let me in her kitchen.' Maddie unwrapped the first gift, a small black velvet box. She snapped the lid up to reveal a beautiful brooch, with a square-cut diamond surrounded by sapphires in the shape of a flower wreath. The morning light caught and sparkled on it, bringing it to vivid life.

'Oh, David,' she whispered. 'It's so beautiful.'

'It was my grandmother's. If it's too old-fashioned, we can have it reset.'

'Don't you dare! It's perfect.' She was so touched he would trust her with an heirloom, that it looked like they were a real family now. 'It's perfect, and it goes with my ring.' She fastened it on her dressing gown, then opened the second package, a small book filled with images. 'Etchings of Rembrandt! I love it. Wherever did you find it? It looks like a Dutch publication.'

'I have a friend who owns a bookshop in Brighton. I asked him to look out for interesting art books for me. I know how much you enjoy this period.'

'You had this book sent that far? You darling!' she cried and hugged the volume to her. 'I'm afraid my gift is rather too practical. But it is something you need, and surely a good wife takes that into much consideration!' She dug a large box from behind the bed. She'd had the devil of a time smuggling it into the house with them.

He laughed. 'If it's from you, it's got to be the best gift ever.' He unwrapped it and found a new doctor's valise, butter-smooth chestnut leather embossed with his initials in gilt and fittings in shining brass.

'Your old one is quite falling apart at the seams,' she said. 'I got it from Mark Cross in New York; they said it's all the fashion right now with these clasps. And they helped me design the print on the silk lining.'

David peeked inside and grinned at the azure-blue printed with fluffy clouds, with a small adobe house dotted along the edges. 'Your own house! And look, Buttercup and Pansy on the portal. I adore it.'

'*Our* house, soon. To remind you at the end of the day we're always waiting for you.'

They kissed again, and it was quite a long time before they came up for air. The daylight was growing brighter, amber edged with pink.

She sighed as she rested her head on his shoulder. 'I only wish poor Katrina and Al could find such happiness. There has to be something else I can do to help them.'

'Once the killer is caught and Al cleared, they can take their inheritance and find a quieter place to stay. That should help for a start. I've been writing to colleagues who have clinics specializing in such cases; I can send them to their offices when we get home and see what they have to say. I'm sure one of them could get him in after the new year.'

Maddie smiled and kissed his cheek. Her kind-hearted

sweetie. 'If he's not in jail first, the poor lamb. I'm afraid something like that would finish him off for good.'

A knock sounded at the door. 'Happy Christmas, my darlings!' Gunther called. Maddie laughed and went to open the door, finding her friend's arms loaded with champagne bottles and chocolate boxes, the gilt labels proclaiming they'd come all the way from Poyet in New York. 'I thought we might need a little bracing holiday pre-breakfast breakfast.'

'You are an angel, Gunther,' Maddie cried. She popped a violet cream into her mouth and sighed happily as David looked for glasses. All he could find were tooth glasses, but that seemed to go well with early Christmas mornings and dressing gowns.

'Is anyone else awake yet?' David asked as Gunther popped open a bottle with a loud fizz.

'Just Marta, setting up the breakfast buffet in the dining room. Everyone else's door is firmly shut.' He poured out the foamy, golden liquid. 'But I did think I heard very lively, i.e. quarrelsome, voices from down the corridor rather late last night, and some pitiful sobs from young Felipe's room.'

Maddie took a gloriously giddy sip of the champagne. 'He did seem awfully upset after church last night. I caught him playing melancholy music on the organ and crying. And I do think the shoe left behind in the cupboard matches the burned sole.'

'It's like a novel, such a puzzle! Or maybe a Restoration stage play, all these sneaky romances and tearful endings, everyone racing hither and yon,' Gunther said. 'What a tangle.' Beyond the windows, they heard the peal of chapel bells ringing out. 'Should we meet at my casita after breakfast to consult? It's rather chilly in there since I moved in here to the house, but it should be quiet enough.'

'That sounds like an excellent idea, Gunther darling,' Maddie said. 'But right now, I want to distract myself utterly with this bubbly, and spend a few heavenly moments with my two favorite fellas.'

Since Gunther had moved into the main house, his little borrowed writing casita was indeed chilly when they stepped inside, but it was cozy and private. The desk was littered with Gunther's precious typewriter and heaps of papers, research books piled everywhere. The only other furniture was a clutch of blue-upholstered chairs gathered near the kiva fireplace, and a rumpled daybed where Gunther had obviously slept. Food baskets lined a table, and empty wine bottles. Maddie pushed open the blue curtains, and saw he had a view of the pond and summerhouse.

'Gunther, darling, I'm afraid we've been keeping you from your work by looking into this murder business,' she said, flittering through the red-marked manuscript pages. She unwrapped her scarf as David started a fire and Gunther cleared away some of the empty glasses.

He waved away mention of *work*. 'My editor is very patient, bless his soul, and this is *murder*, my dear! We can't just let it pass.'

They all chose an armchair as the air finally started to warm, and Gunther found pencils and papers. 'Now,' he said briskly. 'Let's make a nice, tidy list of everyone who was here, get them straight in our minds. Who might have wanted Don Victor out of the way?'

'Where to start!' Maddie exclaimed, accepting a glass of wine from Gunther.

'There is Isabella,' David said. 'The glitz had clearly faded long ago from her marriage . . .'

'If there ever *was* glitz about it,' Gunther said. 'These old families don't care one bit about love or compatibility when they match up their children!'

'Sounds like my family,' Maddie said. 'But yes, I haven't seen one tiny flicker of affection between them since we got here. She seems to miss her old life of parties and wants money to move to town and run an arts salon.'

'Maybe also marry Dr Pierce?' David said. 'That would help his gambling debts. And, if she wasn't strong enough to actually wield the bat, he could do it for her.'

'Mrs Upshaw was angry with Don Victor, too,' Maddie said. 'And she's in love with someone else. Maybe she wants to get out of this relationship without missing out on the money?'

'Who would that be?' Gunther asked, writing feverishly.

'I have no idea. Sam seems unlikely. Ben seems up for anything, maybe, but . . . I can't see it. Someone in town?'

'And what about Sam himself? He seems calm and collected, content to be where he is,' David said.

'Hmm, but is he really? Your heard what he said in the sala,' Maddie mused. 'He's a young man working a hard job. Like Helena, caught by family and custom. Maybe he doesn't really want to run a rancho. Maybe he wants to be free of it, and he's just been making the best of the situation until now.'

'Like Ben, who wants to go off and write plays. Who would take over the rancho, then, with the sons and heirs scarpered off?

'Helena definitely wants to leave, too, and she's in love with someone not quite suitable,' Maddie said. 'Maybe Felipe is secretly scandalous, and she knows he can't be her cover much longer? Or maybe Felipe is holding on to Helena, insisting he get his bride and her inheritance since he's expecting something.'

'Maybe she's even of a sapphic sort,' Gunther suggested. 'Doesn't want to marry at all, but wants the freedom.'

Maddie considered this. 'She isn't. I can't say yet how I know, since it was a confidence, but I know that much.'

'There's Marta Sanchez,' David said.

'The housekeeper who might harbor anger at how Don Victor took advantage of her sister and then left her to raise Rosa,' Gunther said. 'Revenge served cold and all that.'

'She does make such lovely plum pudding, though,' David said sadly.

Maddie laughed. 'It's true Marta loves and would protect Rosa from anything. She probably wants the money to start her teashop and a new life, a place where Rosa isn't haunted by her past. But to kill for it?' She thought of the steely gleam she saw in Marta's eyes sometimes. 'Maybe, yes. But I would doubt Rosa herself.'

'The McTeers?' David asked. 'They're surely tired of living next to some hostile, harassing man and want to get on with their work. The older has that gun with him every time we see him . . .'

'So why steal and use a cricket bat?' Gunther said.

'Shoot him in the head, say it was an accident, done and dusted,' Maddie said. 'But the McTeers and the Luhans do have a lot of bad blood. That Jim McTeer looks young and strong enough to do it, if he's angry enough.' *And if he thought he might lose Helena.*

'There's also . . .' David began, casting a gentle glance at Maddie. 'It could actually have been Al. Blackouts are the very devil, and he's been angry and scared for so long.'

Maddie nodded sadly. 'I know we have to consider Al, much as I hate to do it. His brain just doesn't work right sometimes; he could have done it and not even remembered. But it seems unlikely – no one seems to remember seeing him wandering around that night, and he'd been taking some of your medicines, David. But I know he has to stay on the list.'

'And Katrina,' Gunther said. 'She loves Al; she'd do whatever she had to for him.'

Maddie sighed in frustration. 'That is true. This house is full of dramatic romance. Who would have thought it.'

'There's that first idea of a passing maniac,' David said. 'Unlikely in this weather, but never impossible. And so much easier if it *was*.'

'If only!' Maddie studied the list. 'OK, we certainly have our work cut out here, my lads.'

NINETEEN

'The boar's head in hand bear I . . .' Everyone sang merrily, as Marta marched into the dining room after Christmas dinner. Though it was not a boar's head she carried, but a much more appetizing flaming plum pudding.

Maddie feared she couldn't eat another bite after such a sumptuous feast. Cranberry-orange duck breasts, duchess potatoes with heaps of cheese, minty peas and onions, salmon mousse cups, and a delightful cranberry-studded pudding. Where had it all come from in the middle of a winter storm? Maddie quite hoped Marta really did have nothing to do with the beastly murder business; her teashop would be vastly welcome in Santa Fe.

But when she took a bite of the pudding, rich with cinnamon and nutmeg, she sighed in bliss, and reached out to squeeze David's hand. 'Lovely,' she whispered, and he nodded in closed-eye agreement. 'Are you terribly sad I'm a bad cook, darling?'

'We can hire excellent housekeepers,' he said with a laugh. 'But there is only one you.'

Maddie was still glowing with the romance of it all, and with the beautiful after-dinner sherry, when they all made their way to the sala. 'What shall we do with ourselves this evening?' Ben asked.

'I know!' Helena cried. 'We could play hide and seek. This big, gloomy old place ought to be good for something.'

Maddie laughed, and wondered if Helena would use the 'hide' time to sneak out and see her sweetie Jim McTeer. But everyone seemed enthusiastic in their agreement.

'I really should make sure Al goes to sleep though, it's been a long day,' Katrina said anxiously as she studied her husband. He had grown quiet suddenly, and looked a bit pale.

'No, no. I want to stay here and count everyone down, wait for Papa Noel,' he insisted. 'We deserve some holiday merriness, after all. I'm feeling perfectly well, Katie-kins, I promise.'

As Al began his slow count – 'One, two, three . . .' – they all scattered, footsteps pattering off in every direction, up and down the stairs, along corridors. Maddie pressed her hand to her lips to keep from giggling like a child as she searched for a nearby place to hide.

She went up the stairs to the bedchamber corridor, hearing the echo of others' feet in the darkness. She shivered a bit, thinking of ghosts and killers and illicit lovers, but surely she was safe enough with everyone nearby, even if she couldn't see them. She ducked into a linen cupboard by the bathroom, and it looked wonderfully cozy and quiet, with a tiny bench seat below the tidy stacks of lemon starch-scented towels and sheets.

She quickly slipped inside and closed the door behind her, perching on that shelf with her feet tucked up under her. She wished she had a book and a little light to read by, wished David might find her for a spot of Christmas canoodling. At last, she heard the soft fall of approaching footsteps, and she held her breath.

For an instant, the steps went silent, and she heard nothing. Then a click, and running feet.

'Hello?' she called, her throat starting to close up. She tested the door handle, and found she was locked in. Trapped, like poor Buttercup had been. Fear seized her, colder than the snow outside, and she feared she might faint. 'Hello!'

She pounded on the door for what felt like hours, but must surely have only been minutes before David appeared. His face looked shocked, worried when he swung the door open and Maddie threw herself at him. 'However did you get that key turned in this lock out here, darling?' he asked.

Maddie sobbed roughly and held on to him very tightly indeed.

Maddie couldn't sleep that night, even tucked up tight in her own chamber with blankets pulled up to her chin, a night light burning. Every sound, every creak of the old floors, scratch of a branch at the window, patter of snow sliding off the roof, made her heart pound. She had to resist the urge to leap up every five minutes to test the door handle, but she also didn't want to leave the haven of her bed.

Who had locked her in? Why? Was she somehow getting close to stumbling on the murderer? She couldn't let Al be blamed any longer, no matter what, but she hated the feeling that she could just jump out of her skin. What a beastly coward she was being!

She snuggled Buttercup closer and closed her eyes, imagining the list she'd devised with David and Gunther. Who on that list would be desperate enough to do such a deed? Who would have the nerve? She hated to think it could be someone she knew, but she'd seen too many times that anyone could be driven to mad deeds.

Buttercup started to growl, a rumble low in her throat, and Maddie's heart pounded even faster. She could barely hear anything over the rush of blood in her ears, then suddenly there was a 'crack' right outside her door.

Buttercup growled louder, and Maddie frantically shushed her. She slid out from under the blankets and reached for a large crystal paperweight on the bedside table she could hurl at a villain's head.

A scratch sounded at the door. 'Mrs Vaughn-Alwin? Are you awake? Please!' someone whispered. A familiar someone – Rosa.

Deeply worried something terrible had happened in the house, Maddie rushed to open the door. 'Rosa? Are you ill?'

Rosa looked like a ghost herself in the darkened corridor, her hair loosely plaited over her shoulder, her nightgown bright white. Her eyes were huge in a flushed face. 'I thought I heard someone outside my door. I could swear they stood there for ages and ages! I heard *breathing*. I ran out, and I saw your light on, and I thought . . .'

Maddie glanced down the corridor. 'But they left? Did anyone follow you?'

'No, I don't think so. When I first peeked out my door, I saw a ghost!'

'A ghost!' Maddie pulled her into the room, and they both leaped into bed with the dog to huddle under the blankets.

'Pale and tall, drifting away. I smelled something flowery, too. They say ghosts leave traces of perfume or flowers behind them sometimes.'

'Have you seen things like that before? Los Pintores must be full of creepy crawlies,' Maddie whispered. 'Or maybe it's David's wretched spooky stories.'

Rosa shook her head. 'There are stories like that, of course. The child at the window, the lady on the stairs here wailing. Someone in the trees out there. I've never seen them until tonight. Could it be a ghost that killed Don Victor? Is it after me now?' She shivered.

'I'm afraid the danger is probably all too corporeal,' Maddie said, and wrapped her arms comfortingly around the shaking girl. Buttercup snuggled closer. 'But we'll find them soon, Rosa dear, please don't worry. And be very careful.'

TWENTY

Boxing Day

It was a pearl-gray day outside on Boxing Day morning, but at least no more snow fell. Replete after a huge breakfast, everyone retreated to the sala and the familiar fireside, where Maddie offered to start sketches for Isabella's portrait while Helena played cards with her brothers and Katrina and Al tried to finish a puzzle on the table by the window. David and Gunther had gone for a quick walk, and Dr Pierce and Mrs Upshaw were hiding somewhere.

Maddie etched over the lines of Isabella's sketch as Señora Luhan posed in a ray of pale light from the sala window. She really was a lovely lady, tall and slim with a beautiful milky complexion and dark eyes that contrasted dramatically with her silvery hair. She must have been terribly beautiful when she first married. Yet she fidgeted so much, patting at her pearl necklace, her upswept hair, twitching her bell-shaped Eau-de-Nil chiffon sleeves.

'Where is Dr Pierce?' she fretted. 'I haven't seen him since breakfast. I do feel such tremblings all over. I'm sure it's my heart.'

'You had your tonic this morning, Mama,' Helena said distractedly as she examined her cards.

'And your portrait is coming along beautifully,' Maddie soothed. 'It will be quite elegant when I can get back to my studio and get out my paints! Just tilt your head a tiny bit to the left.'

Isabella obliged, the light catching on her diamond earrings. Even if she didn't get as much money as she hoped from her husband's will, surely her jewels would help her out. 'Just like Catalina Montoya's portrait? It was so highly praised when you showed it at the museum last month. And now she's married again, lucky thing.'

'Would you like to be married again, Mrs Luhan?'

Isabella sighed wistfully. 'It sounds foolish, doesn't it? After being Señora Luhan all these years, though not entirely content with it I must admit. There must be something better out there. Something tender and sweet. Like what you've found!'

'I've been frightfully lucky, yes. There's nothing wrong with looking for a bit of romance in life.'

'Do you really think so?' Isabella shifted on the chaise, stretching her feet under the beaded hem of her chiffon and silk skirt. Inspector Sadler lumbered into the room, and Maddie quickly excused herself to go and see what he had found, leaving her sketchbook on the table.

'Inspector,' she whispered. 'I think I can help you with that shoe business! I found . . .'

He waved her off, his attention never wavering from Al and Katrina by the window. 'We can talk about it later, Mrs Vaughn-Alwin. I've got to speak to Mr Luhan right now.'

'But . . .'

'Now!'

Maddie felt a cold burst of panic that Sadler was about to arrest Al, that this whole thing was about to be over in the worst way. But there was a reprieve.

Marta burst in, her cheeks reddened, her apron rumpled. Maddie was very alarmed to see the unflappable woman in such a state. 'They've gone!' she shouted, far more dramatically than Maddie would have supposed she could ever be.

Isabella sat up straighter. 'Who is gone? What do you mean?'

'Dr Pierce and Mrs Upshaw. Both of them! I went to tidy their rooms, and their luggage is all cleared away. As well as – oh, Señora, you won't like it.'

Isabella jumped up, her hands waving in the air. 'Won't like what? What's happened? Tell me now!'

'Your jewel case is gone from your dressing table,' Marta said, her dramatic panic giving way to a strangely smug look. 'I haven't cleaned that messy room of Mrs Upshaw's yet, but I know I didn't see it there. She must have taken it, along with the doctor.'

Isabella shrieked, and fell back on to her chaise, screaming and kicking. Helena and Ben rushed to her, and Felipe stood up from the card table with a most uncertain expression. He was surely wondering why he'd come to such a wild house in the first place. No sad organ songs would suit this moment.

Amid the tumult, Maddie slipped out of the sala and up the stairs. Could it have been the doctor and the secretary all along? Mrs Upshaw's door was ajar, and she peeked inside to find not the wild clutter of hats and lipsticks and perfumes, but an unmade bed and cleared floor.

She remembered seeing some unsteady stacks of papers on the bedside table. She knelt down on the rug and rooted around behind the table, in the drawers. There were a few dust bunnies, as surely it had been hard to clean in such a place, but Maddie kept digging around.

Just as she'd hoped, a few sheets had fluttered down in the haste of packing up such a mess, along with a green paste earring and a torn stocking. Bills from milliners, dress shops, a perfumier – it seemed Don Victor didn't always pay up on time. A few letters in ripped envelopes. And one at the very bottom, torn in half, but luckily not utterly destroyed. Mrs Upshaw would make a terrible spy.

> *. . . and all our problems, sweetie-bear of mine, will be over! All those lying rats that tried to end your lovely medical practice won't matter one jot, and you can help people again, like you're meant to – if you listen to me. You've done so well with that dumb-bell Isabella so far; she'll do what you say now that we know the truth . . .*

Not the same handwriting as the note left when Buttercup was snatched, but of course that could have been disguised.

Maddie read it over again. Dr Pierce, in league with Mrs Upshaw? Was there no romance left in the world? She almost laughed at it all, but they were thieves and blackmailers – why not murderers, too?

Some lines were scratched out, so fiercely the paper was almost torn, but Maddie turned the paper over and could make out a few more.

. . . we know she's not as lily-white as she pretends, all that swanning around acting like I'm dirt under her little shoe. We sure know better. And that kid young enough to be her son! You've got her just where you want, she's sure to pay up and we can get out of this dump.

That kid. Maddie shook her head in astonishment. She knew she shouldn't be shocked. Hadn't she thought herself that there was way too much crazy romance floating around Los Pintores? But it had to be Felipe, unless Isabella was somehow consorting with Jim McTeer along with Helena, which didn't seem likely. Felipe! Her son's friend, her daughter's purported beau! It sounded very foolhardy. But passion sometimes didn't heed warnings.

The rest of the letter was gone, but Maddie was sure even Sadler could get the idea of it. Had it actually been Dr Pierce and Mrs Upshaw who killed Don Victor, in some kind of blackmail gone wrong? Or was it Isabella and Felipe? Or were Pierce and Upshaw dead now, too? She had to tell Sadler before he arrested poor Al.

Clutching at the letter, Maddie dashed out into the corridor. She could hear a jumble of voices downstairs, shouting about jewel thefts, but it mostly seemed to be Helena and Ben, not Sadler or Isabella. Maddie quickly checked Gunther's room and found him to be out, so she left him a quick note to find her as soon as possible, and she went outside to look for Sadler or Rickie.

She glanced into Isabella's large, luxurious chamber as she buttoned her coat and wrapped her red shawl over her shoulders. No one was there, but a suitcase lay open on the bed, chiffons and silks haphazardly spilling from it. No jewel case on the dressing table, no Isabella. Maddie peeked into the suitcase to study a pair of satin shoes, tiny and beautifully made. Just like the spectator pumps in the fire. She ran down the quiet back stairs toward the back door, but as she stepped out into the garden, Felipe emerged from behind a tree.

He held a small, elegant but dangerous-looking pistol.

'What are you doing here?' he said, his voice shaking in a

way that made her even more afraid. An unsteady hand on a gun was not what one wanted, really.

'So it *was* you,' she whispered, remembering the love nest in the chapel – where Felipe had a key to play the organ. Maybe she could distract him a bit, run away? It was worth a try, until she could scream for someone else. Sadler had to be close by, even if he was just arresting Al. 'Were you the one who did it? Or were you helping your dolly-bird?'

'Don't call her that!' he cried. 'I love her, and she loves me. It had to be this way. It had to . . .'

'OK, just shut up now, Felipe,' Isabella said, coming around the corner of the hacienda with a valise in hand, a fur coat wrapped around her chiffon gown. Her voice was hard now, strong, nothing fade-away or sickly about it. 'And give me that gun for now; you need to get a hold of yourself.' He handed it over and she held it in a too-steady grip trained on Maddie. 'Now, then. Let's just take a little walk, shall we? Get away from this dreadful house.'

Maddie thought she had better just cooperate for the moment, until a new plan presented itself.

TWENTY-ONE

Maddie held up her hands as she walked ahead of Felipe and Isabella toward the pathway to the trees, to the pond and summerhouse. She pushed down that burning touch of panic that was bubbling up inside of her, knowing she had to stay steady, think carefully, keep them talking until she could distract them and get away. She had to learn all she could from them.

'What do you want from me?' she managed to ask hoarsely. 'Why have you been trying to scare me away, locking me in and leaving that note?'

'We never wanted to hurt you! We didn't want to hurt anyone, just be safe and free. But you kept digging and digging. Now we need a guarantee, just until we can get out of this hellish place. You'll do, I'm afraid, Mrs Vaughn-Alwin. Just play hostage for a while, and no one else will get hurt,' Felipe said. He actually sounded rather apologetic, the silly man.

Isabella gestured with the gun for Maddie to start walking along the path that led away from the house gardens, into the trees and closer to the pond and the river. 'I am sorry, really. But we've worked too hard to be together! It can't be ruined now, not after everything.'

Maddie walked as slowly as she could, careful to break branches and leave scuff marks that could be followed. Surely she'd be missed very soon. 'I understand feelings that can't be controlled,' she said, as steady as she could make herself be. 'Love won't be chosen or denied. Have you loved Isabella very long, Felipe?' He definitely seemed the more susceptible of the two.

'Since I came to visit his family with Ben last year, though we'd met before that.' His tone softened, became dreamy and tender – as tender as a man could be while wielding a firearm, anyway. 'I'd never noticed how very beautiful she was before. How sensitive and soft.'

'Sensitive and soft' wasn't quite what Maddie would call Isabella Luhan. A liar and fake, of course. A coward. Not that she would dare say that to the people forcing her to stumble along the wintry path at gunpoint.

'And she loves you, too?' she asked, hoping to distract him while she broke off more branches. Surely someone would come searching soon!

'I dared to kiss her one night, after too many cocktails. I was horrified by what I'd done – I was sure she'd throw me out!' Felipe said.

'But instead, she kissed you back?'

'Of course I did,' Isabella said with a sharp laugh. 'Wouldn't you?'

'Yes,' he said softly, wonderingly. 'It was so beautiful. She said she sensed our connection, too. Didn't you, my angel? I couldn't believe it! Nothing mattered but that we were twin souls, searching for each other through time. I had the key to the chapel, so I could play the organ, and we met there. It was glorious, like a celestial starburst.'

What a load of sheer hooey, Maddie thought, hoping she wouldn't get nauseous. 'How very beautiful,' she said aloud.

'It is! I see you understand, Mrs Vaughn-Alwin, like a real artist would. Stale conventions don't mean anything these days. No one else would see it that way, though. She'd be tossed out by her family, her society; her children would be so angry . . .'

'I couldn't bear it,' Isabella said. 'After all I had worked for! My place in society, my home . . .'

'And there would be no money if you left,' Maddie pointed out. As they neared the end of the path, where the ice-clogged pond and summerhouse lay, she glanced around, searching for something, anything, she could use as a weapon, or a way she could flee. If she just flat-out ran, would they really shoot? She had to get them distracted.

'I would make plenty of money,' Felipe protested. 'Later, after I finish university. Isabella can't live without comforts, though, she's so delicate. Don Victor would have cut her off without a penny if she made a scandal.'

'But with an inheritance, you could move away. Start a new

life, a new identity. Still with your respectability, your good name. It's terribly clever.' Maddie thought of the Christie novels she enjoyed so much. All those characters wanted everything, right away. Their money, houses, love, but most of all they wanted to maintain their respectability, their community.

Maddie turned to face them, the 'tender' lovers. 'You could go now. Just leave me here, at the summerhouse, lock me in, as you did in the linen cupboard. Go now, get what you want, and no one else gets hurt.'

Felipe obviously wavered, glancing at Isabella, glancing behind them, nervous and fidgety. 'Maybe we should do that . . .'

'Felipe! What's this?' Isabella shouted, not so frail and delicate now. 'Are you wavering on me? At this point? Why is she here anyway?'

'I found her with some of Mrs Upshaw's papers, letters to Dr Pierce. She knew, Isabella!' Felipe said beseechingly. Maddie could see who ran this relationship. 'We couldn't just leave her there. Besides, I knew we may need a hostage. You took the gun from me; you brought us out here . . .'

'What was I meant to do?' Isabella scowled. 'This wasn't part of the plan. We need to get away from here, right now. If Upshaw and Pierce could find a way out of here through the snow, so can we.'

Dr Pierce and Mrs Upshaw? Maddie hoped maybe they had gotten away, not been murdered by the love-killers. Even if they were louses, one murder per Christmas was enough.

'Dr Pierce finding out wasn't part of the plan, either,' Felipe said querulously. 'You were the one who insisted on befriending him!'

'How was I supposed to know he'd be a filthy blackmailer? He seemed like a useful fool.' Isabella sent a scathing look over at Maddie, who was backing away in a bid to run off while they had a lovers' tiff. 'Well, come on, then. We have to leave anyway. We can lock her in the chapel or something.'

Maddie didn't like the sound of that *something*. Despite her flimsy indoor clothes and light-set coat in the freezing day, she managed to catch her red shawl on a dried branch as she stumbled off a side path, away from that gun.

'Where is it?' Isabella cried, glancing around frantically. 'The horses were meant to be here! Everything is falling apart.'

'I made the arrangements exactly as you said!' Felipe shouted back. 'They should be here!'

It sounded like the beautiful meeting of twin souls was crumbling at the edges, just like the banks of the pond. Maddie tried to crawl out, to run, but Isabella saw her and grabbed her arm, almost yanking it painfully from the socket. It was shockingly bruising for an invalid. Frantically, Maddie yanked back, wrestling to get away. Isabella pulled too hard trying to keep hold of Maddie and lost her balance, sending them both to the frosty ground and sliding along the bank. Maddie, through sheer force of will, managed to leap up and run, despite her flimsy shoes, and Isabella tried to scramble up and give chase. They ran around the edge of the pond and Maddie aimed for the summerhouse, hoping she could somehow lock herself in there.

'Come back!' Felipe cried, then Maddie heard an enormous crack and splash.

She and Isabella both paused to look back and saw that Felipe had fallen into the freezing water. Maddie remembered he'd said he couldn't swim. The ice kept him from making his way back to the slippery slopes of the banks.

'Isabella!' he screamed, shrill with panic.

'My darling! Wait for me!' Isabella plunged in after him, her cloak and gown splayed around her in the water.

'You'll drown,' Felipe gurgled as he sank like a stone. Isabella's golden head vanished under the murky water, as well.

Maddie frantically searched the ground for something to help, and found a stout branch. She sucked in a deep, fortifying breath and waded down into the ice-edged water toward the struggling couple, whose movement made them drift further and further away. The cold made her gasp and shudder, but she knew she had to try or she'd never forgive herself. She couldn't be like them. She couldn't let someone just die. She called out to them, holding out the branch for them to catch.

But they were too far. She screamed and screamed, until at last shouts answered her, and she heard running footsteps.

'Maddie!' A great splash sounded, and she felt strong arms come around her, hauling her up and out of the pond. Sadler and Rickie swam past her, reaching the place where the couple had gone down. Despite all their heroic efforts, it looked hopeless. Maddie feared they wouldn't be able to find the couple.

Once safe on the snowy banks, Maddie spun around to find David held her. He looked appalled, terrified, and his wonderful, beloved face made her finally collapse into the terrified tears she'd been holding back.

'Oh, David. My darlingest darling! I was so scared I'd never see you again. That we'd never have our wedding,' she cried, catching on a hiccup.

'Maddie,' he said hoarsely, and kissed her, over and over again, as if he'd never stop. 'My brave, foolish, wonderful girl. Whatever were you thinking?'

'I didn't mean to get caught by myself. I was going to find Gunther, to show him the letters I found. It was Isabella and Felipe all along. Mrs Upshaw and Dr Pierce were blackmailing them, and . . . Oh!' A sudden thought struck her, and she stared up at David in horror. 'Are they dead, too?'

'No, they were just found on the road. As could have been predicted, they didn't get far. It sounds like they've been in league for a long time.'

'So, you see, it wasn't Al at all.' Maddie sniffled, desperate to convince everyone. Desperate for Sadler to know it, too.

'Of course not. And now everyone will know that, thanks to you. I know it's probably useless to ask you to stay far away from danger in the future, Maddie,' he said.

Maddie sighed and leaned on his shoulder. 'I do want to, David darling, really and truly. But it does seem to find me now and again. I can't seem to turn away.'

'And that's one of the reasons I love you. Your bravery and kindness.' He kissed the top of her head. 'Just, please, from now on – let me come with you.'

She laughed. 'Oh, darling. I can safely say that's one promise I will definitely keep.'

EPILOGUE

A few months later

It was the most utterly perfect day for a wedding.

The music of bells rang in Maddie's ears all the way along the walk from the church, arm in arm with David – her *husband!* – to her house. Their house. Their home. Neighbors lined the street, cheering, tossing flowers, making her feel she truly was home, not just the house but the people, the sun and sky and stars. She'd never felt more exactly where she was meant to be.

Her cousin Gwennie's gift of a wedding gown (designed by a studio costumer, she declared, and thus very special) was perfect, pale-blue duchesse satin that matched the endless Santa Fe sky, embroidered with pearls and sequins that formed roses and vines along the narrow skirt, a silver lamé train attached at the shoulder. Ruby and Pearl delighted in carrying that train as the little procession marched toward the house along Canyon Road. Maddie wore a crown of flowers on her hair, every bright sprig from her own garden. The twins sported matching garlands with their pink and white lace frocks, while their mother had a corsage for her new green silk dress, and David wore a boutonniere with his newly tailored dark suit. Everything seemed fragrant with those flowers, brilliant with sunshine, a brand-new start.

Maddie held close to David's arm and laughed as a shower of petals fell over her in a stream of pink and white. The drift of pastel colors blended with the beige of the house, the bright skirts and shawls of the people. The cold of winter, the fear of the murder, seemed very far away.

Maddie glanced back to see, walking along with the procession, Helena Luhan and her new fiancé Jim McTeer, the two of them looking nearly as joyful as Maddie felt herself. The freedom of the day was infectious.

Eddie and his pals from La Fonda ran ahead and opened the gates to Maddie's portal, where Juanita and her handsome movie star beau, Frank Altumara, waited for them.

'Welcome home, darlings!' Gunther shouted gleefully and tossed yet more petals.

Inside the dining room was laid a most sumptuous buffet. Amid punch bowls, towers of champagne glasses and tumblers of lemonade, was Juanita's masterpiece, a triple-tiered, white-iced cake bedecked with sugar flowers and blue-tinted marzipan ribbons. Plates of sandwiches and tarts from Marta's new teashop gleamed on silver trays. It was like a royal feast.

'We're home,' Maddie whispered to her husband. She loved to think of the word. *Husband.* Her love. 'Can you believe it?'

'I can't believe it's not all a dream,' David answered. He smiled down at her, attention all on her, as if they were the only people in all the land. 'I never thought I would find such a place. With *you*, my angel.'

'Despite the trouble that always seems to chase me down?' she asked.

He laughed and kissed her. 'My dear. The trouble is one of the best parts.'